"I'll do it. I'll marry Mattie."

Everyone appeared relieved that the decision had been made.

Now it was just a matter of informing the bride about her impending nuptials. Josiah glanced toward the other covered wagons and easily picked out Mattie, even though she was attired in a gown and bonnet for the first time in their acquaintance.

He brought her near the river's edge, a short distance from the wagon train, where they had a measure of privacy. A slight breeze blew across the water and lifted her bonnet strings, setting one fluttering against her cheek. She impatiently brushed it aside. "Well? What's the verdict?"

An infinitesimal pause preceded his response. "Marriage."

Just that one word. Nothing more.

She shook her head in confusion. "Come again?"

"You cannot stay on the wagon train without a man to take responsibility for you, so you need to marry. Miles has insisted that a wedding take place. Today. Before we go any farther."

"You can't be serious! Where does Mr. Carpenter imagine I'll find a husband out here in the middle of nowhere?" She threw her arms wide.

"You're looking at him."

Tracy Blalock lives in Southern California with her family and assorted pets. An avid reader from a young age, it was always her dream to write books of her own. She earned a bachelor of arts in history, and loves researching interesting historical facts. When she's not reading or writing, she enjoys traveling to museums and historic sites, which she uses as inspiration to dream up new characters and stories.

Books by Tracy Blalock

Love Inspired Historical

Wed on the Wagon Train

TRACY BLALOCK

Wed on the Wagon Train

HARLEQUIN® LOVE INSPIRED® HISTORICAL

Recycling programs
for this product may
not exist in your area.

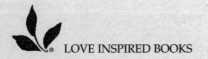

LOVE INSPIRED BOOKS

ISBN-13: 978-0-373-28389-7

Wed on the Wagon Train

Copyright © 2016 by Tracy Blalock

www.Harlequin.com

Printed in U.S.A.

Surely goodness and mercy shall follow me
all the days of my life, and I will dwell in the house
of the Lord forever.
—*Psalms* 23:6

To my family, for always believing in me.

Especially my sister, Robyn.
You were certain I'd receive "The Call"
for this book, though you hadn't even read it yet.
Somehow you just knew.

Chapter One

Independence, Missouri
Early May, 1845

You're supposed to be a man, so stop acting like a girl, Matilda Prescott silently warned herself.

She couldn't afford to be distracted by a handsome cowboy. But there was something vastly appealing about a man so different from the dandies she'd known back in Saint Louis. Her eyes tracked him as he sat straight and tall in the saddle, moving as one with his mount, the sun glinting off his red-gold hair.

With no small effort, she dragged her gaze away from the rider. Hitching up her too-large pants, she concentrated on taking long, manly strides with no eyebrow-raising, feminine hip-swaying, as she headed toward the nearest covered wagon and the man loading provisions.

"Do you know where I can find the wagon master?" she questioned, pitching her voice low and deep.

The man scratched his whiskered jaw. "Miles Carpenter's the gray-bearded gent in the red shirt over yonder."

"Thank you." She touched her hat brim, then headed toward the older man.

He was sitting on an overturned barrel, examining a broken leather harness.

"Mr. Carpenter? I'm Matt Prescott." She extended her hand. "My younger sister and I would like to join your wagon train."

He gave her an assessing look before setting his work aside and returning her handshake. "You'll need a wagon and team and enough provisions to last through four or five months."

"We have all that, sir. Everything's at the livery stable, ready to go."

"I heard a wagon had been left behind by the previous group. Was that you?"

"Yes, sir." She gulped nervously, fearing what else he might've heard. Was her plan about to unravel at the seams?

"Why were you left behind?"

The question eased her mind considerably, proving he didn't know the full story of how another wagon master had refused to take along two unescorted females after their father's death. She couldn't let the same thing happen a second time. Which was why she wasn't giving this man the chance to turn down *Matilda* Prescott.

"Our father took ill after we reached Independence and when he wasn't able to travel, the wagon train left without us." She stayed as close to the truth as possible to minimize the possibility of tripping herself up later.

And prayed God forgave her for this deception.

"Where's your pa now?" Mr. Carpenter asked.

Mattie blinked several times, determined she wouldn't allow any tears to fall. Her father's recent passing was a raw, unhealed wound, but she couldn't show any weaknesses. Men didn't cry. She dug her nails into her palms and closed her eyes, focusing on the physical pain to keep her grounded in the present.

When she had her emotions under control, she lifted her lashes and met the older man's gaze. "Our heavenly Father called him home."

"I'm sorry to hear that, son." He rested his hand on Mattie's shoulder for a moment, giving it a comforting squeeze. But she knew better than to hope his sympathy would extend to accepting the Prescott siblings without question. "How old are you?"

"Nineteen."

He eyed her askance. Should she have shaved a few years off her real age? She lacked the whiskers of a mature man, but the wagon master would surely deny her request if he thought her only a boy.

She waited for his judgment and breathed a sigh of relief when he let the matter of her age drop.

"It's a long, difficult journey, and every family needs to pull their own weight. Can you handle the hardships we'll encounter?"

"Yes, sir. I can take care of my sister and myself." She hoped.

Please, Lord, help me keep Adela safe.

The younger girl was the only family she had left on this side of the Missouri River. But an aunt and uncle waited for them in Oregon Country, if only Mattie and Adela could reach them.

Several tense moments passed without a response

from the wagon master, and Mattie's heart pounded in her chest.

Finally, he nodded. "We leave tomorrow."

"We'll be ready." She turned to hurry away before he changed his mind.

She missed a step when her gaze landed on the handsome cowboy she'd spotted a short time ago.

He was walking in her direction and offered her a cordial nod as he passed. "Howdy."

She returned the gesture, but not the greeting, his intense blue gaze rendering her mute. Her eyes followed him as he continued toward Miles Carpenter.

Dressed in a blue chambray shirt, which contrasted with the red highlights in his hair, the younger man was a strapping figure next to the more portly frame of the wagon master. His angular jaw sported a dusting of cinnamon-colored bristles, and he was handsome enough to turn any woman's head.

Realizing she was staring at him like a brainless ninny, she shook herself out of her stupor, then quickly ducked her head and continued on her way. Before anyone took note of her—pretending to be a *him*—making eyes at the cowboy.

"What can I do for you, Josiah?" she heard Miles Carpenter ask.

She didn't listen to the answer. Instead, she turned her thoughts to the numerous tasks awaiting completion before tomorrow.

A sudden gust of wind caught the brim of her hat, sending it sailing across the ground. The current of air blew the hat into the legs of a horse, and the animal spooked, bucking and unseating its rider.

Mattie rushed forward and snatched up the dangling

reins to control the horse, keeping it from trampling the rider beneath its hooves. "Easy," she soothed the frightened animal.

Scrambling out of danger, the man climbed to his feet and yelled an obscenity at his mount. He drew back his arm to strike its hindquarters with a short leather crop. The horse's eyes rolled and it danced to the side, a sure sign that the crop had been used on him before.

"Stop!" She had no respect for anyone who would mistreat a defenseless animal. Inflicting pain on the horse was the mark of a weak man. In her outrage, she forgot to speak in a deep voice, and she hastily lowered her pitch. "It's not the horse's fault." She stroked the animal's velvet-soft nose to calm it.

The man turned angry eyes toward her. "You are correct," he bit out in a clear-cut British accent. "The fault lies with you."

She trembled inside, but stood her ground. He angled away from the horse, raising his crop toward her, instead.

She had only a moment to regret her impulsive intervention. Ducking her head, she raised her arm in defense and waited for the blow to fall.

Josiah Dawson caught the crop in midair before it could make contact with the slight young man he'd seen talking to the wagon master a short time ago. The kid's shaggy brown hair was cut in uneven hunks, and his baggy clothes appeared two sizes too big for his frame, as if he hadn't quite grown into them, yet.

Josiah could understand why Miles had expressed reservations about allowing this boy to join the group.

Only a few minutes had passed since that conversation and already the kid was mired in a sticky situation, taking on a man almost twice his size.

Josiah was reminded of the Bible story about David and Goliath. Only this boy didn't have even a slingshot for protection.

Deliver the poor and needy; rid them out of the hand of the wicked.

The verse running through Josiah's mind, he faced off against the aggressor. "Not a good idea, Hardwick."

The other man puffed up like a riled rooster. "You will address me as *Lord* Hardwick, as is proper." He paused, allowing time for Josiah to correct the error. But when he realized no bootlicking was forthcoming, his lips pressed together in a thin line. "My father is the Earl of Fenton, and I will not be taken to task by one so far beneath me. I intend to teach this boy to show the proper respect for his betters, and you would be wise to stay out of matters which do not concern you, Dawson."

Josiah didn't back down. "Miles Carpenter has a rule against violence between members of his group. If he hears about this incident he might rethink whether you're the type of person he wants to spend the next several months with."

"I do not answer to him," the other man countered.

If this pretentious Brit didn't know the wagon master's rules were law on the trail, he would soon learn that lesson. "Well, see now, that's where you're wrong. The same rules apply to you as everybody else. You're not in England anymore. Your daddy's name has no sway here—we judge people on their actions, not their family trees. And Miles Carpenter will do what's in the best interest of the group. Now, do you want him to decide that's you finding another way to get to Oregon Country? Or are you going to leave the boy alone?"

Hardwick glared in silence for a moment before jerking the crop out of Josiah's grip. Though they were fairly evenly matched in size, Josiah hoped to avoid a physical altercation. He tensed, waiting for Hardwick's next move. But the Brit didn't raise his crop to strike again. Instead, he snatched his horse's reins from the young man's loose hold, yanking cruelly on the animal's tender mouth. He stalked away without another word to either Josiah or the kid.

Josiah bent down and retrieved the errant hat, knocking it against his thigh to remove some of the dust, then extended it toward the boy.

Miles had confided that he suspected the newest member of their group had exaggerated his age in order to join the wagon train. Josiah was inclined to agree. The boy's beardless chin certainly belied the claim that he was nineteen.

Accepting the hat, he placed it on his head and pulled the brim low to shade his face. "Thank you for that," he offered in a gruff voice.

Josiah understood he meant more than the return of his headwear. "Steer clear of Hardwick from now on."

"I will."

He hoped the kid took his words to heart. Still, Josiah was impressed with a scrappy fighter who waded in against injustice despite the odds. It reminded him of his former self. He'd been orphaned when he was just a few years younger than he guessed this boy to be.

Almost a dozen years had passed since then, but he well remembered getting in over his head and needing someone to step in to help. In his case, his older half brother, Elias, had come to his aid. And though he was now a grown man, Josiah appreciated his brother's continued support. Which was why he'd agreed to join Elias and his wife, Rebecca, on this journey.

Only a few short months ago, Josiah had completely different plans. But things had changed, and those dreams were gone. He'd lost the woman who held his heart and his best friend in the same day—but not to death. There was a wall between them. And though it was of Josiah's own making, he couldn't scale it. It was better that he left.

With nothing for him back in Tennessee, he welcomed the new life that waited out west. And the next few months would be much easier with others to share the load.

But this young kid had no one he could depend on to watch his back. Plus, he had a younger sister to look out for.

"I'm Matt Prescott." The boy stuck out his hand.

He accepted the handshake. "Josiah Dawson."

Matt dug the toe of his boot into the dirt, keeping his head down and his face hidden from view. "So, we'll be traveling together, I guess."

"Looks that way." If the kid could keep himself out of trouble and avoid getting kicked out of their wagon train.

"Don't worry that you'll have to bail me out of any more scrapes. I'll be more careful from now on."

"That's good to hear. Just see that you remember to stop and think before going off half-cocked. Your sister's depending on you."

Matt's head came up and a look of surprise flashed across his face.

"Miles mentioned it's just you and your sister," Josiah explained.

"Oh." He seemed discomfited to find he'd been a topic of conversation. "Well, I better get going now. Thank you again."

Josiah's eyes narrowed as Matt hurried away. With his focus initially on Hardwick, he'd only gotten a brief glimpse of the kid's face before it disappeared beneath his hat brim. And afterward Matt had appeared reluctant to meet his gaze. Maybe the boy was simply shy. But Josiah didn't quite believe that explanation. Not after Matt had confronted the haughty Brit deliberately.

But if the kid *had* lied about his age, would that account for his evasiveness?

Or was he hiding something more?

Mattie glanced back and found Josiah watching her, a speculative expression on his face. Had his blue eyes seen too much? After getting a good look at her face, had he guessed her true gender?

Was that the reason he'd stepped in unasked to defend her? Not because she was smaller than the high-and-mighty earl's son, but because he had realized she was a woman? Though her heart sank at the thought, she tried to remain calm. If he'd worked out the truth about her, surely he would have reported her to the wagon master.

Wouldn't he?

She pushed away the worrying question. She could only assume that her secret was safe. At least for the time being.

But one thing had been made clear to her—she needed to do a better job of taking care of herself. This time, she'd been fortunate not to end up with a nasty welt—or worse. She couldn't expect someone to ride to her rescue every time she ran into trouble. She had to learn to deal with problems on her own. She couldn't risk allowing anyone to get close enough to discover the truth.

With that in mind, she kept her head down to discourage any friendly greetings as she made her way through the town's congested streets, thronged with people preparing for the trail.

It was already nearing noon, and time was in short supply for her to get everything ready for their imminent departure.

Their father had outfitted them well for the journey, but when he'd taken ill their covered wagon and oxen had been left at the livery stable, while the Prescott family took rooms in a nearby boardinghouse.

The livery was her first stop.

Stepping into the dim interior, she searched out the stable master. He accepted without comment her explanation that she was a young man running an errand for the Prescott sisters, and he promised to have the oxen hitched to the wagon and delivered to the boardinghouse first thing the following morning.

Their supplies had remained loaded in the covered wagon, and all that was left for them to do tomorrow was add the trunks of personal items, which still needed to be packed back at the boardinghouse.

She'd left Adela there alone without explanation and had been gone longer than she'd anticipated. The younger girl must be frantic by now. Mattie felt terrible for causing her sister additional fear and worry, after the last ten days of uncertainty they'd already gone through since their father's passing.

As she neared the boardinghouse, her steps slowed. The livery had been easy, but this next part might prove more challenging. While a strange male roused little suspicion in a stable, his presence wouldn't go unquestioned in a genteel rooming establishment.

But she'd come too far to lose her nerve now.

Straightening her shoulders, she turned the knob on the front door. The hinges squealed as the heavy oak door swung open. She winced and swept a furtive look around. Seeing neither the landlady nor any of the other boarders, she quickly headed toward the stairs. All the way up to her room, she expected to hear a voice behind her demanding to know why she was skulking through the house. But she didn't encounter anyone.

She opened the door to her room and stepped inside, a sigh of relief gusting out of her tight chest.

Adela was bent over an open trunk, a silver-backed hairbrush in her hand. She glanced up as the door clicked shut. Her eyes widening in fright, she let out a high-pitched shriek.

"Shh, Adela." The last thing they needed was someone bursting into their room to investigate.

She took a step toward her sister.

But the other girl backed away. "Don't you come any closer, or I'll scream again," she warned, brandishing the hairbrush as if it was a sword.

"Adela, it's me." Removing her hat, she set it on the marble-topped bureau.

"Mattie? You scared me to death!" The hairbrush

slipped from her fingers, and she placed her hand over her heart. Then her mouth dropped open as she took notice of Mattie's altered appearance. "What happened to your hair?!"

Mattie fingered a short lock. She didn't have to look in the mirror to know what she'd see—ragged chunks cut close to her head, instead of the long brown curls that had reached almost to her hips.

Adela plopped down onto the bed. "And why are you dressed like that? Those look like Papa's clothes." Tears filled her eyes at the mention of their father.

"These *are* Papa's clothes." She dropped her hand from her shorn strands, refusing to mourn anything as silly as hair. The loss of their beloved father was much more significant. The pain throbbed like a physical wound, but she kept a tight rein on her emotions. Though they'd buried him little more than a week ago, she couldn't wallow in grief. "I came up with a way for us to reach Oregon Country."

And she'd acted quickly, not giving herself time to rethink the daring plan and change her mind. After hacking off her hair, she'd changed into her father's clothes. He had been taller and broader than Mattie, and the garments hung on her. But the loose material helped to disguise her feminine figure.

Adela wiped a tear away and shook her head in confusion. "How can we do that? Two females can't travel alone, Matilda. You know that."

"You seem to be missing the fact that we *aren't* two females anymore. Matt Prescott, at your service." She executed an exaggerated bow.

"Do you really think you're going to fool anyone with that ridiculous getup?"

"I fooled you, didn't I? Or was it someone else who screamed and threatened me with a hairbrush when I entered the room?"

Adela colored at the reminder. "You surprised me. I would have realized it was you in a moment or two."

"True. But you're my sister. A stranger won't know me from Adam. I was out most of the morning dressed like this, and nobody doubted I was a man." Though to be completely honest, Josiah Dawson was a disturbing question mark on that point. However, he hadn't confronted her, and that was good enough for now.

She hoped her disguise would hold for the whole journey, but once they were out on the trail, surely the wagon master would have to let them stay, even if her gender was revealed.

"I still don't think your plan will work," Adela argued.

"It already has." She opened a bureau drawer and started pulling out garments, then moved to her trunk and tucked the items inside. Though she'd have little use for the feminine clothing in the coming months, once they reached Oregon Country she'd be glad to have them. Her father's clothes, except for the pants and shirt she wore, were packed away in another trunk. "The wagon master's agreed to let us—or to be precise, 'Matt' and his sister—join his group."

"So that's why you left the table in the middle of breakfast. I did wonder over your abrupt departure, but I never imagined you'd come up with such a harebrained scheme."

Mattie turned toward her sister. "Do you have a better idea? We're paid up through the end of the week, but after that we don't have the money to pay for this room."

"We could sell the covered wagon, oxen and supplies, couldn't we?"

"Yes, but the cash we'd receive wouldn't last forever. When it ran out, what would we do? How would we support ourselves?"

"One of us could find a husband and get married." Adela's curls bobbed up and down as she nodded her head, the chestnut strands shimmering in the stream of sunlight spilling through the window.

She made a stark contrast to Mattie right now.

"I doubt any man would want to take me as a wife, looking like this."

But it was no great loss since she didn't particularly want a husband anyway. At least, not right now. If circumstances forced her to marry in haste, she wouldn't have a chance to truly get to know her bridegroom first. To place herself and Adela completely under a man's power without being absolutely certain of his character was unthinkable.

Mattie had made a narrow escape back in Saint Louis and wouldn't make the same mistake again, judging a man by outward appearances without taking the time to discover if the inside matched his outer facade.

Hopefully her fifteen-year-old sister had learned from Mattie's error, as well. "Do *you* want to marry a strange man and put your trust in him?"

The younger girl shook her head, clearly recognizing the pitfalls in that arrangement.

Mattie grasped her sister's hands. "This is the only way."

But Adela still looked doubtful. And with good reason.

Though their biggest obstacle—convincing the wagon master to let them join the wagon train—had been overcome, any number of other things could go wrong in the coming days.

Even if no one else knew it, they were two women alone, with only God's protection against whatever dangers they faced.

Would she and Adela be up to the journey ahead?

Chapter Two

"It's not too late to change your mind, Mattie."

Adela's words echoed Mattie's inner doubts as she surveyed the wagons and oxen teams lined up at the Missouri River's ferry crossing.

Was she making a mistake?

She hadn't thought so a short time ago when their covered wagon had arrived at the boardinghouse as promised. While Mattie stayed out of sight, Adela had overseen the loading of their trunks without incident, and they were quickly under way.

Now, however, Mattie's earlier confidence was suffering a decided downturn.

She shifted her gaze to focus on her sister. Adela certainly didn't look like a girl about to embark on an arduous four or five month journey. She was decked out in a fancy costume complete with frilly parasol, as if going for a casual jaunt around the park.

Before his passing, their father had purchased practical garments suitable for travel for himself and his daughters. Mattie, seeing little sense in hanging on to remnants of the past, had gotten rid of anything she wouldn't need in her new life. But Adela had flatly refused to part with so much as a lacy hankie from her wardrobe, despite the fact that wagon space was limited and expensive fabrics had no place on the trail.

It wasn't surprising she'd dug in her heels over the issue, however, since she'd been against this trip from the start. She hadn't wanted to give up their life in Saint Louis.

And Mattie felt personally responsible for her unhappiness. The family's financial decline was a direct result of choices Mattie had made.

But neither her guilt nor Adela's objections could restore what they'd lost. That life was gone, whether they returned to the city or not. Adela would have to come to terms with their changed circumstances.

Their best hope for a bright and joyous future lay ahead in Oregon Country.

Taking a deep breath, Mattie stiffened her own flagging resolve. "We can't go back. And remember to call me 'Matt.' No one can know the truth." She didn't want to consider what might happen if Adela accidentally called her Mattie in front of anyone.

"I'm sorry. It just slipped out. But I'll be more careful. I promise."

Mattie steered the oxen toward the end of the line and drew them to a halt behind the last wagon. The lowing of cattle and whiny of horses mixed with the sound of people shouting and whips cracking, creating a cacophony of noise.

Several minutes passed without any movement forward.

Adela fanned herself with one lace-gloved hand and

huffed out an impatient sigh. "How long will we have to wait for our turn to cross the river?"

Scanning the dozen or so covered wagons waiting ahead of them, Mattie shook her head in answer. "I don't know."

"Hours, most like," a male voice interjected.

Mattie turned toward the speaker and recognized the bearded man who had pointed out Miles Carpenter to her the previous day. Of medium height and build, he looked to be in his forties or fifties.

He nudged the brim of his hat up to scratch his temple. "It'll take the better part of the day to get all twenty-five wagons across the river. But it gives folks a chance to get to know each other. The name's Jed Smith."

Mattie hesitated to reply. Each encounter with other travelers held the potential for disaster if her ruse was exposed. But living in such close quarters over the next few months looked to make any attempts at completely dodging conversation an impossibility.

Grudgingly, she accepted Jed's outstretched hand and again introduced herself as Matt Prescott, knowing she would be called on to do tasks so many times over the next several days.

The deception was already wearing on her, and it had only just begun. Would it get any easier in time? Probably not. But she couldn't let that discourage her.

Jed squinted against the glare of the sun as he surveyed Mattie and Adela. "Seeing as how you joined the wagon train only yesterday, I'd guess you haven't had occasion to meet many of our fellow travelers yet."

"No, we haven't," Adela replied. "Are all these people making the journey?"

"Yep." Jed hooked his thumbs under his suspenders and shifted his stance, indicating he planned to stay and chat for a while. "All told, our group's about two dozen families. Mostly farmers, like myself and the Bakers with their brood of six, and Thomas Malone, a widower with a pair apiece of teenage offspring—two boys, and two gals about your age, missy."

"By any chance, would that be the two tall, blonde girls standing by the covered wagon near the head of the line?" Adela questioned.

Jed glanced in that direction and nodded. "That's them."

Mattie reached for Adela's arm and gave it a slight squeeze as a subtle signal to shush her.

The younger girl simply shook off her hold, however. "And who is that man on horseback, wearing a brocade waistcoat and starched cravat? He certainly isn't a farmer."

"That's Phillip Hardwick, a fancy British lord. He's brought along a pair of servants. We also have a doctor and a preacher traveling with us. Then there's our trail guide, a mountain man and trapper." Jed fell quiet, his expression expectant.

Clearly, he was hoping the Prescotts would volunteer information about their own background.

And Adela obliged him, despite Mattie's none-too-subtle elbow to her ribs. "We're from Saint Louis originally. Now, we're traveling to join relatives. Our uncle owns a hotel in Oregon City. The Prescott. Perhaps you've heard of it?"

Jed shook his head. "I can't say that I have."

Mattie cleared her throat and spoke before Adela had a chance. "It was nice meeting you, Mr. Smith—"

"Jed," he inserted.

"Jed. We won't keep you any longer."

He tugged his hat brim down lower on his forehead. "Well, I'll just mosey along and say howdy to some other folks."

Once he was out of earshot, Mattie turned toward her sister. "You shouldn't encourage conversation. We must be especially careful that no one discovers the truth."

Adela pursed her lips. "We'll draw more attention to ourselves if we refuse to speak to anybody. That will make it seem as if we have something to hide."

"We *do* have something to hide."

"Yes, but we don't want the others to suspect that."

Mattie had to concede her sister made a valid point.

Adela waved to a passing woman, who offered them an affable smile. "Besides, chatting helps pass the time."

"Fine. But please, watch what you say."

Adela held up one hand as if making a pledge. "I promise not to let words come tumbling out of my mouth with no prompting from my brain. Will that satisfy you?"

"Thank you."

It quickly became apparent that Jed wasn't the only person who viewed the delay as an impromptu social gathering. Several others approached her and Adela, including a couple who turned out to be Josiah's brother and sister-in-law.

Elias Dawson looked to be half a dozen years older than Josiah, but the family resemblance between the two was strong. Blessed with similar good looks, both men were tall and well built. But Mattie estimated Josiah stood an inch or two taller, and his frame carried a bit more muscle than the older man. It was difficult to judge for certain, however, without the pair positioned side by side.

Although a redhead like his brother, Elias's hair was a darker chestnut than Josiah's light red-gold hue. The most notable difference between the siblings was that the elder didn't share the same intense blue eye color that had so struck Mattie the day before. Instead, the older man's eyes were an ordinary shade of brown.

Rebecca, Elias's wife, was a petite blonde in her early twenties. She seemed a pleasant woman, with her friendly manner and twin dimples bracketing her charming smile.

Mattie extended the bare minimum of courtesies. Adela, in contrast, chattered on merrily. "You'll have to excuse Matt. He's a bit tongue-tied around strangers," she offered at one point.

Mattie's stomach was in knots as she agonized over all the things Adela might let slip. But the younger girl skirted around any dangerous topics and steered the conversation toward inconsequential chitchat.

Still, Mattie breathed a sigh of relief when Josiah's relatives eventually departed.

Time crept by, the minutes turning into hours as they waited their turn to ferry across the river. Mattie's tension coiled tighter and tighter until she was almost sick with it. If only they were already out on the trail she would feel slightly more at ease. Sitting here, however, she was all too aware that it would be a simple matter for Miles Carpenter to order her and Adela back to Independence. The town was still much too close for her peace of mind.

And it didn't help that the line of covered wagons inched ahead at a snail's pace. Every so often she prodded the team into motion and the wagon rolled forward, only to come to a standstill again after a few short feet. This pattern was repeated again and again as morning gave way to afternoon. Until, finally, there was a single covered wagon left in front of them.

"You're beautiful," a child's voice piped up, snagging Mattie's attention.

She shifted her gaze and spotted a little girl of about five standing beside their wagon, staring at Adela in rapt awe. "Are you a princess?"

Adela laughed in delight. "No. But thank you for the lovely compliment."

"Sarah Jane Baker, come away from there!" A woman with the same light brown hair and hazel eyes as the little girl rushed over and caught the child's arm in a firm grasp. "Don't bother the fine lady."

"But, Mama," Sarah Jane protested, tugging against her mother's hold.

Adela offered mother and daughter a wide smile. "She's not a bother."

Mrs. Baker seemed momentarily stunned by Adela's dazzling expression, but quickly recovered her wits and hastened her child away.

A piercing whistle rent the air, drawing Mattie's attention to the man waving her forward. It was their turn to board the wooden ferry, at last.

But she immediately hit a snag when she tried to get the oxen in motion. After countless starts and stops, they weren't inclined to budge any farther. And she had no idea how to persuade them. Though plenty of men used whips to control their teams, she hesitated to do so.

"Get up," she urged, but to no avail.

One animal stamped his foot, but the team didn't move forward.

Climbing down from the wagon seat, she walked to the head of one of the oxen and tugged on the U-shaped metal piece encircling his neck. Still nothing.

She didn't have the strength to muscle him where he didn't want to go. To make matters worse, he shook his head as though silently scoffing at her puny efforts.

"You're making me look bad," she scolded the recalcitrant beast. "Come on, cooperate. Please?"

All she got in response was an ear twitch.

"Hurry up!" a man yelled behind her, his British accent instantly recognizable.

Couldn't he see she was trying? If he was in such an all-fired rush, he should offer his assistance instead of just shouting orders. But he no doubt considered it beneath him to help others.

Mattie wished her father had chosen horses to pull the covered wagon. She prided herself on her ability as a horsewoman. They would have given her no trouble. But horses couldn't live off prairie grasses like oxen. And oxen were supposed to be more reliable—though, apparently, someone had forgotten to tell *her* team.

Lord, please move these oxen.

Josiah appeared at her side as if in answer to her prayer. "Need some help?"

Though it wasn't what she'd meant when she'd appealed to the Lord, she wasn't going to question His ways. "Yes, please," she accepted in relief.

He gave the animal's rump a light tap, which was

enough to get him moving, and the rest of the team followed behind as docile as lambs, trailing Josiah onto the ferry.

Her cheeks heated.

What had she done wrong? She had no experience with driving a wagon. Had the oxen sensed that? If she couldn't control her team, she'd be subjected to dangerous scrutiny. It felt like dozens of eyes were focused on her even now, and she pulled the brim of her hat lower over her face.

Once the wagon wheels rolled onto the wooden planks, Josiah hopped back down to the ground. "There you go."

"Thank you." Mattie stepped onto the ferry then glanced back in time to see Josiah heading toward an area where several horses were penned.

When he reached the fence, he paused to stroke the nose of one animal. It was a different horse than the one she'd seen him riding yesterday.

The wind tousled his bright hair, causing a lock to fall over his forehead. He was one of the most handsome men she'd ever met.

But good looks could hide a multitude of sins, as she knew from personal experience. Even months later, she still sometimes had nightmares about what her life would be like if she'd married Charles Worthington back in Saint Louis. She touched her cheek, where a tiny scar served as a permanent reminder to look beneath the surface.

Josiah appeared to be a truly good man—stepping in on two separate occasions to help her out—but she'd been fooled before and wouldn't naively trust that he was everything he seemed.

Too much was at stake.

And she still didn't know whether he'd seen through her disguise. Had he discerned more about her than he'd let on? The thought left her unsettled, but she scolded herself not to borrow trouble.

Nonetheless, she had to keep her guard up. Around him and everyone else.

The river current suddenly rocked the ferry, pulling her focus away from the far bank. She tightened her hold on the wagon frame and turned to face west.

It was midafternoon by the time all twenty-five wagons were across the river, and their group made it less than two miles before the wagon master called a halt for the night. After their earlier obstinacy, the oxen seemed to take pity on her and hadn't balked once on the trail.

At their campsite, the covered wagons were arranged in a circle, and the area inside quickly became a hive of activity and movement. Mattie had to take special care to avoid being trampled by a nervous animal. Or getting in someone's way. Observing the chaos, she noted that everybody seemed to know what to do.

Except her and Adela.

She didn't want to stand out as a novice, but belatedly realized she had no idea how to unhitch the oxen. Or what to do with them once they were free of the wagon.

She wasn't living up to the promise she'd made to Miles Carpenter.

Glancing around, she spotted Josiah. He was occupied with a group of horses, so there would be no help from that quarter.

She'd have to do this on her own. Somehow.

Circumspectly, she watched the other drivers' actions in order to imitate them. As she moved toward her oxen, she noticed Adela still sat on the bench seat, where she'd insisted on riding all afternoon, despite the uncomfortable jostling as the covered wagon bounced over the rough trail.

"Are you going to get down?"

Tilting her parasol to shade her eyes from the slanting rays of the setting sun, she shook her head. "No. This is the only place to sit."

Mattie reached for the metal pin securing the nearest oxen's neck thingamabob to the wooden doodad, which connected him to a second animal. "You don't need a place to sit right now. You need to get busy starting a fire and cooking supper." She abandoned her task for a moment to give her sister her full attention. "I can't do everything myself, Adela. And since I'm taking over the jobs Papa would have handled, it's up to you to see to the chores around camp that you and I originally planned to share."

"But I don't know how to cook," the younger girl protested. "I don't even know how to start a fire."

"You'll learn." She wasn't unsympathetic toward Adela's plight, but coddling the younger girl would set an unwise precedent. "There's some wood in that box strapped to the side of the wagon, and the matches are in Papa's copper tin."

But still, her sister sat motionless.

"The chores aren't going to do themselves, and you're wasting daylight," Mattie prodded. "Things will be even more difficult to do in the dark."

Snapping her parasol closed, Adela tossed it into the wagon and clambered down from the high seat.

Mattie breathed a sigh of relief. "Thank you."

"Save your thanks until we see if I can make anything edible," the younger girl advised.

After constructing a temporary enclosure to house his horses for the night, Josiah headed toward the circle of wagons. Slipping between the tailgate of one and the tongue of another, he entered the ring and recognized Matt and his sister at the nearest campfire.

The boy squatted, feeding a piece of wood into the crackling flames, while Adela stirred a boiling pot.

"Evening," Josiah greeted.

Adela turned toward him, the action sending her skirt swinging into the fire.

"Watch out!" Josiah reached forward, intent on pulling her out of harm's way. But it was too late. The flames ignited the edge of the material.

A series of shrieks filled the air, and the girl's frantic movements hindered Josiah's attempts to extinguish the fire by smothering it.

Grabbing a large pan from the tailgate, Matt yanked the cover off the water barrel and filled the container, then tossed the water over his sister's burning skirts, dousing the flames. "It's out."

Silence fell as Adela finally stopped screaming.

Several people had hurried over to see what all the commotion was about, but with the danger now past, they returned to their own campfires.

Everyone except Josiah's brother and sister-in-law.

Rebecca's eyebrows knit in concern. "Are you all right?"

Adela looked down at herself. "My dress! It's ruined." No pain showed in her expression.

Was that because she was unharmed? Or was she in a state of shock?

Matt grabbed his sister and gave her a slight shake. "Never mind about your dress!" Fear raised his voice an octave higher than normal. "Are you burned?" Not waiting for a response, he lifted the sodden, fire-damaged edge of her skirt, wincing at what he saw. "You already have blisters forming."

A moan slipped past Adela's lips as the pain finally registered. "It hurts."

Elias knelt for a quick look. "I have some salve that will help. I'll go get it." He stood and hurried away.

Rebecca took Adela by the arm. "Let me help you into the wagon. I'm sure you'd prefer some privacy while Elias tends to your injury."

By the time the two women disappeared between the canvas flaps, Elias had returned, and he followed them inside.

Anxiety crossed Matt's face.

"Don't worry. My brother's a doctor. Adela's in good hands."

"It's my fault she got hurt. She's never cooked over an open fire before, but I made her do it." Moving toward the pot suspended above the flames, he lifted the spoon.

"She's not used to this kind of life, but she'll adapt."

Matt tipped the spoon, and a large blob plopped back into the pot. "I guess it's pretty obvious all of this is new to us."

"Well, her attire was a bit of a clue." The picture Adela Prescott had made perched on the bench seat, like a queen on her throne, still had Josiah shaking his head.

Though sensibly dressed, in contrast, it was clear Matt was just as much a greenhorn as his sister. But Josiah wouldn't hurt the boy's pride by mentioning it.

Yesterday, he'd wondered if the kid was hiding something. Today, he'd gotten his answer. Matt was trying to disguise the fact that he didn't know how to handle life on the trail.

But he was smart—observing others to learn the skills he lacked—and had successfully unhitched the oxen on his own and herded them to the area where the other animals grazed.

Now he stirred the contents of the pot, poking at the charred chunks floating in a thick, mud-colored liquid.

It wasn't recognizable as food—at least not to Josiah. "What's that supposed to be?"

"I'm not sure. It's Adela's first attempt at cooking. We had servants back in St. Louis, and she never learned to prepare meals."

"She'll get the hang of it once she's had a bit more experience." Although, right now, it was a toss-up whether she would improve enough to produce edible meals before the Prescotts starved.

"Well, this is definitely past saving." Matt dropped the spoon, and the wooden handle landed against the edge of the pot with a dull thud.

"What's past saving?" Rebecca questioned as she climbed down from the covered wagon, followed by her husband and his patient.

"In all the excitement, their dinner was ruined," Josiah excused, seeing no need to mention the food had been inedible even before it was scorched.

Eyeing the contents of the pot, Rebecca's eyebrows arched, but she didn't challenge his claim. "I left a delicious stew simmering over the fire, and there's enough to share."

"That's very kind," Matt began. "But we couldn't—"

"We'd love to join you," his sister cut across him.

His cheeks reddened. "Adela, we can't impose on the Dawsons."

"It's not an imposition," Rebecca assured. "It will give us a chance to get better acquainted."

A moment of silent communication passed between the siblings, but finally Matt turned away from his sister's pleading eyes and nodded his assent. "Thank you for your kind offer, Mrs. Dawson. We appreciate it."

"Please, call me Rebecca," she invited. "Come on over whenever you're ready."

Josiah walked with Elias and Rebecca back to their covered wagon. By the time Matt and Adela arrived, Rebecca had five bowls of mouth-watering stew dished up.

Everyone took seats around the campfire. Elias said grace, and they dug in.

Matt offered Rebecca a compliment on her cooking.

Adela added her agreement with an appreciative smile. A moment later, the happy expression slipped from her face. "I'll never be able to make anything half as good as this."

"Of course, you will," Rebecca encouraged her. "It simply takes a little practice."

Adela looked unconvinced, but she didn't argue, and the conversation turned to other topics.

"Did you get your horses bedded down for the night?" Elias questioned.

Josiah nodded. "One of the mares is a bit skittish with so many other animals around, but Miles asked me to take first watch, so I'll be able to keep an eye on her and make sure she settles."

Elias turned to the Prescotts to explain, "Josiah plans to start a ranch and has a string of horses he's taking to Oregon Country."

"They're only green broke and have a tendency to spook at unfamiliar noises," Josiah elaborated. "But they come from hardy stock and will make good saddle horses with a little more training."

Elias clapped his hand on Josiah's shoulder. "He's already got them eating out of the palm of his hand, just like the high-strung bloodstock he worked with outside Nashville."

Josiah didn't want to be reminded of the past, and all he'd left behind in Tennessee.

He was determined to focus on the future, instead. "Thoroughbred racers are best left in the East. Practical mounts are what's needed out west."

"My baby brother has a special knack with animals. Like your oxen. They followed him like great big puppy dogs this afternoon. And I bet they were much better behaved for you afterward, too."

Matt's head bobbed up and down. "It's a handy skill to have."

"It's a way to earn a living," Josiah conceded. "But not like Elias, here, who can use his medical skills to help people. Now, that's a talent in short supply in Oregon Country."

Rebecca nodded. "My parents and sister moved out to the Willamette Valley two years ago, and they arranged a doctoring job for him in Silver Springs." She beamed with pride at her husband. "The townspeople are building a clinic and house for us that should be completed by the time we arrive."

Finished with his stew, Josiah set the bowl aside. "While the rest of us will have to scramble to put up some sort of makeshift shelter before winter sets in."

"Being a doctor does have some perks," Elias allowed.

Just then, a small dark-haired boy raced past their campfire. He giggled in glee as if playing a game, while his frazzled mother, the preacher's wife, chased after him.

"Henry Linton, slow down," she called out. "And watch where you're going!"

But the little boy paid her no heed. He was still going full speed when he reached his father, a man in his late twenties with a neatly trimmed beard.

The preacher snagged his young son and swung him up into his arms to prevent Henry from barreling over his little sister, who was sitting on the ground playing with a doll. "Whoa there, young man. I think you and I need to have a talk about minding your mama. And having a care around Lizzie." He sat down with the boy on his lap and spoke in low tones, his expression stern.

Tessa Linton brushed a straggling lock of red hair off her forehead. "I apologize for my son's behavior. He's been dashing around all day. I expected that he'd have tuckered himself out by now. I'm certainly worn-out from running after him."

"Then you deserve a rest." Rebecca glanced toward the dark-haired preacher. "It looks like David has things well in hand."

"For the moment, at least." Tessa's expression was wearily resigned, but it was edged with affection. "I'd best take advantage of the calm while it lasts." She moved toward her own campfire and sat down next to her husband.

"What adorable children." A soft smile tugged at Adela's lips as she watched the Lintons, her opinion plainly unaffected by the boy's misbehaving.

The corner of Elias's mouth curled up in a lopsided grin, then he picked up the thread of their interrupted conversation. "What are your plans for when you reach Oregon, Matt?"

"We have an aunt and uncle in Oregon City and will stay with them to start."

Adela nodded and her eyes lit up. "Our relatives own an elegant hotel. The dining room's paneled in solid mahogany, and the lobby has a large crystal chandelier ordered from New York. Although I've never seen it, I imagine it's magnificent."

"It certainly sounds lovely," Rebecca acknowledged. "So, you'll be living in the hotel, then?"

"Oh, no. Uncle Ephraim has a grand two-story house a few blocks from the hotel." Adela twirled a lock of dark hair around her finger. "The drawing room is big enough for social gatherings, and the dining table can seat a party of twelve."

"You're looking forward to a lifestyle similar to what you had back in Saint Louis." Josiah didn't bother to phase it as a question since the answer was obvious.

Adela immediately concurred. "Of course. There will be entertainment and music, and we'll have a string of handsome beaus—"

"We?" Rebecca's brow pleated in puzzlement.

"Oh! I meant me. And the friends I'm sure to make," Adela hastily clarified, with an overly bright smile.

Matt spooned the last few bites of stew into his mouth as if suddenly in a hurry. "It's getting late. Adela and I better head back to our wagon." He placed his empty bowl in Rebecca's outstretched hand. "Thank you for a delicious meal, Mrs. Dawson—Rebecca," he quickly corrected.

"You're welcome," Rebecca replied with a smile, then moved to collect Adela's bowl and stack it with the other one. "Why don't I come by in the morning to give you some pointers on how to prepare breakfast?"

Adela's mouth dropped open at the words. "I have to make breakfast, too?"

"Certainly. Our men need food to fuel them through the long day of travel and work. But don't worry. I'll show you how easy it is."

Adela offered a weak smile, clearly not looking forward to another cooking attempt so soon after tonight's disaster. "Thank you."

Josiah's eyes followed the Prescott siblings as they crossed to their own dying campfire, and yesterday's conversation with Miles replayed in his mind. The wagon master had expressed concern that the Prescotts might prove a burden to others.

To ensure that didn't become an issue, Matt and his sister had to be self-sufficient. Though it wouldn't happen overnight, a little guidance might speed up the process.

Whatever you did for the least of My brothers, you did for Me.

If he accompanied Rebecca on her visit in the morning, he could offer his assistance should Matt encounter any problems rounding up his oxen or hitching them to the covered wagon.

* * *

Dusk had fallen, and a cold wind blew into the camp, cutting through the thin fabric of Mattie's cotton shirt. But worse than the chill in the air was the creeping uncertainty she couldn't shake. Had she and Adela revealed too much to the Dawson family?

Glancing back, she found Josiah's gaze on her and quickly turned away to build up the fire.

A yip sounded in the distance.

Adela jumped and peered into the gathering darkness. "What was that?"

"I'm not sure." It wasn't a sound she'd ever heard before.

Several answering cries followed, seeming much closer than the first.

"Are they going to attack us?"

It would only add to Adela's fright if Mattie admitted to her own. "I'm sure they won't come near this many people. And the guards will keep them away from the livestock. You should try to get some sleep. We have to be up early in the morning."

"I don't think I can sleep."

"You'll be safe in the wagon."

Once Adela was gone, Mattie felt completely defenseless. Though the younger girl's presence wasn't any sort of protection, concern for her had served to keep the worst of Mattie's fears at bay.

Now, they rushed in to attack without mercy, setting her heart pounding.

She shivered, and though it was only partly due to the dropping temperature, she pulled on her father's coat. Inhaling his familiar cologne and the smell of the peppermint candies, which he'd been so fond of, made her feel he was still with her in some small way.

Would he disapprove of what she was doing? Or would he understand her reasons for persisting on this journey?

Out here, shifting shadows dominated, with only the stars to light the landscape. Though they appeared to shine brighter without the illumination from houses and businesses, the night conversely seemed darker, hiding unknown dangers from sight.

Yea, though I walk through the valley of the shadow of death, I will fear no evil: for You are with me.

She took courage from the remembered verse, determined to be strong for her sister.

Still, the responsibility weighed heavily on her. Daunting days and weeks loomed ahead. And she didn't have anyone to share her fears and doubts with.

Her deception stood as a barrier between her and others.

Chapter Three

It seemed to Mattie that she'd barely slept when the camp was roused early the next morning. Exiting the wagon, she noted there was nothing more than a faint lightening of the sky over the distant horizon to herald the new day. But with animals in need of tending and a wagon to pack up before the call to move out, she dared not delay.

Rebecca arrived at the Prescotts' campfire as promised to help Adela prepare the morning meal. Unfortunately, she wasn't alone—Josiah had accompanied her.

His presence sounded alarm bells in Mattie's head. What reason did he have to be here? She could only speculate—and none of the possibilities flooding her mind brought any reassurance.

"I should see to the oxen," she said to no one in particular.

"Go ahead," Rebecca replied, waving Mattie on her way. "Adela and I will be fine here while you're gone. And we'll have food waiting for your return."

Mattie had taken only two steps when Josiah appeared at her side and kept pace with her. She opened her mouth, though she wasn't sure what she intended to say to him.

He spoke before she could form any words. "I'll walk with you. I need to take care of my own animals."

Despite his perfectly reasonable explanation, she fretted over his motives for joining her. Was it truly as he'd claimed? Or something else, as yet unrevealed?

He didn't say anything more before they parted ways to see to their own chores.

When Mattie bent to her task, she felt a curious prickling sensation at the back of her neck, as if she was being watched. Glancing up, she found Josiah looking in her direction. She ducked her head, hiding her face beneath the shadow of her hat.

There was no mistaking the fact that he'd shown a marked interest in her over the past two days. The question was, why? What was his true purpose? It likely didn't bode well for her, whatever it might be.

Hurrying through the job, she finished up before Josiah and gladly left him behind. Once out from under his worrying silent regard, she breathed a sigh of relief.

She returned to the circle of covered wagons and found Adela alone at the campfire, stirring a skillet of scrambled eggs and bacon, Josiah's sister-in-law nowhere in sight. "Where's Rebecca?"

Adela pushed a lock of hair off her forehead as she glanced up. "She went back to her own wagon to cook breakfast for her family. But don't worry, she showed me what to do and gave me strict instructions to stir the eggs so they wouldn't burn. I haven't stopped for even a second."

While Mattie doubted constant stirring was precisely what the other woman had meant, she didn't say as much to her sister. She was simply glad to see Adela had been receptive to the cooking lesson. It was clearly helping already.

"It certainly smells good. Let's find out how it tastes." Mattie wrapped a towel around the handle of the skillet and lifted it from the fire.

Two tin plates sat waiting on an overturned crate that had been set up to serve as a table of sorts. After spooning out equal portions, she took a bite and hummed in approval. "Do you think you can make this on your own tomorrow?"

The younger girl worried her bottom lip between her teeth. "I can try." But her tone lacked confidence.

That was a worry for another time, however. Mattie had more immediate concerns, such as the myriad obstacles she would face during her first full day on the trail. Not the least of which was maintaining her guise as a male.

The sky grew lighter as they ate, giving Mattie a better view of the activity going on around the wagon circle. Small clusters of men stood at various camp-fires, nursing mugs of steaming coffee. Women tended to sleepy-eyed children who grumped over being roused at such an early hour. The little ones would undoubtedly be full of boundless energy as soon as the group got under way again, a short time from now.

There was no opportunity to enjoy a leisurely break-fast, and Mattie urged her sister to hurry after noticing her taking small, measured nibbles the way their gov-erness had taught them. The younger girl wrinkled her nose and muttered about behaving akin to a heathen, but thankfully did as Mattie requested.

Once the meal was finished, Adela handled the

cleanup and packed everything back into the wagon while Mattie retrieved the oxen. Upon her return, she was brought up short by the sight of Josiah, standing with his back to her, just a few feet from her wagon.

On the surface, his presence seemed perfectly innocent. Nothing more than a man pausing for a moment of quiet reflection as he enjoyed a mug of coffee before taking on the day ahead.

But she couldn't help suspecting him of deliberately loitering nearby.

She quickly pushed the troubling thought aside. She'd drive herself quite mad searching his every action for hidden meaning. And she needed her wits about her.

Josiah glanced over his shoulder and spotted her, then turned and moved closer. Patting the lead oxen, he subtly urged it in the right direction. "I'm happy to help, if you need a hand."

"Thanks, but I can handle it." She wanted to prove— no, she *needed* to prove that she could do it on her own.

Wordlessly accepting her refusal, he stepped back and gave her some space to work. But he didn't leave.

She preferred to do this without an audience and attempted to prod him on his way. "Shouldn't you be getting your horses ready?"

"I have plenty of time yet. It won't take long." He finished his coffee, then tossed out the dregs.

But still, he remained.

Fortunately, the oxen didn't give her any difficulty as she worked to hitch them to the wagon.

Josiah crossed his arms over his chest, a slight grin stretching the corners of his mouth. "I see the oxen are behaving for you today."

"I was worried they might turn stubborn again after stopping for so long overnight, the way they did yesterday before the ferry crossing," she admitted aloud, now that possibility hadn't come to pass.

"You'll be an old hand at this in no time," he predicted.

That was her hope.

Once the team was in position, it was a simple matter to reverse the process of the previous night.

Now, if only the rest of the day would prove as trouble-free.

Once out on the trail, Josiah stuck close to the line of covered wagons despite the fact that his horses could travel at a much faster pace than the slow-moving oxen teams.

He kept an unobtrusive eye on the Prescotts. Although Matt had done all right so far, Josiah wasn't quite ready to leave the kid completely on his own. This was a foreign environment to the boy and his sister. One filled with obstacles that could easily spell injury or worse for the unwary.

Miles from the nearest town or settlement, their group had nobody to depend upon other than one another. It was only right that Josiah should watch out for all his fellow travelers and, even more so, for a pair of siblings without any other family to back them.

His eyes swept along the line of wagons stretched out a goodly distance across the prairie, cutting a swath through the tall grasses. There wasn't a tree in sight. Or anything else that cast a shadow big enough to offer a moment's relief from the rays of the sun, climbing steadily higher in the sky. The day had turned warm already, and it would grow even hotter by the time the sun reached its zenith.

Josiah returned his gaze to the Prescotts' covered wagon, near the end of the line. Doubtless, neither Matt nor his sister were used to spending hours out of doors with little protection from the unrelenting elements. But Matt trekked gamely ahead without complaint.

His sister had again taken up a position atop the wagon seat, parasol in hand. Tugging free the lace-edged handkerchief tucked at her wrist, she placed the material over her nose and mouth and daintily coughed into it. "Isn't there anything you can do about this dust, Mattie?"

"Nope." Matt reached under his hat brim and wiped a trickle of moisture from his temple, then adjusted the hat to shield his eyes from the glare of sunlight reflecting off the pale canvas wagon bonnets in front of him. "But if you get down and walk you'll stay out of the worst of the dust cloud."

Adela flapped her handkerchief in front of her face, but she wasn't waving it as a white flag in surrender. "Walking in this heat would be even more miserable."

"The other women clearly don't think so," Matt pointed out.

"All the same, I'll stay here."

"Suit yourself."

Adela lapsed into silence. A few minutes later, her expression suddenly brightened when she sighted a small girl walking alongside their covered wagon. "Hello again," she greeted the child. "I remember you from yesterday. I'm Adela."

The little girl trailed her hand through the high grasses as she moved forward. "'ello, Dela."

Adela's smile stretched wider at the shortened version of her name. "And this is Mattie." She indicated her brother with a flutter of her handkerchief.

"Matt," he interposed, plainly not liking his sister's nickname. Perhaps he thought it made him sound like a child rather than a man.

"'ello, Matt." The child's eyes shifted from the boy back to his sister, her little face tilted upward as she focused on Adela perched high above her on the wagon seat.

But she wasn't paying proper attention to how close she was getting to the wagon wheels, which were taller than she was. And neither Matt nor Adela seemed to comprehend the deadly hazard the wagon presented to the little girl.

Josiah was all too aware of the danger, however. Moving quickly, he scooped up the child and settled her in front of him on the saddle.

She tipped her head back and looked at him with big, surprised eyes. Though her name escaped him at the moment, he recognized her as one of the Bakers' brood. She was a miniature copy of her mama, unlike the rest of her siblings who took after their father in coloring. A large heavyset man, George Baker had black hair and a thick beard that reached halfway down his shirtfront.

Urging his horses to a faster pace, Josiah traveled up the line to reach her family's covered wagon. After depositing her next to her mother, he cautioned Edith Baker to keep a closer watch on her child. The woman expressed effusive gratitude, but he waved it off and led his string of horses back down the line.

As he neared the Prescotts' wagon, Matt called out to him.

Reining in next to the kid, Josiah matched his horse's pace to Matt's on foot. From his greater height atop his mount, he couldn't see much of the boy's expression, blocked as it was by the wide brim of his hat.

But Matt's stiff posture telegraphed his discontent. "Why did you whisk that child away? You acted as if you feared we might taint her somehow."

"It was nothing against you," he refuted, stunned at the conclusion the kid had drawn from his actions. "I was simply trying to keep her safe."

"Safe from what? I don't understand." Though Matt tipped his head up toward Josiah, half his face remained in shadow.

"A fully loaded wagon is hard to stop, and if that child had ventured too close to the wheels, she would've been run over and crushed."

Adela gasped, her face contorting into a mask of horror. "Dear God, no." She leaned to the side in an attempt to see down the line of wagons in front of her, but the canvas cover immediately ahead blocked her view.

"She's safely back with her mother now," Josiah reassured her. "But that type of accident's all too common out here on the trail."

"How do you know that?" Matt questioned. "Have you completed this trip before?"

"No, but when Rebecca's family made the journey two years ago, her sister wrote dozens of letters about the experience. Rebecca shared several of them with me." They had given him a firsthand account of the many perils another group of travelers had encountered along the trail. "Most people have no idea what they're in for. But they soon learn. Just as you will."

Matt ducked his head and his face disappeared completely beneath the brim of his hat. "Well, thank you for what you did. I'd never forgive myself if my ignorance was the cause of a child's death." Strong emotion roughened his voice.

Josiah shifted in the saddle. "No harm done this time. And now you'll know to be careful in the future."

Matt bobbed his head and didn't say anything more.

With their conversation at an end, Josiah guided his string of horses a ways from the dust kicked up by the oxen teams and covered wagons.

The remainder of the morning passed uneventfully. At midday, Miles called the wagon train to a halt, allowing people the opportunity to eat a cold meal while the animals took a short rest.

And after the noon stop, Adela opted to walk instead of continuing to ride in the wagon. Though her parasol remained very much in evidence, it drew fewer stares and sniggers than it had the day before—most likely because she'd volunteered to help keep an eye on the smaller children now that she knew about the potential dangers.

Several little ones surrounded her as she strolled along at the plodding pace set by the oxen. She led one toddler by the hand, and a handful of other children trailed behind while she regaled the group with tales of daring adventure. Judging by her expression, Adela plainly found as much enjoyment in the pastime as the youngsters did.

Which served as proof that both she and her brother

had begun to adjust to trail life. Admittedly, Adela at a significantly slower rate than Matt. But it was progress.

There was hope for the Prescotts yet.

The fourth night on the trail, Mattie perched on a slight rise overlooking their campsite. She was in the company of Josiah—though not by her choice. Miles Carpenter had put them together for guard duty.

She suspected Josiah might have had something to do with their pairing. But, despite that, there was no denying his presence calmed the worst of her fears about leaving the safety of the wagon circle.

Unfortunately, after settling at their post he'd seemed bent on passing the time in conversation.

The need to watch her every word made silence easier, but imprudent, as Adela had pointed out a few days ago.

Since staying mute wasn't the wisest course, she might as well make the most of this opportunity to learn all she could, given that Josiah was more knowledgeable about life on the trail. Besides, if she was the one directing the discussion, she could keep the focus away from thorny areas, such as "Matt's" past.

Her fingers flexed around the barrel of her father's rifle. "I know we're guarding the wagons and livestock." That much was obvious even to her. "But what exactly are we guarding against?" She hoped the darkness hid the flush that heated her cheeks at voicing a question that so starkly revealed her ignorance.

"Coyotes and other critters. They might go after the smaller animals, or search for scraps of food around the campfires. Also, sounds travel far out here, and any sudden noise could spook the livestock and make them bolt. If they do, someone needs to be close by to round up the animals before they get too far." He tilted his head back and glanced overhead. "The sky looks clear tonight, but a sudden thunderstorm could cause a stampede if we're caught unawares. Trouble's more easily averted when you see it coming."

She fiddled with the bottom button on her father's coat. "Just out of curiosity, in any of those letters did Rebecca's sister write about a catastrophe befalling the group because somebody performed poorly during guard duty?"

Josiah turned his head, his gaze coming to rest on her again. "She didn't mention it. Are you worried something like that might happen?"

Her hand curled into a fist, and the button she'd forgotten she was clenching popped off. She hastily stuffed it into her coat pocket. "Well, it's possible, isn't it?"

"I suppose. But don't brood overmuch about it. As long as we keep our eyes open, it's a simple enough job. Most nights the most difficult task you'll face is ensuring you don't nod off." Josiah's teeth flashed white in the darkness. "But talking helps with that. Plus, wild animals are more likely to keep their distance if they hear voices."

"That's good to know."

A few hours later, Mattie turned up her coat collar to ward off the chill in the air and tucked her chin beneath the heavy material. Scanning the darkened landscape, she kept a lookout for any signs of trouble. All was quiet in the camp as the crescent moon tracked across the sky toward midnight.

Once again, she glanced toward the covered wagon

where Adela slumbered. At least, Mattie prayed her sister wasn't lying awake, too scared to sleep. The younger girl had begged not to be left alone. But there wasn't any other choice. Every able-bodied man was expected to take a turn at guard duty. And that included "Matt." But Mattie had departed with the promise that she would watch over Adela from her guard post.

Suddenly catching movement at the edge of her field of vision, she shifted her gaze. A shadow detached itself from the others near the livestock enclosures. Were her eyes playing tricks on her? She didn't want to seem an alarmist, spooking at harmless shadows.

But her gut told her she wasn't wrong. "I think there's someone down by the horses."

Josiah focused his attention where she'd indicated. "I see him. No, wait, there are two of them."

Though her eyes strained for a better view, it was impossible. "I can't make out who they are. But what reason would anyone have for being near the horses in the middle of the night?"

"No good reason that I can think of. Let's go check it out." He pushed to his feet. "We'll approach them quietly until we get close enough to identify them. Best to be cautious when we don't know the lay of the land. If they're strangers up to no good, I can guarantee they're armed."

Panic spread through Mattie at his words, but she fought against it. Others were counting on her to do a job. Innocent people, sleeping blissfully unaware of any trouble that might be visited upon them. And if Mattie couldn't handle it, then Adela was correct that they should never have begun this journey after their father was gone.

Mattie refused to accept her decision was a mistake. It couldn't be. Not when any other choice would have placed her and her sister in a worse situation.

This moment was one of many tests she would face. But she had faith that the Lord would help her through it. And all the others to come.

With that conviction shoring up her shaky courage, she followed Josiah's lead and started down the hill.

She cradled her father's rifle gingerly in her arms, praying she wouldn't need to use it. She'd never fired any type of gun in her life. She had only brought the rifle with her because showing up for guard duty unarmed would have raised questions. But she was more likely to shoot herself in the foot by accident than anything else.

Best not to think about that—though the thoughts which then rushed in to fill her mind weren't any more comforting.

There was nowhere to hide on the vast open prairie, no convenient boulders or shrubs to offer concealment, as she and Josiah worked their way toward the livestock enclosure. All it would take was one of the men down below glancing in their direction, and she and Josiah could find themselves in the middle of a gunfight.

Her mouth ran dry and her heart pounded behind her ribs. *Please, Lord, let there be a perfectly innocent explanation for those two men.* Though their furtive movements unquestionably roused suspicion.

As she drew closer, their purpose became evident. They were tying ropes around the necks of several horses.

And she could now confirm that neither man was a member of their wagon train. "I don't recognize them." She kept her voice low, ensuring it carried no farther than Josiah.

"Horse thieves." Though the words were a bare whisper, his anger clearly bled through.

"What should we do?" she questioned in a quiet murmur.

"We have the element of surprise and can use that to our advantage. We'll—" The rest of his words were drowned out by a camp dog's barking.

"What's that mutt yapping about?" one of the thieves growled as he glanced around. A second later, he spotted Mattie and Josiah. "Someone's coming!"

His partner fired a shot, the sound cracking through the still night air.

Though conscious of Josiah ducking next to her, Mattie stood frozen in place. But in the next moment, her arm was grabbed as Josiah pulled her down to the ground with him.

"Hold your fire," he commanded. "I don't want to risk hitting one of the horses."

"You half-wit!" the first thief growled. "Now the whole camp knows we're here! Let's get out of here." He tried to grasp the ropes.

But the loud noise of the gunshot had unnerved the horses. They danced out of reach, thwarting his efforts. He glanced over his shoulder in the direction of the wagon circle, where several men were emerging with lanterns in hand.

Muttering a curse, he abandoned all attempts to regain control of the skittish animals. "Forget the horses. I'm not sticking around to be caught and hanged!"

He beat a hasty retreat, his partner in crime hot on his heels.

Josiah and Mattie climbed to their feet. After quickly assessing that neither of them had been injured, Josiah moved toward his horses.

"Whoa, easy." His tone soft and gentle, he climbed between the ropes forming the temporary enclosure.

But calming a half dozen horses at once was more than any one man could handle on his own, and Josiah's animals were in danger of breaking through the flimsy barrier.

Here at last was a way Mattie could be useful. She had plenty of experience with horses—unlike most other aspects of trail life.

Despite her worry for the animals and Josiah, her heart felt lighter as she stepped forward to lend him a hand.

Josiah cast a sidelong glance at Matt as the boy waded into the mass of milling horseflesh. It took less than a handful of seconds to determine that this was one area where the kid could hold his own. He plainly knew how to navigate around unsettled horses.

While showing proper caution and respect for their size and strength, he displayed no signs of hesitation or unease. Though one wrong move could see him kicked or even trampled.

As Matt advanced toward the head of one horse, he spoke in low, soothing tones. Fuzzy ears cocked in response. Reaching for the rope encircling the horse's neck, he held the animal in place and stroked her side. The chestnut mare visibly calmed under his gentle ministrations.

The instinctive fear Josiah had felt over Matt's safety vanished, and he wordlessly accepted the boy's assistance.

More men started to arrive then, but they were clearly made wary by the other horses' rolling eyes and stomping hooves, and none braved the space inside the makeshift corral.

"What happened?" the wagon master demanded, breathing heavily after his dash from the wagon circle. "Who fired that shot?"

Matt remained silent, leaving it to Josiah to explain. He did so in a few succinct words and jerked his head toward the two retreating figures, now barely discernible in the darkness.

"Will they come back and try again?" nineteen-year-old Frank Malone asked, as he watched the would-be thieves hightailing it across the prairie.

"It's unlikely," Jed Smith volunteered. "They'd be fools to try anything else tonight, with the entire camp on alert."

Frank's younger brother, Cody, cleared his throat, his blond peach fuzz gleaming in the lantern light. "Shouldn't we go after them? Form a posse or something?"

"There's no need," Elias countered. "They didn't take any of the horses. Besides, they have too much of a head start, and tracking is near impossible at night."

Several men voiced their agreement.

Miles Carpenter moved closer to the rope fence encircling the horses. "Good work running off those thieves, Josiah."

"I didn't do it alone. Matt had a hand in it. In fact,

he's the one who first spotted them." He flicked a quick glance toward Miles.

The news plainly caught the wagon master by surprise, but he quickly recovered. "Job well done, Matt."

The kid was practically hidden behind the large bulk of one horse. Almost as if he would've preferred that no one took any notice of him.

He kept his head down as he replied, "Thanks."

Miles held his lantern aloft to read the face of his pocket watch. "It's almost midnight. Since you men assigned to the second watch are already here, we may as well change the guards now." No one uttered a protest, and he continued, raising his voice to be heard by the small crowd that had gathered. "The rest of you folks head on back to the wagons and get some sleep."

The group dispersed and soon only Josiah and Matt remained, still tending to the horses.

Josiah removed a hastily tied rope from around one horse's neck. "I'm grateful to you for spotting the thieves when you did, Matt. If not for your vigilance, they might have succeeded in stealing the horses before we could stop them." And that would have meant his livelihood. All his plans for starting a ranch in Oregon Country hinged on these horses. He patted the neck of the closest one. "Then you helped keep the animals from bolting. That puts me in your debt twice over."

The kid's back remained turned toward Josiah as he answered. "You've helped me a time or two. So, why don't we call it even?"

"Fair enough." Judging the horses sufficiently calmed, Josiah exited the enclosure, but moved no farther. "You should head back to the wagon circle."

"Aren't you coming?"

"No. I'm going to bed down here for what's left of the night." This patch of dirt was just as comfortable as the spot where he'd intended to sleep near the covered wagons.

"Do you expect more trouble?" Though darkness masked Matt's expression, a hint of worry sounded in his voice.

Josiah shook his head. "But I'll rest easier if I stay close."

"Well, then, good night."

"See you in the morning," Josiah returned.

The boy's nod seemed stiff as he walked away.

Watching his retreating back, Josiah contemplated the puzzle that was Matt Prescott. Just when he thought he had the kid figured out, Matt did something to surprise him.

But perhaps the boy's expertise with horses wasn't so unexpected. After all, back in Tennessee Josiah had encountered his fair share of well-to-do gentlemen who were accomplished horsemen, though sadly inept in other respects.

Several of them had been willfully ignorant besides, with no desire to learn. That didn't appear to be the case with Matt, however. Was it because he had no alternative but to adapt to a different life than the one he'd been raised to lead?

What was his story? The kid was strangely close-mouthed about himself.

Leaving Josiah to draw his own conclusions. How close those were to the actual truth, he could only guess.

Chapter Four

The wind gusted across the prairie as Mattie staked the oxen out at the chosen night campsite more than a week later. Clapping a hand to her hat, she jammed it farther down on her head to prevent it blowing away.

Once the oxen were settled, she started back toward the wagon circle, passing the horse enclosure on her way. One mare stepped forward, her head stretched over the rope fence, seeking attention.

Josiah had ridden out on one of his other horses, as was his habit after the group made camp. He spent a good bit of time each day working with the green-broke horses on a rotating basis, furthering their training.

Mattie paused to stroke the mare's soft nose, then saw the horse was favoring one leg, not putting any weight on it. She couldn't see Josiah ignoring something like this—he cared too much about his animals to ever neglect one of them. The problem must have escaped his notice before he departed.

While she could wait and bring it to his attention upon his return, she could just as easily take a look at it herself.

Despite her words to Josiah several days ago, she didn't consider them even. She'd simply spotted the thieves a few moments before they would have caught Josiah's eye anyway. The balance was still tipped against her, and the fact that she owed him made her leery. A debt could be used to ruin a person, as she'd learned back in Saint Louis.

She never again wanted to be trapped in a position where she was beholden to anyone for anything. And seeing to Josiah's horse right now would help serve as repayment, at least in part.

Her decision made, she ducked under the rope and moved to the mare's side. Running a hand down the leg, Mattie didn't find any signs of injury and lifted the hoof to examine it.

She discovered a rock lodged in the underside and worked to remove it. "You poor baby. Little wonder you didn't want to stand on this hoof."

Once the stone popped free, she released the mare's hoof and straightened. The sound of approaching hoof-beats reached her ears, and she turned to see Josiah atop his mount.

Reining to a stop, he slid to the ground and stared at Mattie's position inside the fence with his horses.

She shifted nervously under his regard and rushed to explain. "I was just removing this rock from her hoof." She kicked the offending object out of the corral.

"I know. I saw what you were doing."

Her palms grew moist, and she wiped them against her pant legs. "Then why are you looking at me as if I'm an undiscovered species of bug you've pinned to a board in order to study?"

The corner of his mouth turned up in a crooked

smile. "Perhaps you *are* a previously unknown species, at that. You're certainly not what I expected."

"What do you mean?" she asked, then wondered whether she truly wanted to hear his unvarnished opinion of her—or rather *him*? Was she prepared for whatever Josiah might say? Probably not. But it was too late for her to call back the question.

"Well, it's been my experience that most high-society gents leave the dirty work to others. Take Hardwick, for example. While he's arguably a competent rider, I have yet to witness him caring for his own mount. Odds are, he's never even considered removing a rock from a horse's hoof, beyond ordering someone else to see to it. But you? You plainly have the know-how. I find that rather unusual."

If he thought it unexpected in a male, he wouldn't imagine for even an instant that a gently bred lady possessed such skills. Thus, she could be relatively certain he would never deduce her true identify. That was a relief. But he still seemed to be waiting for an explanation, and she had no idea what to say.

She supposed she could have told him that after her mother's passing the stables had become her refuge when she needed to escape the oppressive atmosphere of mourning inside the house. Surrounded by the horses, she'd found a measure of peace. And the long hours spent in the barn meant she knew the grooms' and stable hands' jobs almost as well as they did.

But she only said, "A little work's never bothered me. I like knowing I can take care of myself without the need for servants. It's a sorry state of events when a body can't even get dressed without assistance."

Josiah cocked his head to the side. "You're full of surprises, kid."

He had no idea just how true his words were. And that's the way it had to stay.

"Well, I'd better get back to Adela now." She exited the enclosure and started toward the wagons, then abruptly turned back. "It's probably a good idea to keep an eye on that hoof tonight, check that the rock didn't do any damage that might be exacerbated by further travel."

"I'll do that."

Nodding once, she spun on her heels and walked away.

As she neared the wagon circle, the wind picked up, flapping the canvas bonnet material of the wagons against the arched wooden supports. Flames from the campfires leaped higher. Dirt flew into her eyes, making them water, and the cold air stung her exposed cheeks.

Arriving at her covered wagon, Mattie spotted Adela struggling to weave a little girl's brown hair into braids while the wind did its best to whip the strains out of her hands. The child's presence no longer came as a surprise—it had taken mere days for little Sarah Jane to become Adela's shadow.

And Edith Baker's youngest wasn't the only child who was often underfoot. The smaller children seemed irresistibly drawn to Adela, who had stood by her promise to keep them entertained and occupied. Often with the aid of another girl about her age, Charlotte Malone.

The mothers appreciated the help riding herd on their little ones, while Adela in turn benefited from the support of other females. Since Mattie wasn't in a position to fill that role herself, she could only be grateful for the women's acceptance of her sister.

Despite the fear that it might put her secret at risk.

She simply had to trust that Adela was ever mindful of the danger and guarded her tongue around the others. Just as Mattie did with Josiah and the other men.

"Supper's going to be full of grit," Mattie commented, noting the uncovered pot suspended above the cooking fire. The cast-iron lid clinked into place as she remedied the situation.

"Sorry." Adela grimaced and brushed aside loose tendrils of hair the wind blew across her eyes. "I forgot to replace the cover after I stirred the food. But at least I didn't let it burn this time."

Mattie made a noncommittal sound in response.

Despite Rebecca Dawson's instructions, Adela's cooking ability hadn't improved much over the past fortnight. More often than not, Mattie returned to camp after completing her own chores only to find the food burned or otherwise unappetizing. But at least Adela's complaints had decreased. With all the challenges they faced, Mattie supposed that small victory was enough for now.

After supper that evening, Josiah and Elias worked together to stake their covered wagon to the ground, to prevent it tipping over in the high winds that hadn't abated as the sunlight waned.

The task complete, Josiah glanced around the wagon circle to see that most other families had done the same. Or were making a start on it, at least. Including Matt Prescott.

The past couple weeks had proved that the kid was adept at learning what to do by observing those who were more experienced. He had conquered many an obstacle in that way.

But this job looked to be getting the better of him. Though he clearly understood what needed to be done, he struggled with the heavy iron chains. And his slight frame didn't have the sheer weight required to swing the unwieldy mallet with enough force to drive the stakes deep into the hard-packed earth.

Josiah started forward, and as he neared the Prescotts' wagon, he caught Matt muttering, "This would be a lot easier if I had a third hand."

Squatting down next to the kid, Josiah held out his palms. "How about one of these?"

Matt gasped and narrowly missed smashing his thumb with the mallet.

Josiah curled his hands into fists and let them drop. "Sorry, kid. I didn't mean to startle you. But you're right—this will be quicker work with an extra set of hands. Why don't you thread the chain between the spokes and over the iron rim of the wheels, while I pound in the stakes?"

The boy hesitated a moment before nodding. "Thank you."

Accepting the proffered mallet, Josiah shifted back slightly to give Matt space to maneuver. Links of chain clinked together as he positioned the heavy iron. Then Josiah swung the mallet, filling the air with a series of dull thuds.

The temperature had dropped in the last hour, and his hands felt numbed from the cold even inside a pair of leather gloves. He flexed his fingers as he followed behind Matt, who had already moved on to the next wheel.

Gusts of wind buffeted the covered wagon while they worked to secure it. Josiah prayed it didn't tip over in the meantime and crush either of them. And he sent fervent thanks heavenward when the job was done.

Soon afterward, he left the Prescotts and headed in the direction of his horses. He was greeted by a chestnut mare prancing along the edge of the enclosure.

Patting her neck, Josiah glanced back over his shoulder toward Matt. "What do you make of him, Flame? He's a puzzle, sure enough. Still, I can't help but like the kid."

The mare bobbed her head up and down as if indicating approval.

Josiah didn't consider it the least bit outlandish that he was consulting a horse for a second opinion. He'd found they were excellent judges of character, better than most people at sensing when an individual possessed a cruel streak. Or perhaps it was simply that men didn't feel any need to hide their true selves from animals.

The horses had never displayed any hints of fear or aversion toward Matt Prescott. In fact, they always moved forward, eager for his attention, whenever he approached.

"I reckon he's a good kid at heart, Flame." With a final pat to the mare's glossy coat, he checked on the other horses before rejoining Elias and Rebecca by their campfire.

His sister-in-law greeted him with a smile. "It was kind of you to go over and help Matt." Her mouth turned down slightly. "The poor boy's in over his head, with no male family members to support him."

"A bit, perhaps," Josiah acknowledged as he took a seat and stretched his legs out in front of him. "But sooner or later every young man has to step out into the world on his own for the first time. I was no different, years ago. Only in my case, I had an older brother who rode to my rescue." Though admittedly, the time between his mother's death and Elias's arrival had been tough.

At thirteen, Josiah had already been working odd jobs for years to help his mother as much as he could. But the money he made wasn't near enough to cover room and board for himself once she was gone. And the townspeople who had looked down on Louisa Dawson hadn't stirred themselves to offer charity to her orphaned son.

He didn't want to think about what his life would be now, if his half brother hadn't shown up. When he'd been at his lowest point, the Lord had sent Elias to him. To lift Josiah up.

Now that he was in a place where he could, he felt called to help others less fortunate. It was his small way of showing thanks for the blessing he'd been given when his brother had appeared in his life just as Josiah needed him most.

"And now you're doing the same for another boy." Rebecca reached over and placed her fingers on Josiah's arm, her expression beaming with approval. "You're a good man."

He drew his legs up and folded his hands together between his bent knees. "I try to be."

Elias clasped Josiah's shoulder and gave it a squeeze. "That's all any of us can do."

Half an hour later, Josiah covered a yawn with his hand. "It's been a long day, so I'm going to call it a night. I'll see you both in the morning." He left the pair sitting by their campfire and headed back toward the horse enclosure.

Since he wasn't scheduled for guard duty, he opted to bed down near his horses, fearing the turbulent weather might unsettle them.

Somewhere around midnight, rain began to fall. It made for an uncomfortable night out in the open. But the oilskin cloth on the outside of Josiah's bedroll kept the worst of the dampness from soaking into his clothes. At least until he got up to check on his horses.

The storm suddenly seemed to gain intensity, as the rain blew sideways, pelting him with fat drops. He regretted his lack of forethought, that he hadn't retrieved his rain slicker from the covered wagon earlier.

But he was nowhere near as wet and miserable as the horses standing huddled together. Rainwater sluiced off their coats, and the wind blew their sodden tails out behind them like streamers. The drenching wasn't likely to cause any lasting harm to such hardy stock, but they looked pitiful all the same.

Near dawn, the deluge let up at last—leaving behind a soggy quagmire even hours later. While the group enjoyed a welcome respite from the dust, the mud added a new hindrance. Over the course of the morning, several wagons became mired along the trail. It slowed their progress, and tempers were short.

Especially when Hardwick's overloaded wagon got stuck tight, and he simply stood back, expecting others to assist his servants in doing the physical labor required to free it.

Josiah, along with Matt and half a dozen other men, put a shoulder against the tailgate, while the oxen strained at the front. But whereas lighter wagons had been freed with relative ease, it was no use this time. The wheels had sunk deep and refused to budge.

"This isn't working," the man to Josiah's right grunted in frustration. In his early forties, Thomas Malone was tall and thin with pale blond hair—traits he'd passed down to all four of his children.

"Stop pushing for a minute," Miles instructed. "We need to come up with a different plan."

Glad for the opportunity to take a breather, Josiah relaxed his muscles and propped an arm against the wagon box.

Jed Smith rubbed his jaw as he studied the covered wagon, then turned toward the wagon master. "If we unload some of the heavier items, then we might be able to push it forward."

Several heads nodded in accord.

But Hardwick took exception. "You dare to suggest that priceless antiques be placed in the muck?" Pinching a tiny dot of mud from his trousers, he cleaned his fingertips on a monogrammed handkerchief. "I will not hear of it!"

His words were greeted by angry retorts from many of the others, all of whom were mud-splattered from head to toe.

A piercing whistle cut through the ruckus, halting the grumbles of discontent. "Does anyone have any other ideas?" Miles inserted into the silence.

Matt used the back of his hand to wipe a trickle of

sweat from his temple, leaving a streak of grime behind on his skin.

Josiah didn't expect the boy to say anything, since he'd noticed that Matt seemed shy to open his mouth around the others.

It caught him by surprise when the kid piped up with a suggestion. "What if we added more oxen to the front?"

"You mean unhitch a team or two from another wagon and hook 'em up to this one?" Thomas Malone checked.

Mattie prayed she hadn't made a mistake by speaking up, but it was too late for second thoughts now. With everyone's attention focused squarely on her, she had to brazen it out. "Sure. Why not?"

"That's not a bad idea, actually," the wagon master mused, his fingers stroking his gray beard. "With more pulling power, that just might work. It's certainly worth a try."

Josiah stepped forward to volunteer. "I'll handle the oxen, get them in position."

"Much appreciated," Miles Carpenter replied. "Jed, why don't you go along with him?"

"Sure thing."

"And the rest of you men, get ready to push once the oxen are in place," the wagon master finished.

"We're all set up here," Jed called a few minutes later.

"Josiah!" the wagon master raised his voice to be heard. "You stay at the head of the oxen and get them moving." He turned to the group standing at the back of the covered wagon. "And everyone else—on the count of three, we push. One. Two. Three."

Mattie added her efforts to the others struggling to push the wagon from behind. Her muscles strained to equal her determination.

"Put your backs into it, men!" Lord Hardwick ordered from his vantage point well away from the worst of the mud.

Mattie would've shot a glare at him over her shoulder if she could have spared the energy. But all her concentration had to stay focused on the task at hand.

When the wagon remained stuck for several seconds, she worried that this wasn't going to work, after all. But just as she'd concluded they would have to give up, the mud released its grip with a sucking sound, enabling the wheels to roll forward.

A cheer went up among the men on either side of her.

"Good thinking, kid." Elias Dawson clapped her on the back.

The action sent her stumbling forward a step and knocked her hat over her eyes.

Straightening, she repositioned the headwear. "Thank you."

Despite the dull throbbing above her shoulder blade, she was warmed by his praise. It felt as if she'd made a worthwhile contribution, for a change. Done something that benefited the entire group.

Finally, she was pulling her own weight and proving an asset, not a hindrance to anybody.

And that lessened her guilt slightly over the deception she was perpetrating against these good people.

But only slightly.

Chapter Five

"Elias and I are going hunting. Why don't you come along?" Josiah invited Mattie a few days later.

Hunting? Her heart raced in panic.

Though she felt more comfortable holding her father's rifle now—at least enough so she no longer feared accidentally shooting herself—there was a world of difference between carrying a gun around and actually firing it. She had little faith in beginner's luck, and the likelihood of her hitting a specific target was practically nil.

But she didn't want to admit that aloud. "I should stay here, near Adela."

"There's no need. Rebecca will keep an eye on her while the women wash clothes. And Miles already has enough volunteers working on the repairs to Hardwick's wagon." Undoubtedly overtaxed while battling the mud three days ago, a broken axle had forced their group to stop early.

And though sunset was still several hours away, the camp was already set up. She couldn't think of any other excuse. Still, she hesitated.

"Are you game?" Josiah prompted. "I don't know about you, but I'd sure like to add some fresh meat to our stores."

He made a valid point. She and Adela could certainly use an additional food source. Cooking mishaps had dwindled their supplies faster than anticipated. And while Mattie lacked any hunting skills, she was sure the Dawson brothers did not. If she went along with them and they were successful, would they share with her?

Even if they didn't, she could gain some valuable knowledge that might prove useful later. "Let me get my rifle."

On the way to her wagon, Mattie glanced toward the river to check on her sister and spotted Adela near the water's edge. She was attired more practically in a simple calico dress at last, after several of her fancy gowns had been ruined by fire, mud and the rigors of day-to-day trail conditions.

Numerous small children scampered around Adela, and she kept them occupied while the older women focused on scrubbing mud-stained clothing. The smile on Adela's face matched those of her young charges, and their laughter rang out in joyous peals.

As Mattie watched, two-year-old Lizzie Linton, the preacher's daughter, took a tumble, which had been aided by a shove from her five-year-old brother, Henry. She started to cry, and Adela was there in a flash, scooping up Lizzie and inspecting her for injury, then soothing her tears. Though her sister's words were indistinguishable to Mattie from this distance, her tone was easily recognizable. When she admonished the boy for his naughty behavior, she was patient and kind.

Turning away from the scene, Mattie ducked inside her wagon to retrieve her father's rifle, then returned to where Josiah waited with Elias.

The three set off, and she paid close attention to everything the brothers did, then tried to mimic them. They kept their eyes on the ground, and she guessed they were looking for tracks or other indications of animals. One patch of dirt looked much the same as another to her, however.

After several minutes of walking, Josiah stopped and squatted down to take a closer look at…something.

Elias glanced over his brother's shoulder. "Looks like antelope tracks."

Josiah nodded. "But no telling how old they are. The last rain might have been days ago. Or longer, if the storm that drenched us missed this area."

Elias's eyes swept over the surrounding vicinity. "I don't see anything from here, but there's a depression out toward the east that's probably big enough to hide a large animal. We'll follow the tracks for a ways and see if they head in that direction."

Josiah straightened and led the way along a deliberate but winding path.

Taking her gaze off the ground, Mattie looked out across the landscape, trying to spot any animals. The wind sighed through the tall grasses, setting them rustling, a wheat-colored sea of motion that could easily conceal an animal of similar coloring.

Although the prairie appeared flat, Mattie had learned over the past few weeks that it actually rose in slight hills then descended into lower spots in seemingly endless succession.

She looked behind her, in the direction they'd come

from, and noted they had traveled a good distance. From here, the wagon circle looked small and insignificant on the vastness of the plains.

As she took a step, the toe of her boot caught and she stumbled.

Josiah glanced back at her. "What happened?"

"I wasn't watching where I was walking," she admitted. "And I stepped in a hole."

"You need to keep your eyes on the ground."

She nodded in understanding. "I don't want to twist an ankle."

"Or step on a rattlesnake," Elias added.

"Rattlesnakes?" She froze in place.

"Yeah. They'll usually let you know when you're getting too close, but you don't want to sneak up on one and surprise it."

"No, I definitely don't want to do that." Before taking another step, she scanned the nearby clumps of grass for any slithering serpents intent on ambush.

Josiah stretched out his arm to bar her way. "Stay still."

She froze a second time. "Why? Is there a snake?" Her eyes darted around the ground again.

"No. A jackrabbit. Over there."

Her breath gusted out as her gaze followed the direction he was pointing.

"Why don't you take the shot, Matt?" Elias invited.

Her eyes flew to him in horror. She couldn't shoot a poor, defenseless bunny!

But "Matt" wouldn't be plagued by any feminine hesitation. She schooled her expression before either of the men could read her true feelings.

She had to play her part.

Assuming her unmanly snake panic hadn't already given her away.

She raised her rifle, but didn't bother to aim at the rabbit, only pointed the gun in its general direction. She doubted she could hit it even if she *was* trying. That would take practice, surely. So the sweet little bunny rabbit would be safe.

She'd watched her father handle the rifle a time or two and knew he kept it loaded. Firing it should be a simple enough matter, since hitting a target wasn't her goal. Reloading would present a problem, however, as she hadn't even thought to bring the shot and powder necessary. But she'd worry about that later.

When she pulled the trigger, the wooden end of the gun slammed into her shoulder with unexpected force, knocking her to the ground.

The loud blast left her ears ringing and the rabbit fleeing.

Raising his own rifle, Elias took aim. But his shot also missed, and the rabbit disappeared from sight.

Though hunting was a necessity, she couldn't help feeling relieved it had escaped unscathed.

But she wasn't as fortunate. Her shoulder throbbed.

Josiah reached down, hand extended. "Are you all right?"

"I'm fine." She grasped his hand, and as he pulled her to her feet, she had to stifle a groan behind gritted teeth. The movement had sent pain shooting through her injured shoulder. But she couldn't let the men know she was hurting.

If Elias insisted on examining her, he might discover her secret.

She couldn't risk that.

As she'd feared, Josiah's brother moved toward her. "Let me take a look."

"No!" Shying away from his touch, she sidestepped out of reach. "I told you, I'm fine."

She hoped it was true. But what if she'd broken a bone? Her shoulder certainly hurt enough for that to be a possibility.

If the injury didn't heal on its own, she'd have no choice but to reveal the truth to the doctor.

Josiah wondered over Matt's behavior. Why didn't he want Elias to check him over? It was clear the kid wasn't "fine," as he'd claimed.

Was he embarrassed that his inexperience with the firearm had been revealed?

Josiah could see how the boy's pride might prevent him from admitting to a weakness, but he should have owned up to it. If he had, he would've avoided injuring himself.

Not to mention, his shot had gone a yard wide, and they'd lost the rabbit.

Josiah acknowledged that he wasn't just upset about losing the chance for some fresh meat—he was hurt that the boy still didn't trust him enough to ask for help. After realizing Josiah had seen through his ruse that first day on the trail, by now the kid should've known that Josiah wouldn't betray his confidence.

Over the past several weeks, they'd become better acquainted. The boy didn't say much about his past, but his actions spoke well of him. He wasn't afraid of hard work, and though his size was a handicap on occasion, his determination saw him through. That said a lot about his character.

Despite his privileged upbringing, he had grit. Instead of whining about his change in circumstance, he pressed forward and did what needed to be done. And no one could ask for anything more from him than that.

How could the kid not realize that he'd already earned Josiah's respect? That Josiah wouldn't think any less of him if he admitted his inexperience?

"We should head back." Elias's words broke into his brother's thoughts.

Checking the position of the sun, Josiah noted it was edging toward the horizon.

He nodded in agreement and retraced his steps, keeping an eye on Matt as they made their way toward the wagon train.

The boy carried his rifle in his uninjured arm and appeared to be taking special care with his other shoulder, holding it as still as possible. But he kept pace with them, never asking for allowances, even when a grimace briefly twisted his features.

How bad *was* his injury? Everyday tasks on the trail were physically demanding, and the kid could hurt himself worse if he tried to do too much.

As they reached the circle of covered wagons, Miles waylaid Josiah, and Matt took the opportunity to speed ahead to his own wagon.

Waving his brother to continue on without him, Josiah turned his attention to the wagon master. "What can I do for you, Miles?"

"I wanted to talk to you about Matt Prescott. I had my doubts about his capabilities at the start, but I just didn't have the heart to leave those two young'uns behind. The boy's done better than I was expecting. Still,

I'd like to thank you for stepping in to help on occasion." His words brought a verse to mind.

Let each man look out not only for his own interests, but also for the interests of others.

"I was glad to do it."

The older man clapped Josiah on the back. "Well, I'm sure you have things to do, so I'll let you get to them." He headed off to see to his own duties as wagon master.

As long as Matt didn't pose a threat to the group or slow them down, Miles seemed satisfied. Hopefully, that wouldn't change due to the kid's recent self-inflicted impairment.

Josiah recalled one particular letter from Rebecca's sister, in which Abigail wrote of a wagon left behind when the family took sick and couldn't keep up with the rest of the group.

The hard truth was that while the pioneers pulled together to support one another when a job required additional hands, someone in need of ongoing assistance—and lacking a handy pair of servants to take up his slack—most likely wouldn't be tolerated.

Say, a young man hobbled by injury, for instance.

The only way to find out whether it was a baseless fear or serious cause for concern was to convince Matt to let Elias take a look at his shoulder.

With that in mind, Josiah went in search of the kid.

Arriving at the Prescotts' wagon, he found Adela by the campfire, but her brother was nowhere in sight. "Where's Matt?"

The girl pointed behind her. "She's in the wagon."

"Thanks." He moved toward the tailgate, then paused as her words replayed in his mind. He turned back to face her. *"She?"* Surely, he couldn't have heard right.

But one look at Adela's expression—her eyes widening in horror as she clapped a hand over her mouth—convinced him there was nothing wrong with his hearing.

He spun on his heel and ripped open the wagon's canvas flaps.

An attractive female stared back at him, her guilt-filled amber eyes fringed by thick lashes.

"I don't believe it." But he was looking at the proof with his own eyes.

Her face was clearly visible without the wide-brimmed hat she always wore. Hid behind, he now realized. But he'd seen her without it a time or two and hadn't recognized the truth. How had he missed it?

Now that he knew, it was obvious she was a woman, despite her short hair and masculine attire. She was too pretty to be a boy.

He *had* harbored some suspicions. But he'd been on the wrong track. Though certain the kid was hiding something, Josiah had believed it was inexperience on the trail. Not a much bigger secret.

Viewed through his changed perception, he suddenly had a whole new picture of the past several weeks. The reason the boy rarely looked people in the eye might not be due to shyness, but the fear of discovery. That would also account for why "Matt" had been sparing with details about his past.

So many clues that Josiah had noticed, only to come up with other ways to explain them away, never guessing the truth. It was small comfort that no one else had seen it, either.

She'd fooled everyone.

But why? What would lead a young woman to masquerade as a boy?

He climbed inside the wagon to confront her, but before he could open his mouth, a noise behind him drew his attention. He turned to find Adela poking her head between the canvas flaps.

"I want to speak to your *sister* alone."

Adela didn't take the hint, her gaze focused intently on her sister. "Mattie?"

"It's okay, Adela," she assured. "Everything will be fine."

The younger girl hesitated for a moment more before retreating, her head disappearing from sight.

He pivoted back toward Matt—no, *Mattie*.

She shrank away from him. "What are you going to do?"

Her question hung suspended between them.

Mattie felt sick with tension at suddenly finding herself alone with a man—a very angry one, if his thunderous expression was any indication. He knew she was a female, and he was clearly riled up by her deception. Riled enough to hurt her?

Was Josiah about to prove her impression of him up until now was wrong? Regardless, she wouldn't cower, no matter the fear that filled her heart.

But he didn't move any closer, and his face relaxed into softer, less intimidating lines. "I just want to talk."

Her muscles remained knotted as she waited in uneasy dread.

Taking off his hat, he placed it on his knee and ran

his fingers through the damp strands of his red-gold hair. "Why the deception?"

"It was the only way Adela and I could get to our relatives in Oregon City. One group had already left us behind when we no longer had a man traveling with us after our father's death. I couldn't give anyone else the chance to make the same decision."

"The rules are there for a reason," Josiah pointed out, no doubt remembering every time he'd been forced to step in and help her over the past few weeks.

He couldn't understand what it was like to be in her position.

Here or back in Independence, she and her sister were still women alone without the protection of family. They needed to reach their aunt and uncle in Oregon Country—but they never would if no one allowed them to join a wagon train.

That hadn't seemed to trouble the wagon master who'd abandoned two women in a strange town. Other than ensuring she and Adela weren't *his* problem, he hadn't cared what happened to them.

"My gender doesn't make any difference in whether I can do the job, and I think I've done pretty well."

"You have," he agreed, surprising her. "But I still have to tell Miles about this." He made a move to exit the wagon.

"You can't!" Grabbing his arm, she stopped him from leaving. "Who knows what he'll do? Please. Don't give me away."

Chapter Six

Josiah grasped her hand to move it from his arm, but he paused when his finger brushed across a ridged scab. Turning her hand over, he found her palm marred by several healing cuts and painful-looking ruptured blisters.

She was a petite woman, and from what he knew of her background it was clear she'd been raised as a lady—but she'd done the work of a man. He wouldn't have credited it if he hadn't seen it for himself.

No wonder she had run into difficulties a time or two. He was amazed it hadn't happened more often. The only help she'd received had come from him, and it had consisted mostly of offered advice and verbal instructions. There had been no reason to mollycoddle a boy by performing tasks for him.

His thumb stroked the center of her palm, over the white line of a freshly healed cut. Though it was irrational, he felt personally responsible for every nick and scrape, as if he had inflicted the wounds himself.

She snatched her hand away and curled it into a fist,

hiding the damage from sight. "Mr. Carpenter can't find out the truth. There's no telling what he'd do."

Josiah shifted position in the cramped space and braced a hand on his knee. "He might surprise you. You didn't give him a chance before."

Skepticism shone in her eyes. "Do you honestly believe that would have made any difference?"

He started to nod, then paused. *Did* he believe it? He wanted to. But Mattie and her sister had been left behind by a wagon train before, which meant she had valid cause for her concern. He couldn't simply dismiss it out of hand, without giving due consideration to the possible consequences.

If presented with the truth, would Miles make accommodations to aid the sisters? Or would he put the needs of the group as a whole over his sympathy for a few individuals? Josiah didn't know, but either way the Prescotts wouldn't be allowed to continue on the same as they had been previously. Things would change.

Some of what he was thinking must have shown on his face.

Mattie's expression set in stubborn lines as she shook her head. "I can't risk it. If Miles Carpenter refuses to allow us to continue with the wagon train, Adela and I will be abandoned here, in the middle of nowhere. It's nearly impossible for anyone to survive on their own in this rugged land. What chance would my sister and I have?"

Josiah was reminded of the family mentioned in Abigail's letter. She hadn't written a word about what had happened to them after they were left behind by the wagon train. Most likely, she'd never learned their fate.

How would he feel, never knowing what had become of the Prescotts? Being left to wonder if they had perished somewhere along the trail? It would remain a troubling torment for the rest of his days.

He didn't want it to come to that.

But even if he agreed to keep Mattie's secret, someone else would inevitability learn the truth just as he had. "Others are going to find out long before we reach the end of the journey," he felt compelled to point out.

"Not if you don't tell anyone."

Was she really that naive? They would be on the trail for another four months or so. How could she possibly think to maintain her disguise for that length of time?

"Don't you think people will catch on when Adela calls you 'Mattie'? She's slipped up in front of me more than once and will doubtlessly do so around others, as well."

"No one will think twice about Adela calling her brother by a nickname. You didn't, did you?"

He had to concede her point. "You're right." But that wasn't what had tipped him off. "What *will* grab their attention is if she refers to you as a 'she' again."

Mattie seemed momentarily dismayed by this revelation, but her expression quickly cleared. "I'll talk to her. I'm sure she'll be more careful from now on."

Though he had doubts, he didn't press that particular issue. "Even if she does guard her tongue, that still leaves any number of other ways for your secret to get out. What if an unscrupulous man learns the truth and demands payment for his silence?"

Her back stiffened. "And how would he have learned the truth? From you?"

His words weren't meant to be a threat, and it caught

him by surprise that she'd taken them as such. "No, of course not."

She folded her arms across her stomach. "You haven't made any promises yet. Maybe it's *you* who expects payment."

"No, I don't." It rankled that she would suspect him of such appalling motives, but he couldn't really fault her when he was the one who had brought up the subject. "I was just trying to show you what kind of problems you might encounter." For all the good it had done him.

He should have saved his breath. The warning hadn't given her pause.

"Does that mean you'll keep my secret?" The woman could give stubbornness lessons to a mule.

He slapped his hat against his thigh in frustration. She'd met all his arguments with resistance, refusing to surrender her position. And he couldn't think of anything else to say that might convince her to change her mind.

Could he give her the assurance she wanted?

Lord, help me to make the right decision.

There was no immediate answer.

Josiah could only guess at how Miles would react to this situation. And if he was wrong…? Mattie and her sister would be the ones to pay for his error in judgment. He couldn't gamble with their lives like that. Someone needed to look out for them.

Since there was no one else, he guessed he was it.

As long as Mattie's pretense didn't endanger her physical safety or that of any others, he wouldn't talk to the wagon master about it. And he prayed that no one else found out the truth, either. Though it seemed like asking for the impossible.

"I won't tell Miles. But your shoulder needs to be looked at. Let me get Elias—"

She was already shaking her head before he got all the words out. "I won't be able to keep the truth from him if he examines me. The fewer people who know, the better."

Josiah wanted to insist, but if Mattie felt so strongly about it, he would honor her wishes.

He reluctantly nodded his agreement. "We'll do it your way." For now, at least. "But you have to be completely honest with me about something." He caught her gaze to judge the truthfulness of her answer in her eyes.

Dread coiled in Mattie's stomach. "Honest about what?"

He was already privy to more than she felt comfortable with. Especially given the fact she wasn't sure she could trust him. She wouldn't hand him potential weapons that could be used against her.

"Your shoulder." Concern darkened his eyes. "How bad is it hurt?"

Her apprehension calmed by several degrees, but she couldn't relax completely. "I'm not sure," she admitted.

He glanced away, his expression troubled. Would he go back on his word?

She couldn't allow him the opportunity. "But it will be fine in a few days," she quickly assured him, praying it wasn't a lie.

There was no blood spurting out, or bones sticking through her skin. No signs of something in need of immediate attention. So, it wasn't anything serious, surely?

But what if she was wrong? Not letting the doctor look at her could have devastating consequences later on. She pushed the worrying thought aside, however.

Protecting her secret was more important than coddling a minor injury. She wouldn't allow irrational fears free rein, causing her to make a decision that might all too easily prove disastrous for her and Adela.

Josiah captured her gaze again. "Does it hurt to move your arm?"

She rotated her shoulder, demonstrating that her range of motion wasn't hindered. "It's sore, but not the sharp pain from when it first happened. It's more of a dull ache now."

"And your shoulder's the only thing that hurts?" he checked. "You don't have any pain anywhere else?"

She shook her head. Her derriere, where she'd hit the ground hard, was a bit tender, and sitting down would be uncomfortable for the next few days. But that wasn't something she'd ever mention in front of him.

He was silent for a minute before he seemed to reach a decision. "Well, I'm no doctor, but I suppose I've managed to pick up enough from my brother and from working with horses to make a decent estimation of whether an injury's serious or not." His tense expression eased somewhat. "It doesn't sound like anything's broken. It's probably just bruised."

She gaped at him until she realized he was talking about her shoulder and not another part of her anatomy. "I'm sure you're right."

"But we don't want it to become a bigger problem.

I'll get some medicine from my brother that will help it heal." He held up a hand as she opened her mouth to speak. "It's not up for debate." The determined set of his expression made it clear he wouldn't budge.

Snapping her mouth closed, she nodded.

He settled his hat back on his head and moved toward the rear of the wagon. "I'll be back." Climbing to the ground, he disappeared from sight.

Though he had agreed to her request, she remained uncertain of his true intent. He'd been kind and decent to her thus far—but he was still little more than a stranger. Could she trust his word?

He wouldn't be the first man who made false promises to her. Charles Worthington, her ex-fiancé, had been the son of her father's boss. They'd been acquainted for years, and he had appeared all that was good and honorable. But his entire character was a lie.

After she'd discovered the truth and called off their marriage just days before the wedding, her father was left with a mountain of debts to cover the costs for a ceremony that never happened. Even though the elaborate and expensive preparations had been done at her future mother-in-law's insistence, the Worthingtons had directed all bills to Mattie's father. But he was unable to pay them, as he'd been fired from his job and blacklisted by his former employer for the embarrassment Mattie had caused by calling off the wedding.

With the loss of income and mounting demands for payment from countless local business owners, the situation had become grim. Especially when several of her father's investments failed to bring the returns he was counting on. He'd been forced to sell the family home to cover the debts, and afterward he had no desire to stay in Saint Louis. Their remaining money had gone toward the wagon and supplies, with the hope of a better life awaiting them in Oregon Country.

Mattie thanked the Lord every day that she'd escaped from her ex-fiancé, a man who was a sinner to his core. But she never forgot that her loved ones had paid the price for her freedom.

Was trusting Josiah yet another mistake that would hurt her family?

She hadn't known him for very long. Only a couple weeks. It was entirely possible he could have fooled her for that length of time. Though she couldn't imagine why he would put up a front for someone as insignificant as "Matt," that didn't mean he hadn't.

Her anxiety level rose at the thought.

Now would be the perfect opportunity for Josiah to go running to Miles Carpenter. His promise might be nothing more than a smoke screen, allowing him to catch her by surprise.

Please, Lord, show him to be a good and honest man, that I haven't misplaced my trust again.

She waited, her ears straining for any noises that would tell her what was going on outside the wagon. But all she heard were the typical sounds of the camp settling in for the night. Still, when the canvas flap was suddenly pulled back she expected the worst.

It was only Adela, however. Mattie willed her heart to return to its normal rhythm, but she was too on edge.

The younger girl climbed into the wagon, her face revealing her consternation. "I'm sorry, Mattie. I didn't mean to do it. Please, say you believe me!"

She appeared so contrite that Mattie didn't have the heart to scold her. "I do."

Adela wrung her hands. "What is he going to do?"

Mattie placed her hand over Adela's, stilling their nervous movement, but before she could answer, a knock sounded on the covered wagon's wooden frame and both sisters jumped.

Giving Adela's fingers a comforting squeeze, Mattie moved past her to lift the flap, dreading who she'd see there. But it wasn't the wagon master, or even Elias.

Only Josiah. "Here's the liniment for your shoulder."

She accepted the jar he held out.

Adela came up beside her. "If you don't need me, Mattie, I'll check on dinner."

"Go ahead." She moved aside, allowing Adela to exit the wagon.

Josiah offered his arm and helped the younger girl to the ground.

Mattie didn't immediately retreat back inside. "Did you have any problems getting this?" She indicated the jar.

He shook his head, but a shadow crossed his expression. He didn't offer anything more, however.

It appeared he had kept his word. Thus far.

She immediately felt ashamed for assuming he might yet break her trust. Was she doing him an injustice, judging him on another man's actions and not his own merit?

Josiah hadn't given her any reason to doubt his integrity. Instead of using the knowledge of her inexperience against her—as he'd had ample opportunity to do—or simply leaving her to flounder alone, he'd provided assistance. And from the start, when he'd spared her from a beating at Hardwick's hands, Josiah had helped Mattie without expecting anything in return.

Though it was difficult for her to take any man at face value, she had no option other than to put her faith in Josiah.

"Thank you for the liniment."

He nodded in acknowledgment, but didn't say anything more.

She released the flap and the material fell back into place, cutting off her view of him.

Josiah moved to the far side of the wagon circle, hoping to avoid questions about why he was loitering here. It seemed like nothing went unnoticed in the close proximity on the trail.

He was amazed that Mattie had avoided detection this long. But somehow she had.

And he couldn't do anything that would draw undue attention to her now.

He scanned the rapidly darkening landscape. Though there wasn't likely to be many people wandering outside the circle of covered wagons, the men assigned to guard duty would be heading to their posts soon. For now, Josiah didn't see any movement, nor did he hear anything other than the normal sounds of night closing in on the prairie. Everything seemed peaceful and harmonious for the wagon train. Yet he knew they'd all be thrown into turmoil if Mattie's deception was revealed.

After the experiences of his childhood, he couldn't help worrying about what might then befall the Prescott sisters. And imagining the worst.

His mother's life hadn't been easy after her husband learned her second son was another man's child.

Samuel Dawson wasn't a forgiving man. Refusing to take responsibility for the fruit of his wife's indiscretion, he'd abandoned her and cruelly kept their son, Elias, from her.

Left with no choice but to live with a man not her husband, both Louisa and Josiah had suffered the derisive remarks and disdainful looks of self-righteous people as far back as he could remember.

Though his father was gone more often than not, at least the arrangement had offered Louisa a measure of financial support and security. After his death, however, she'd been preyed on by men more than willing to take advantage of the situation.

Now, Josiah feared the same happening to Mattie and her sister if they were ejected from the wagon train.

His hands clenched into fists at the thought. He'd been powerless to do anything to help his mother, but he was grown now and wouldn't let the same thing occur this time.

No man would be given the opportunity to take advantage of either Prescott sister.

And Mattie was right that secrecy was her best protection right now. The more people who knew her true identity, the more likely it wouldn't remain a secret.

Josiah was absolutely certain Elias would never betray her, but he felt he had no choice other than to keep this from his brother since he'd given Mattie his word.

Elias had been sitting with Rebecca by their campfire when Josiah arrived at their covered wagon to collect the medicine. And after stating his intention, it had been all he could do to convince the doctor that it wasn't necessary for him to personally examine Mattie.

Although no false words had passed Josiah's lips, his conscience wasn't untroubled.

But, for Mattie's sake, he'd simply have to live with it.

Mattie finished rubbing liniment into her shoulder, then refastened the top two buttons on her father's shirt. She replaced the cover on the jar and moved to the back of the wagon. Intending to ask Josiah to return the medicine to his brother, she poked her head outside only to find that he wasn't waiting as she'd expected.

She turned her eyes toward his family's covered wagon and spotted Elias and Rebecca sitting by their campfire. Josiah wasn't with them, and a quick glance around didn't reveal him anywhere else. It wasn't his and Mattie's night for guard duty, so where was he? Perhaps he had gone to check on his horses. In which case, he should return soon.

Unless he didn't plan to come back past here.

Her fingers tightened around the jar in her hand. She shied away from delivering it to the doctor personally, preferring to avoid the possibility of probing questions. She drummed her free hand against the top edge of the wagon frame and debated what to do.

A noise on the far side of the wagon drew her attention. She turned her head and strained to peer through the darkness. Was it Josiah? But what would he be doing in that direction? The horse enclosure was out past the opposite side of the wagon circle.

An unnerving possibility occurred to her. What if it was someone skulking about, up to no good? Nightmarish images flooded her head. She quickly slammed a mental door against the onslaught. She was letting her imagination run away with her. Except for that one brief sound, she hadn't heard anything suspicious.

Still, it would be prudent to investigate. She'd rest easier once she assured herself there was nothing sinister lurking in the dark.

She climbed to the ground, careful to move slowly and silently to keep the element of surprise. Her heart pounding, she rounded the corner of the covered wagon. And barreled straight into a solid object.

She stumbled back, and the forgotten jar of liniment slipped from her fingers. A scream rose in her throat as a pair of hands grabbed her arms. A second before she let loose a screech sure to bring the whole camp running, she recognized Josiah in the faint light cast by the moon. At the same time, she realized he'd taken a hold of her only to steady her.

She put a hand over her heart to slow its racing. "What are you doing out here?" Besides scaring her half out of her wits.

"I was waiting for you." He released her and stepped back, then bent to retrieve the liniment, which had come to rest against the toe of his boot.

The small jar wouldn't have done much good as a weapon if she'd run into someone dangerous, but she hadn't thought to bring anything else with her. Thank the Lord it was Josiah she'd encountered.

He balanced the jar of liniment on the wagon wheel and reached into his coat pocket, pulling out a roll of cotton bandages and a small container. "I brought these for your hands." He tucked the bandages under his arm and opened the container. "This salve will keep the cuts and blisters from getting infected."

She bit her lower lip in consternation. She'd known

it wasn't wise to leave the wounds unattended, but hadn't wanted to draw attention to her soft, white hands. She'd hoped to avoid giving anyone reason to think she couldn't do her share of the work. It could have proved a very foolhardy decision, however, had they festered, making it impossible for her to use them at all.

She extended a hand to take the salve. Instead of passing it to her, he grasped her wrist and pulled her palm toward him.

At the realization that he intended to apply the salve himself, she tried to tug her hand away. "I can do it."

He shook his head and didn't relinquish his grip. "It's easier if I do it. Then you won't have to struggle to wrap a bandage with only one hand."

Left with a choice between an undignified tussle over possession of her hand or giving in, she subsided and allowed him to spread the salve across her palm. Though his touch was feather-light, she flinched.

He glanced up, concern darkening his eyes. "I'm sorry, I didn't mean to cause you pain. I'll be as gentle as I can."

She breathed a sigh of relief that he'd misunderstood her reaction. It hadn't been due to physical discomfort; instead, it was in response to the way her heart had contracted at his tender care.

"You just surprised me, that's all," she excused. "It doesn't hurt."

She silently urged him to hurry up and finish so she could put some distance between them. But he took his time dabbing salve on each wound, checking that even the tiniest scratch wasn't overlooked in the pale wash of moonlight. Finally, he seemed satisfied and released his grasp to reach for her other hand.

Once he'd given it the same careful inspection and treatment, he capped the salve and placed it next to the jar of liniment. He wrapped a strip of cotton around one palm and then the other, tying off the ends to hold them in place.

He stepped back and pulled a handkerchief from his pocket to wipe his hands. "There you go. All finished."

"Thanks." She picked up both containers of medicinals and tried to hand them to him.

He refused to take them. "You keep those for now. You'll need to reapply both tomorrow morning. I'll come by and help you rewrap your hands in clean bandages."

"That's not necessary," she hastily declined. "Adela can do it."

"In that case, I'll leave this with you, too." He added the diminished roll of bandaging to the other items in her hands. "If driving the oxen is too much for you, I'll take over for a day or two."

She'd already taken advantage of his good nature as much as she intended to. "You don't have to do that."

"You need to go easy," he persisted. "It's to everyone's benefit that you avoid overtaxing your shoulder—otherwise you risk making your injury worse. Then you'd be laid up for more than just a few days."

"I can handle it."

"But you'll ask for help if you need it," he pressed.

"If I need it." But she wouldn't. Instead, she'd prove she could function without his help.

She would rest her shoulder tonight, and by tomorrow morning it should be improved enough that it wouldn't hinder her on the trail. She hoped. Or her lofty ambition would turn to ashes.

Chapter Seven

The next day was Sunday. Their morning departure was delayed by an hour—as had become the group's custom since setting out from Missouri—to allow the preacher to deliver his weekly sermon to any who desired to hear the Lord's word.

Mattie stood next to Adela, their father's Bible held open between them, while David Linton's powerful voice boomed across the gathered people.

Mattie usually enjoyed this time of worship, finding peace and strength in the scriptures, while the preacher focused on sermons that lifted up the weary travelers as they faced the trials and hardships of long days on the trail. But today's scripture selection was different.

Her gaze rested on the page in front of her, but the words blurred out of focus. She didn't need to see the passages, however, to hear their message.

The preacher was reading them out loud.

"'Keep thy tongue from evil, and thy lips from speaking guile. Depart from evil, and do good, seek peace, and pursue it. The eyes of the Lord are upon the righteous, and His ears are open unto their cry. The face of the Lord is against them that do evil, to cut off the remembrance of them from the earth.' We must follow the path of righteousness in all ways."

It seemed as if his words were targeted directly at Mattie. She didn't believe what she was doing was truly evil, but there was no denying her actions didn't honor the Lord.

She imagined that her shortcomings were visible for all to see. But it was only her guilty conscience making it seem that way. Wasn't it?

When she glanced up, no one appeared to be paying her any attention, not even the preacher. She looked behind her, scanning across the back of the gathering. When she reached the spot where the Dawsons stood, her eyes collided with Josiah's unreadable gaze.

What was going on inside his head? Did he hold her in contempt? How could he not? After lying to him for weeks, she'd then forced him to become part of her deception.

Gasping at the realization that she'd been so focused on her own culpability she hadn't given a thought to him, shame filled her and she turned away. She couldn't bear to see accusations burning in his eyes. Or, worse, him silently prodding her to come clean.

Lord, I know what I'm doing is wrong. But I don't have a choice. Please, forgive me, Lord.

Would He heed her prayer when she wasn't able to change her ways? At least, not now. But she would.

She just couldn't do it yet.

Instructing the congregation to turn to another passage, the preacher again read aloud. "'Who shall ascend into the hill of the Lord? Or who shall stand in His holy place? He that hath clean hands, and a pure heart; who hath not lifted up his soul unto vanity, nor sworn deceitfully. He shall receive the blessing from the Lord, and righteousness from the God of his salvation.'"

Finally, he closed his Bible and led them in singing hymns, but she didn't join in. The words flowed around her as her mind circled endlessly, allowing her no peace. As soon as the final prayer was spoken, she worked her way to the edge of the gathering while the amens were still echoing.

She didn't wait for Adela as she normally would, her determination to get away pushing common courtesy to the wayside. And she didn't slow down to exchange a few words with anyone, fearing that Josiah would use that opportunity to approach her. She didn't want to hear anything he had to say just now.

Leaving the others behind, she hurried to her wagon. She understood that hiding wouldn't resolve the issue and that if Josiah was of a mind to speak to her, she couldn't avoid the confrontation forever. Still, she admitted she'd much rather postpone it.

Even though daily life on the trail didn't afford many chances for him to catch her for a private word, she spent the next few days feeling as if her insides were tied up in knots. Then it was their turn for guard duty.

He didn't come around to walk with her to the lookout spot, as he'd done on previous nights. Was he waiting to pounce on her out in the darkness?

As she made her way to the slight rise a short distance from camp, the light from the full moon allowed her to easily pick her way over the uneven ground. Yet she felt the urge to drag her feet.

She could already imagine the bite of Josiah's words, and she longed to scramble back to the safety of her wagon. But it was past time for her to abandon avoidance tactics and face up to her transgressions.

Josiah had no sooner taken up his position for guard duty than he heard someone approaching. With the moon temporarily obscured by passing clouds, he couldn't immediately identify the figure climbing up the hill toward him. But then the clouds drifted away and the moonlight revealed Mattie's face.

Where did she think she was going?

He waited for her to draw closer before he spoke, and he kept his voice low so it wouldn't carry beyond them through the still night air. "What are you doing out here?"

Her eyes widened in surprise at his question. "Why wouldn't I be here? It's my turn for guard duty."

"You shouldn't be doing guard duty. Besides, it isn't proper for us to be alone together like this." Though he and Mattie had never discussed it, Josiah hadn't expected her to continue with the charade when it was just the two of them.

She propped her hands on her hips. "We've been doing it for weeks already. To paraphrase one of Mr. Carpenter's favorite sayings, it's too late to close the barn door after the horse gets out."

If Josiah had known she was a woman from the start, they would've had this conversation on their very first night at guard duty. To his mind, it was now long overdue. "We shouldn't compound the error by letting the cow and the sheep escape, too."

"Huh? What cow and sheep?" She looked around

as if expecting to see the Bakers' milk cow making a break for it.

"What I'm trying to say is just because we did it before, that doesn't make it any less wrong. And we should remedy the situation now."

"But there's no harm in it as long as no one else knows I'm a woman."

Why was she being so obstinate? He couldn't imagine she actually *wanted* to be here, that she enjoyed sitting out in the cold for hours, losing sleep.

"Besides, how would you explain me suddenly skipping guard duty?" she queried.

It was a valid question, and he considered it for a moment before he hit upon the perfect excuse. "Your shoulder. You shouldn't tax it."

She wasted no time shooting him down. "Keeping an eye out for trouble and watching over the animals isn't physically taxing. Other than that one time when we spotted the thieves, night watches have been wholly uneventful. And anyway, that explanation would only work for a short while until my shoulder mended. What then?" She didn't give him a chance to answer before she rushed on. "No, we'll just have to continue as before. Someone would be bound to notice, otherwise. I can't do anything that might arouse suspicion."

He had to concede her point, and with all his arguments neatly dispatched, he lapsed into silence. What other choice did he have? His promise to keep her secret had tied his hands.

He nodded in acknowledgment to her words.

Turning up her coat collar, she tucked her hands into the pockets and settled in for the duration.

At least she wasn't hiding under her hat any longer when it was just the two of them.

He studied her face as she looked out across the dark prairie. Moonlight gilded her delicate features, highlighting her cheekbones and making her skin gleam like the finest alabaster, while her eyes remained still pools of mystery beneath the concealing shadow of her lashes. But he knew her biggest secret now.

He'd respected the boy on the brink of manhood, but he was in awe of the resourcefulness and determination of the woman, despite her stubborn refusal to give an inch. Her dogged attitude was no doubt responsible for the way she'd handled everything that was thrown at her over the past few weeks. Even things that should have been impossible. Just thinking about it, his admiration for her went up several notches higher.

She was strong, and not just in a physical sense. He'd met few females with her fortitude. Though he knew from her snippets of conversation that she'd been raised in a home with servants, never by word or deed had she indicated any resentment at her diminished circumstances. She'd made no complaints about the calluses on her hands or the dirt under her fingernails.

But the fact remained that she wasn't used to this kind of life. "Why would a prosperous man uproot his two daughters and take them on a difficult trek they might not survive?" He spoke his thoughts aloud.

"The same reason others make this journey." She didn't look at him as she answered. Instead, she stared off into the distance. "For the promise of a new life."

"Was there something wrong with the old one?"

"Was there something wrong with *yours*?" she shot back, turning her head to skewer him with her gaze.

"I worked for someone else back in Tennessee, but out west I can build something of my own. Like most, I hope to find something better than what I left behind. Elias and Rebecca are moving to be closer to her family. Even Hardwick is trying to improve his situation as a second son with neither title nor fortune of his own. But then there's you and Adela." Her eyes dropped from his as he shook his head. "Despite your uncle's affluence, Oregon City is by no means a bustling metropolis of high society. What's waiting ahead can't compare with what you knew in the past."

He couldn't deny he was curious about her. She'd always been so close-mouthed about herself—an understandable precaution when she was concerned with keeping her secret. But now that he knew the truth, surely there was no reason for her to hold back. Would she open up to him, trusting him at last?

Oregon City couldn't compare to the life she'd left behind? A year ago, that might have proved true. But not any longer.

Admitting as much to Josiah, however, could lead to questions about parts of her past she'd rather not dwell on. She was still embarrassed to admit how close she'd come to marrying a man so undeserving of her affection and respect.

"After my mother died, life in Saint Louis wasn't the same." She left it at that and let him draw what conclusions he may from her words.

His jaw worked as his thoughts turned inward. "My life changed, too, after my mother's passing." He didn't offer any other details.

"I guess we have that in common."

The wind suddenly picked up and gusted around her, cutting through the fabric of her father's coat. The cold seeped into her injured shoulder and made it ache. A soft gasp slipped past her lips as she shifted in an attempt to find a more comfortable position.

Josiah turned toward her. "What is it?"

If she voiced the truth, she knew he would insist she abandon her post and return to the wagons. She'd refuse, and then they'd spend the next few minutes going over the same ground they'd already covered once.

"I thought I saw something for a minute," she fabricated.

He scanned the surrounding area. "I don't see anything."

"It was probably just a shadow cast by the moon." Huddling deeper into the coat, she was careful not to make any other telling movements or sounds.

She expected him to bring up the subject she'd been dreading for days. But as the seconds ticked past without him speaking, she realized it wasn't going to happen, that all her fretting and fussing had been for naught. He hadn't denounced her for her failings or placed blame.

His actions reminded her of a Bible verse. *He that is without sin among you, let him cast a stone.*

This wasn't the first time Josiah's behavior suggested a steadfast integrity. Though she remained wary of trusting him completely, her heart whispered that he seemed exactly the type of man she hoped to one day marry, after she reached Oregon Country and threw off the bonds of her deception.

Surely, she couldn't be the first woman to think as much. Why then was Josiah unattached? He looked to be in his midtwenties, an age when most men had already taken a wife. Yet he remained a bachelor. Was that proof he must have a major character flaw tucked away somewhere out of sight? Or was she judging him too harshly?

She similarly doubted every other man she met. So, how could she ever let one close enough for her to feel confident that marriage to him wouldn't be a mistake? Would her past always stand in the way of her future?

Hours later, when it was time to return to camp, she still hadn't reached an answer.

"I'll walk you back."

"That's not necessary," she protested. "After all, I got here on my own."

He waved his arm for her to go ahead. But if she'd imagined he would so easily acquiesce, she was soon set straight as he fell into step beside her.

She sped up, and he kept pace. She slowed down; he did likewise.

"I doubt I'll get into trouble walking such a short distance by myself," she pointed out, hoping to shake him.

But he stuck to her like a burr. "We're going the same way. It only makes sense to walk together."

Finally, she gave up. She couldn't outdistance him, even if running pell-mell through the night wasn't a foolish thing to do.

Though she'd never admit it to him, she felt safe with his warm, reassuring presence nearby. There was nothing to fear in the shadows when he was around.

The wind blew clouds across the moon, and she stumbled in the sudden darkness.

Josiah was there to catch her, his fingers wrapping

securely around hers to keep her upright. "Steady now."

She regained her footing and shook off his hold. "I didn't need your help."

His eyebrows knit together in confusion. "Why are you so quick to take offense at a simple gesture of kindness?"

"Because you didn't do the same for Matt. When we went hunting, I tripped in a hole, and you didn't rush to my aid then." She took off toward the covered wagons again.

He hurried to catch up. "I get it now. You think I'm treating you differently because I know you're a woman." He moved in front of her, then turned and walked backward, facing her, and placed his hand over his heart as if making a solemn vow. "I won't let it happen again. Next time, I'll let you land flat on your face. But don't worry—your broken nose should only take a few weeks to heal, and I'm sure it won't be too crooked or unsightly. It might even make you look more manly."

Throughout his discourse, her eyebrows arched higher and higher at his nonchalant attitude. Then she caught the gleam of merriment twinkling in his eyes and the suspicious twitching of his lips.

She stuck aforesaid nose in the air, determined to suppress the answering smile trying the stretch the corners of her mouth. "You do that. And watch where you're going, or you'll be the one taking a spill."

"Yes, ma'am—uh, Matt. Sir." He saluted then executed a smart about-face and moved to walk beside her again.

She could only shake her head at his clowning. But the brief moment of shared humor wouldn't weaken her resolve to maintain an emotional distance from him. He affected her too strongly already.

When he'd held her hands, it had felt as if there was more than just a physical connection between them, though it had only lasted for the space of a heartbeat before she'd pulled away. Allowing such feelings free rein would bring only misery.

If she gave her heart unwisely for a second time and it was broken once more, she feared it would be impossible to stitch the shattered pieces back together again.

A week later, the wagon train reached a harrowing river crossing. Mattie stood overlooking the water, which rushed past in a raging torrent that spelled danger for any who ventured too close. Their group had to cross it as soon as they moved out following the noon stop.

Her stomach knotted at the thought of driving her oxen and covered wagon through the swift-moving river, and she needed these moments to shore up her courage. Breathing deeply in an attempt to restore some calm, she turned her eyes away from the churning waters.

All hope for peace of mind was shattered when she encountered two pairs of eyes focused in her direction, displaying expressions of varying unease. Josiah and Elias stood together in conversation a short distance from her, and when they both quickly looked away as soon as they saw her watching, an immediate suspicion sprouted in her mind that she was their topic of discussion.

There was no reason for them to talk about her, however. Other than Josiah divulging her true identity to his brother. And he wouldn't go back on his word. Would he?

The men were too far away for her to hear their words over the roar of the river, and it would be unfair to convict Josiah on so little evidence. She cautioned herself not to instantly assume the worst. Surely, she'd simply gotten a hold of the wrong end of the stick. After all, given her position near the water's edge, it was entirely possible they were merely looking past her while considering the potentially hazardous crossing.

Her confidence in that explanation diminished somewhat when the two men parted ways and Elias appeared to be heading straight toward her.

He came to a halt at her side, his eyes focused on the river. "Our trail guide has judged this the best spot, but even he's concerned about the higher-than-normal water level. It'll be tough getting all the wagons safely across. Why don't I drive yours for you?"

He clearly thought she couldn't handle it. Was that because he knew she was a woman? There didn't seem to be any other logical conclusion.

So much for Josiah's word being worth anything. She'd been correct in her original distrust.

Her jaw clenched in frustrated fury, but she contained her vitriol. "No, thank you."

Elias shifted to face her, compassion shining in his gaze. "There's no shame in feeling uneasy about crossing a river that's overflowing its banks. The most stalwart of men would find it intimidating." His attention was diverted by the covered wagon rolling past.

Mattie remained silent as they both watched its progress.

The oxen entered the river and strained to pull the

heavy load as the current buffeted them on one side, threatening catastrophe. It was a tense few minutes until the team reached the other side.

Elias turned back to Mattie. "You're certain you won't change your mind?"

"I can handle it." Her anger had chased away all traces of fear.

"All right, then. I'd best make certain my team is ready—it'll be our turn soon." He tipped his hat to her and moved off in one direction.

She headed in another, toward the area where she could see Josiah occupied tending to his horses. She planned to tell him exactly what she thought of a man who broke his word.

She never should have put her faith in him. Never mind that she hadn't really had a choice. He'd betrayed her confidence, and she was only deluding herself when she gave him the benefit of the doubt. He clearly hadn't deserved it.

Again, she had been taken for a fool.

Why did she continue falling for men's lies?

Chapter Eight

"I'd like a word with you, Josiah." Mattie's curt tone conveyed agitation, but her closed expression gave away nothing of her thoughts.

One of Josiah's horses shifted restlessly, and he moved a few steps to the side, out of boot-stomping range. "What can I do for you?"

"You can keep your mouth shut from here on out," she gritted through clenched teeth.

His head jerked back at her vehement attack against him. "What is that supposed to mean?"

"Don't try to feign innocence. Your brother just offered to drive my wagon across the river. Now, one might ask why." She put up a hand, forestalling his explanation. "And before you try to use my shoulder as an excuse again, let me remind you that he already knows it's all healed up, since I returned the liniment to him the day before yesterday."

"I wasn't going to use your shoulder as an excuse," he refuted. "I was just going to say that Elias's offer wasn't my doing."

"Stop lying to me! I saw you two talking, then not

two minutes later he approached me. There's only one reason why he would feel compelled to make an offer like that." Her hands balled into fists at her sides. "Did you think I wouldn't work it out that you'd told him the truth about me?"

Only now did Josiah fully comprehend what had sparked her fit of temper. "Stop hissing and spitting at me and retract your claws, little tiger. I didn't tell him."

But his words didn't mollify her. She paced a few steps, agitation evident in every line of her stiff posture, and then pivoted back toward him. "Were you or were you not discussing me with your brother a few minutes ago?"

"Yes, I was," he admitted, then rushed on before she let him have it with both barrels. "But not *you* you."

Her eyebrows scrunched together in confusion. "What?"

Little wonder she didn't understand; he wasn't explaining this very well. "What I mean is that we were talking about 'Matt.'"

Doubt remained heavy in her features as she crossed her arms in front of her. "Why?"

"Elias saw you looking at the river and believed you were apprehensive about making the crossing. He said he could see it in your expression. That's why he took it upon himself to offer his aid."

She stared him down. "So, you had nothing to do with it? You didn't say something to him that put the thought in his head that I couldn't handle it myself?"

"No, I didn't," he stated with absolute honesty.

He'd said he wouldn't reveal her secret, and he hadn't. And that included any sneaky maneuvering that, while technically following the letter of his promise, would have been in violation of its true spirit.

Mattie couldn't have made it any more clear, however, that she didn't trust him to keep his word, even though he'd given her no cause for doubt. The thought struck a nerve, mirroring too closely the way his good deeds as a boy hadn't made a lick of difference in people's opinions of him.

He strove to be a man others could respect and admire, but every now and again, doubts about his worth ambushed him when he least expected it. But he pushed his wounded pride aside. It didn't matter what Mattie thought of him. He'd never held with living down to others' low expectations of him.

Still, he wouldn't allow her misconceptions to stand. "Elias sees you as a young man with a heavy weight of responsibility on your shoulders. He was simply trying to lighten the load." Just as he'd done for Josiah years ago.

Elias was likely reminded of Josiah's younger self when he looked at "Matt" and the result was Elias treating "him" like a younger brother.

The older man hadn't realized how Mattie would misconstrue his well-meaning kindness. "I told him you'd likely refuse, but he wouldn't be swayed."

When his explanation failed to smooth her bristling fur, Josiah decided to try humor, instead. It had worked the other night, after all. "You shouldn't blame Elias. It's not his fault. He has what I like to call Big Brother Syndrome."

She looked askance at him. "And what is that, exactly?"

"Nasty disease." He shook his head and tsked. "Its

symptoms include taking charge without an invitation and sticking one's nose where it isn't wanted. Sadly, it's incurable. Though, thankfully, nonfatal."

The corners of her mouth curled up, although she tried to fight it. "And, apparently, it's contagious."

"Excuse me? Surely, you don't mean me. I don't have any younger siblings."

"And yet, you seem to have caught it, regardless."

"Well, then, you can't hold it against me—I'm not at all well."

She huffed out a laugh and unbent enough to offer an apology. "I'm sorry I jumped to conclusions."

"Apology accepted."

But he couldn't forget the fact that she'd questioned his honor in the first place. It left a familiar ache deep inside his heart.

If he was a fine gentleman, like the ones she'd no doubt grown up with, perhaps she'd believe him trustworthy. But a fine gentleman wouldn't have been able to help her on the trail the way Josiah had. And that counted for more in his book than fancy clothes and pretty manners.

It shouldn't matter to him that Mattie didn't appear to share that view.

Mattie sat on the wagon seat next to Adela, who gripped Mattie's arm with one hand and the edge of the wooden bench with the other. Her nails dug into tender flesh as their heavy covered wagon lumbered down the bank and the water level rose up the wheels. Mattie gritted her teeth against the pain and focused on her task.

She'd made numerous river crossings in past weeks,

though this was the most difficult one she'd faced thus far. About twenty families, including the Dawsons, had already made it without incident and now waited on the opposite side. There was no reason to imagine she wouldn't soon join them, unharmed and with the wagon intact. No reason to expect she'd encounter problems when others hadn't. To do so was merely borrowing trouble.

Still, she had to fight against mounting panic when the oxen reached a point where their hooves couldn't touch the bottom, and they began to swim. Caulking the covered wagon had made it watertight and allowed it to float, but it bobbed on the rough current like a ship in storm-tossed seas.

She gave a thought for the wisdom—or lack thereof—in refusing Elias, but quickly pushed such musing aside. Her present situation required all her concentration.

Water splashed up over the sides of the wagon and soaked into her clothes, leaving large damp patches. Adela let out a terrified moan, but Mattie didn't glance her way.

Instead, she kept her eyes pointed straight ahead toward dry land. Why did it suddenly seem farther away now than it had when she was standing at the river's edge a short time ago?

"Look out!" a voice shouted over the roar of the water.

Mattie saw people pointing upriver, and she turned her eyes in that direction.

But it was too late.

She had only a second to watch the large tree branch hurtling at her and Adela. Only an instant to realize there wasn't nearly enough time for them to get out of its path.

Then the branch slammed into the side of their wagon.

The jarring impact overbalanced Mattie. She made a wild grab for something to hang on to, but she couldn't arrest her fall and plunged into the churning waters.

"Matilda!" Adela shrieked in terror.

Then the water closed over Mattie's head, muffling sounds.

Had Adela fallen in, too? The thought sent panic racing through Mattie's veins. Adela couldn't swim! Neither could Mattie, but that didn't stop her from thrashing her arms and legs as she fought her way to the surface to check that her sister wasn't battling, too.

Though water blurred her vision, she caught a glimpse of Adela still safely atop the wagon's seat— clinging so tightly that Mattie doubted a full-blown gale would dislodge the girl. She snatched in a relieved breath of air before the current pulled her under again.

She flailed her arms and legs, but she couldn't break free of the current's power, and the struggle sapped her energy. Her limbs felt heavy as she grew weak and her lungs screamed for oxygen. Fear, unlike any she'd ever known, took hold. Was she going to die? Was this how her life ended? How could this be what God intended for her?

Despite her sins, she refused to believe this was His punishment for them. He was a merciful God.

She sent a silent prayer heavenward. *Please, Lord, help me.*

Simply thinking the words brought her peace and the strength to keep fighting.

Fear not, for I am with you. The verse echoed through her mind.

Her fingers brushed against something. She grabbed it like a lifeline and used it as leverage to pull her head above water. Locking her arms around the object, she gasped and coughed as she gulped in huge lungfuls of precious air.

When her head cleared a bit, she looked down and registered the floating object was a tree branch. Was it the same one that had put her life in peril to begin with? She didn't know or care. It had been used to save her from certain death.

But she was still caught in the current, being carried ever farther downriver. *Lord, I could use just a little more heavenly intervention.*

The branch suddenly snagged on some rocks, and it was all she could do to maintain her grip on it as the force of the river tried to drag her away. Her fingers ached from the strain. How long would she be able to hold on?

Her eyes darted around and she noticed the nearby rocks seemed to form a bridge of sorts, offering a way to get out of the deepest part of the river and closer to safety. But she would have to let go of the branch first. An act that required more daring and strength than she seemed to have at the moment.

Though she was losing her grip, the rest of her body had frozen and refused to follow the dictates of her brain.

She heard shouting and turned her head to see men running along the bank toward her. Josiah was in the lead, several paces ahead of the others. But even he was still a ways off. She couldn't count on him for rescue. He might not get there in time. If she didn't do something to save herself, she very likely wouldn't survive.

Would anyone take in her sister, if Mattie drowned? What would become of poor Adela, out here without any family to sustain her? Mattie couldn't leave the younger girl all alone facing an uncertain fate.

This last thought gave her the courage to do what she must. Letting go of the branch with one hand, she reached out and gripped the rock. The sharp edges dug into her fingers, and she feared she wouldn't be able to maintain her hold. Ignoring the pain, she quickly transferred her other hand to the rock.

The force of the water pushed her toward the rough surface, and she fought to avoid being slammed into it as she pulled herself close enough to the next rock to get a handhold on it.

Working this way, hand over hand from one rock to the next, she slowly towed her body toward the riverbank. Once out of the fast-flowing current in the middle, she was able to gain her footing on the sandy bottom. Still, she maintained her hold on the rocks to keep her balance as she waded through the water.

Josiah was the first to arrive on the scene. He jumped down from the bank and splashed through the shallows, reaching out toward her. "Here, take my hand."

She released the rock and latched on to him with relief, finding immense comfort in his warm fingers wrapping hers in a strong, sure clasp. He hauled her out of the deeper water that reached to her waist and pulled her right into his arms.

The embrace only lasted a moment before he moved

to put some distance between them. Though she wanted to cling, she let her arms drop to her sides.

He didn't set her away, however. His hands remained at her waist as he looked into her eyes.

Jumbled emotions swirled in the blue depths of his gaze, too many for her to pick out any single one. "Are you all right?" he demanded.

At her nod, he breathed a deep sigh and lifted his fingers to brush a strand of wet hair off her cheek. Her skin heated beneath his touch, warmth spreading out from the small point of contact.

A throat cleared behind Josiah, and he quickly lowered his arm.

She peeked around him to see that other men had arrived and were standing on the bank.

Josiah shifted to the side. "Come on, let's get you out of here." With a hand braced at the back of her waist, he helped her climb the slight incline until the others could grasp her hands and pull her the rest of the way up to solid ground.

Her knees suddenly gave out, and she collapsed onto the grassy slope. Sitting back on her heels, she bowed her head and braced her hands on her thighs, laboring to catch her breath and slow her heart rate. She shivered, but it was more in reaction to stress and residual fear than from cold.

Thank You for sparing my life, Lord.

She felt a touch on her back, rubbing up and down along her spine, and shifted her gaze to the side without raising her head. A pair of pant legs, wet past the knee, identified Josiah as the one squatting next to her. But though his caress was soothing, she saw a dozen pairs of boots crowding close, and it felt as if they were pressing in on her, cutting off her air.

"All right, everyone, back off and give him some space," Elias's voice commanded.

Once the others moved back, the doctor dropped down beside her and took her wrist to check her pulse. "A little fast, but that's only to be expected under the circumstances. Does anything hurt? Did you hit your head or get scraped on any of the rocks?"

She shook her head.

"You were fortunate. You don't seem any the worse for wear. But the adrenaline could be blocking the pain right now. If you notice any problems later on, you're to come straight to me. Understood?"

She was in no fit state to argue just now. "Yes, Doctor," she meekly replied.

Finally, feeling somewhat recovered, she straightened and climbed slowly to her feet.

Josiah placed a hand under her elbow to steady her. "Are you up to walking back to the covered wagons yet, or do you need a few more minutes?"

"I'm—Adela!" she gasped, suddenly realizing she didn't know what had happened to her sister after that one brief glimpse she'd managed, when the younger girl was out in the middle of the river, clinging to the wagon seat for dear life. "Is she all right?" Mattie fisted her hands in Josiah's shirtfront, fearing he'd tell her the worst.

Guilt and shame filled her that she'd put her sister's safety at risk when she refused to accept Elias's offer. Had Adela been forced to pay the ultimate price for Mattie's stubbornness? If anything had happened to her, Mattie would be solely to blame. She was supposed to protect Adela. How could she live with herself if she'd failed in that duty?

Josiah placed his hands over Mattie's and stroked her white knuckles.

"Adela's fine," he assured her, indicating back upriver with a nod of his head. "See for yourself."

She turned to look in that direction, but her fists remained bunched in his shirt.

Though not yet safe and sound on dry land, the Prescotts' team had reached the shallow, slow-moving part of the current near the end of the river crossing. By this point, the water only reached halfway up the wheels, and even as Josiah and Mattie watched, the oxen plodded up the slope, pulling the covered wagon onto the bank.

"Thank You, God," she breathed, her hands relaxing against his chest.

And thank God you're all right, too, Josiah silently added. He'd prayed to the Lord to protect Mattie, and He had delivered her from harm.

The possibility of accidents was ever present on this journey, and it was an accepted fact that not everyone who started out from Independence would make it to Oregon Country. People got sick or injured, sometimes fatally, and grave markers were a common sight.

For a terrifying eternity Josiah had believed that Mattie would become another cross on the side of the trail. His heart had been in his throat when he'd feared he wouldn't get to her in time. That she'd be swept away, carried beyond his reach as the river claimed her. It was gut wrenching to think of how close she'd come to losing her life.

His eyes rested on her face, soaking up the details he'd feared never to see again.

Through God's grace, she'd escaped tragedy. Josiah was both relieved and grateful.

But he reminded himself that he would have experienced the same emotions for anyone in the same situation. His reaction certainly didn't mean he felt something special for Mattie. It couldn't. There was no room in his heart for another woman. And a lady such as Mattie wasn't meant for the likes of him anyway.

Mattie abruptly dropped her hands to her sides and moved away. He wondered if she'd somehow sensed his thoughts, until he noticed that Adela had gotten down from the wagon seat and was rushing to meet her sister.

Josiah trailed behind Mattie. With Elias's earlier words replaying in his head, it didn't seem wise to let her roam too far yet. At least not until he was reassured that she would take it easy for a while and try not to overdo things. But that was merely the concern he would show for anyone who had been through such an ordeal.

Adela threw her arms around her sister. "Thank the Lord you're all right, Matilda!"

A gasp sounded behind Josiah. Glancing over his shoulder, he found that several of the other men were only a few steps away from him. And every one of them had heard Adela's revealing remark.

Their expressions showed varying degrees of surprise and confusion while they struggled to make heads or tails of the mortar shell that had exploded without warning in their midst.

Josiah turned back toward Mattie and Adela. Neither sister seemed to notice anything amiss as yet.

They embraced for long moments, while additional people arrived from upriver and joined the men already gathered.

Word spread quickly from there. Everyone seemed shocked as they realized the full import of what had transpired.

When Mattie suddenly stiffened, Josiah guessed that she'd caught the muttering going on around her. In that instant, she seemed to cling to her sister all the tighter as she faced up to the fact that everyone knew the truth.

It was only after Rebecca approached with a blanket that Mattie reluctantly let go of Adela.

Rebecca draped the woolen fabric over Mattie's shoulders. "Let's get you back to the wagons so you can change into dry clothes, Matilda. May I call you that?"

"I prefer Mattie." She pulled the edges of the blanket closer around her and allowed Rebecca to steer her in the direction indicated.

The others moved back to clear a path for them. But despite this delay before being called to answer for her actions, it was plain that a reckoning was coming.

Would Miles and the other men show her leniency? Or had her deception sealed her fate? The thought of a harsh judgment befalling Mattie sent a dart of pain arrowing through Josiah's chest.

Was there anything he could do to influence the outcome? Or would all efforts on his part be in vain? No matter the uncertainties, he had to try.

Mattie spared a glance over her shoulder at Josiah before she climbed into the covered wagon at Rebecca's urging.

"If you only have men's clothing, I have some dresses that should fit you," the older woman offered, apparently calculating with a quick look that Adela's clothes would be too small for Mattie. "They're nothing fancy, but much more appropriate than what you're wearing now."

"Thank you, but I have a trunk full of my own things. Dressing in men's clothing was a late-minute decision," Mattie explained, and reached to take Rebecca's hand. "I'm sorry I deceived you, especially after you were so kind to Adela and me."

Rebecca squeezed Mattie's fingers in return. "There's nothing to apologize for. I believe I understand your reasons, so don't worry on my account. I'll leave you now, but I'll be by my wagon. Come on over when you're ready. Elias will want to double-check that you didn't suffer any ill effects from earlier." She released Mattie's hand and moved away.

Adela followed Mattie inside the covered wagon. "I'll help you find your trunk."

As they shifted items, Mattie noticed some felt a little damp. They had likely gotten wet when water splashed over the sides of the wagon. Still, she made a mental note to check the outside for damage or any signs of a leak, after she changed her clothes.

It took some effort to locate the trunk, but once they'd unearthed it, Mattie pulled out a dark blue cotton dress with cream cording at the collar and wrists. It was badly winkled from being folded away for several weeks, but at least it was clean and dry. And it smelled of the lavender that she'd pressed between the layers of fabric, a fragrance that always calmed her. She also selected a bonnet to cover her short hair, and once she was properly attired, they exited the covered wagon.

Mattie noted that the last few families were now safely across the river. No doubt they'd already been informed of her scandalous secret. It never took long for word to spread in situations like this. But she wouldn't let herself think about that just yet.

She moved to the side of the wagon where the branch had hit. Running her hand over the area, she inspected it for damage. There was a gouge in the wood, but the structure was intact.

Adela came up beside her. "I was so frightened when you fell in, Mattie. The oxen just kept swimming as you were washed downriver. I didn't know what to do other than pray. Then, when I saw you were all right, I was just so relieved that I spoke without thinking. I'm sorry! You were depending on me, and I let you down." Her expression clouded over with worry. "What's going to happen now?"

Mattie could only shake her head. She didn't know the answer.

Tears shimmered in Adela's eyes. "This is all my fault."

"Don't blame yourself." Mattie hugged her sister close for a moment, then released her. "It wasn't fair that I asked you to keep such a secret. In my heart I always knew it was wrong to deceive the others, but I felt we had no choice." Taking a deep breath, she straightened her spine. "It's time for me to face up to my own wrongdoings."

Please, Lord, forgive me for acting in a manner that didn't honor You. Forgive me for not trusting in You to show me the way. I tried to make my own way through deceit and dishonesty, and now I ask Your forgiveness, Lord.

She felt a weight of guilt lift off her, knowing that her sins were forgiven as she repented them.

But remembering the expressions on the men's faces earlier, she'd hazard a guess that they weren't inclined to be so forgiving. Would they sit in judgment of her, finding her crimes unpardonable and deserving of banishment from their group?

Although, she could do the job of tending to her wagon and livestock just as well now as she had yesterday, when she was "Matt" to everyone but Adela and Josiah, that might not make any difference to the other men. The simple fact of knowing she was female would irrevocably change their perception of her, and she feared what that would mean for her and Adela.

As they walked together toward the Dawsons' covered wagon, she spotted a gathering nearby comprised entirely of men, including Josiah. The mood of the group was serious, and it didn't take much of a leap to guess that she and Adela were likely the topic under discussion.

"Wait for me with Rebecca," she instructed her sister.

While Adela continued on their previous course, Mattie changed direction and headed toward the men. But Rebecca called her name, stopping Mattie in her tracks. She turned toward the other woman.

Rebecca waved her over. "Come sit with us."

Mattie glanced back at the group of men, who clearly hadn't waited for her to start their meeting. "I can't. I need to go—"

"It's men only," Rebecca interrupted. "Women weren't invited to join them."

"But it's about me and Adela, isn't it?" At Rebecca's nod, Mattie continued. "Then I should have a say. It's our future they're discussing."

Compassion shone in Rebecca's eyes. "You know it doesn't work that way. Such matters are for the men to decide."

Mattie shook her head in frustration. She'd grown accustomed to being accepted as someone who had a say in the decisions, too. For more than a month, she'd acted like a male—and been treated like one. Now, suddenly she was barred from a conversation when she was the one with the most at stake.

Didn't she at least deserve the opportunity to defend herself and her actions? Even a criminal was granted that right. But clearly the men weren't interested in her explanations.

Though she wanted nothing more than to demand they hear her out, it wouldn't help her case to force her way in where she wasn't welcome. And if she was completely honest with herself, she couldn't fault the men for refusing to listen to her side after discovering that she'd been lying to them from the start.

Would Josiah argue in support of her? Or hold his silence?

Or, even more damaging, would he reveal how she'd rejected the opportunity to come clean with the wagon master when Josiah had presented it to her?

A knot of foreboding settled in her stomach.

She felt as if her life had been derailed for a second time in the space of a few weeks, only on this occasion it fell to others to put her back on track. Would she be permitted to continue on to her original destination? Or would they switch the direction she was heading?

Chapter Nine

Miles Carpenter glanced around the group of men. "I'm sure no one here will argue in favor of leaving the Prescott sisters to fend for themselves in this wild country, no matter what they've done. But the fact remains that we can't have unescorted females traveling with us."

Josiah shifted restlessly from one foot to the other.

This wasn't sounding good for Mattie and Adela. If they couldn't continue with the rest of the group, what was the alternative?

The wagon train was traveling through unorganized territory, with no homesteads or towns. Only a few far-flung forts dotted the landscape. Frequented by rough men, the frontier outposts were no place for women alone and unprotected.

"Surely, you're not saying we have no other option but to abandon them at a fort?" Josiah protested.

Assuming the wagon train maintained the same pace as in previous weeks, they would reach Fort John on the Laramie River in a matter of ten days or so. A fortnight at most.

If the Prescotts weren't permitted to travel with the wagon train beyond that point, they would be stranded hundreds of miles away from their relatives in Oregon Country. What would become of the sisters, then?

Worst-case scenarios flooded Josiah's mind as he was sharply reminded of his childhood, watching his mother struggle—and ultimately fail—to provide for herself and Josiah without the assistance of predatory men. He hastily slammed a mental door against the onslaught of painful memories.

"No, that's not what I'm saying," Miles assured. "What I meant is that one of the single men here will have to take responsibility for the Prescotts by marrying one of the sisters."

"Which sister?" Cody Malone piped up, his voice cracking at the end.

"Never you mind, boy," his father retorted. "You're too young to take responsibility for two females."

David Linton folded his hands together at his waist. "We'll just leave the choice of bride for the groom to decide."

"Do we have a volunteer?" Miles queried.

As a married man, the wagon master was out of the running. So too were the majority of the other men standing around the circle. Husbands outnumbered the bachelors in this group by roughly three to one. Besides Josiah, there were the two teenage Malone boys, their widowed father, Hardwick, and just a handful of others without wives.

Up till now, Josiah had never once turned away when he saw someone in need of aid. And that was true in Mattie's case especially, as Josiah's past gave him an undeniable empathy for the elder Prescott's situation.

But getting hitched? That went far beyond a simple helping hand.

Marriage was a serious commitment, and he hadn't pictured himself ever entering into it. At least not since the woman he loved had married his best friend, William Montgomery. It wouldn't be fair for Josiah to take a wife when his heart belonged to Georgiana.

But how could he stand by and do nothing when Mattie's need was the greatest, praying for someone else to step up, instead?

"What happens if no one volunteers?" George Baker, husband and father of six, asked the question that was doubtlessly on the minds of most everyone else.

They looked to the wagon master for an answer.

Miles cleared his throat. "Then the single men will have to draw straws to determine the groom."

"Now, see here," Hardwick objected. "I have no desire to acquire a wife beneath my station, nor shall I allow my family lineage to be sullied in such a manner. I refuse to take part in this."

Elias spoke up as the voice of reason. "In order to be fair, all the men not already spoken for need to be included."

Hardwick turned on him. "Why should any other man be made to pay for your brother's misdeeds?"

Josiah stiffened in indignation. "What do you mean by that? Just what are you accusing me of?"

The corner of Hardwick's mouth curled up in a sneer. "I am surely not the only one here with suspicions regarding the time you spent alone with that woman."

"But he didn't know she was a woman then," Jed Smith disputed.

"Did he not?" Hardwick slanted a narrow-eyed glance at Josiah. "Are we to believe that during long hours in her company, he never realized the truth? I, most assuredly, doubt it! He did not appear surprised by this day's revelation, as the rest of us were. One can only surmise that he has compromised the Prescott chit quite beyond ruin!"

All eyes turned in Josiah's direction, and he noted numerous gazes shadowed with suspicion and distrust even before he had a chance to answer Hardwick's charges. Judging Josiah on another's say-so, without benefit of a fair hearing.

Though they'd been strangers when they started out from Independence, Josiah had imagined that after the past several weeks these men knew him well enough to recognize he was an honorable man. Learning that they were so quick to doubt him felt as if a horse's hoof had kicked out and connected with his chest.

"Nothing improper happened between us," he defended.

Disdain spread across Hardwick's features. "We only have your word for that. And what worth is the word of a man who acted as willing party to that woman's deception?"

Josiah couldn't refute the last part of that statement without speaking a lie. He scanned the other men's expressions to gauge their thoughts and found that Hardwick wasn't alone in his harsh opinion. Skepticism lingered on quite a few faces, in spite of Josiah's denial.

He never doubted he could count on his brother. And Elias didn't let him down, speaking in defense of Josiah. Several others voiced their support, as well; yet, an equal number appeared firmly on Hardwick's side.

Their lack of faith stung. But if his childhood had taught him anything, it was that some people were only too happy to believe the worst of those they considered beneath them.

In this case, however, maybe the doubts *were* justified. He had lied by omission. And noble intentions didn't absolve him.

Only You can do that, Lord.

"For his part, Dawson must be called to account." Hardwick's overdeveloped sense of importance seemed even more inflated now he'd found that others were backing him. He tugged on the bottom edge of his coat and straightened his cravat, taking great enjoyment in this opportunity to lord it over another. "And, thus, he is the man to remedy the situation through marriage. No one else."

"He's right," one of Hardwick's supporters seconded.

"Josiah?" Though Miles hadn't jumped to judgment against him, the wagon master plainly hoped Josiah would agree for the sake of keeping the peace.

A wedding would take place—one way or the other. And it seemed as though nearly half the men here were of the opinion that Josiah should be the designated bridegroom, willing or not. But was that right or fair to Mattie? Forced into a loveless marriage, with no hope that it might one day grow into something more. Tied to a man with a frozen heart and limited resources.

What am I to do, Lord?

Suddenly, a thought occurred to him. A solution to his dilemma, so simple he should have considered it from the first.

The marriage need not last forever.

It wouldn't be a true joining of heart, mind and body, merely a temporary measure to protect Mattie and Adela until they reached Oregon Country. After that, the union would be quietly annulled. And Mattie would be free to find a husband worthy of her. One who could give her the love and the social position she deserved.

Josiah wasn't that man. Could never be that man.

Mattie would recognize this was a necessary means to an end, not a lifelong commitment.

That steadfast certainty finally served to silence his conflicted thoughts. "I'll do it. I'll marry Mattie."

Everyone appeared relieved that the decision had been made, especially the single men who had neatly sidestepped any possibility of being drafted into duty in Josiah's place.

"We'll have the wedding immediately," Miles pronounced.

Now it was just a matter of informing the bride about her impending nuptials. Josiah glanced toward the covered wagons and easily picked out Mattie, even though she was attired in a gown and bonnet for the first time in their acquaintance.

Her altered appearance was striking. The cut of the dress flattered her feminine figure while the navy color contrasted with her skin, giving it the pale luster of a pearl. From the first moment he'd realized the truth, he had recognized she was a beautiful woman. Now, it was plain for everyone to see.

He searched her face, trying to guess how she would react to the news he'd soon impart. Her gaze was focused in the direction of the men, her expression a mixture of anger and frustration.

What thoughts occupied her mind? Did she have any inkling of what was to come? Did she suspect that she would be compelled to wed before the day was done? Or was she upset merely because she disliked having her fate decided by others?

Either way, her disposition wouldn't be improved by the knowledge that she was obliged to take a husband not of her choosing.

Josiah didn't expect meek acceptance of dictates. Not from Mattie.

But he never doubted she would cooperate. Eventually.

There was no other option open to her.

Mattie stood with Josiah near the river's edge, a short distance from the circle of wagons, where they had a measure of privacy as he'd requested. Scanning his face, she searched for an indication of what had been decided, but could determine nothing from his expression. While he didn't appear particularly content, neither did he seem as troubled as she would expect if the men had come to the decision to expel her and Adela from the wagon train.

A slight breeze blew across the water and lifted her bonnet strings, setting one fluttering against her cheek. She impatiently brushed it aside. "Well? What's the verdict?"

An infinitesimal pause preceded his response. "Marriage."

Just that one word. Nothing more.

She shook her head in confusion, certain she must have misunderstood him. "Pardon me?"

"You need a man to take responsibility for you and

Adela while we're on the trail, and Miles has insisted that a wedding take place. Today. Before we go any farther."

"You can't be serious! Who am I supposed to marry? Most of the men in this group are already married or otherwise spoken for, in case you haven't noticed. Matrimonial prospects aren't exactly thick on the ground. So, where does Mr. Carpenter imagine I'll find a husband, out here in the middle of nowhere?" She threw her arms wide.

"You're looking at him."

Her arms dropped to her sides. "You? Why would you agree to this?"

He rubbed the back of his neck as if a knot of tension was centered there. "We don't really have time for long explanations right now. Miles is anxious to see this matter settled and get back on the trail."

"Well, he will just have to wait." She first needed to understand Josiah's motivation before she would even consider placing herself and Adela into his keeping. "I'm not moving from this spot until you answer my questions." Gathering her skirts, she took a seat on a rock, emphasizing her words.

He mumbled something under his breath that sounded suspiciously like "I knew this wouldn't be easy—the woman's stubborn enough to sit here all day," then raised his voice to address her. "I suppose you won't be satisfied until you know everything that was said."

"If I'd been included in the meeting, I wouldn't need you to tell me anything," she pointed out, then winced at the self-inflicted jab to what remained a sore spot for her.

"You can take that up with Miles later, if you want, but for now I hope you don't mind if I give you the short version to speed things along."

"For someone who claims to be in such a hurry, you're sure coming at this from the long way around." The question was, why? She cocked her head to the side. "Are you deliberately delaying?"

"No." But his expression seemed to say otherwise. Sighing in resignation, he settled on a rock adjacent to hers. "After Miles made it clear there was no alternative other than marriage, I was…elected to fill the position as husband."

There was obviously more to it than he was voicing aloud, and she wouldn't let him sidestep a full explanation. "Why you?"

He picked at his pants' seam with his nail, his eyes focused on the movement of his fingers instead of on her. "I was deemed the obvious choice. You've spent more time with me since we left Missouri than with any other single man."

"I can see why the others might choose you, but that still doesn't explain why you agreed to it."

His head came up as he crossed his arms over his chest and raised one red-gold eyebrow. "Would you rather I'd refused?"

She opened her mouth to tell him that wasn't what she'd meant, but he waved her off.

"Never mind. It doesn't matter. The fact is there's no other alternative. But don't focus on the marriage aspect of this. Nothing will change between us." The corner of his mouth quirked up. "Well, nothing except that you need not worry about how others might view the help I offer. Nor fear that you'd inadvertently give something away by accepting."

Surely, he realized it could never be as simple as that. They weren't talking about some inconsequential little thing here, after all. "You want me to forget that we're discussing marriage? Forget that we would be bound together in holy wedlock, as husband and wife? How do you suggest I do that?"

He shifted at her pointed questions and pushed to his feet. "Well, for starters, don't think of me as a husband. I would merely be a friend lending a hand. Nothing more."

The pieces finally clicked into place as to the reason behind his agreement. This was a way for him to help by giving her the security of his name and protection. But that was it.

He simply wasn't the kind of man who could stand idly by while anyone was in dire straits. As she and Adela most assuredly were at this moment.

Though she was loath to admit it, they needed his help now, more than ever before.

But that didn't mean she intended to accept without first giving it careful consideration. Too many times in the past, impulse had led her into trouble. And she wouldn't make the same mistake again now, when so much depended on her next actions. Not just her future and Adela's, but Josiah's, as well.

She stood up and moved past him toward the river, her thoughts racing as fast as the water.

She'd convicted Josiah unfairly when she had jumped to conclusions earlier and, likewise, all the other times she'd made unwarranted assumptions due to self-doubts about her own ability to correctly discern a man's character.

Josiah was kind, considerate, always willing to lend a hand. When judged on his own merits, he had proved himself trustworthy in countless different ways over the past several weeks. His every action supported the belief that he was exactly the man he appeared to be. Without hidden agendas or ulterior motives for his benevolence.

Never once had he displayed a temper, not even when she'd provoked him past most other men's limits. Her father certainly wouldn't have responded with humor if faced with some of her more recent behavior. But Josiah had, ever ready with a teasing comment to calm her heightened emotions.

Now, he was riding to her rescue by offering marriage, a course with no benefit to him personally. Quite the opposite, in fact. She and Adela would only be an additional burden on top of his other responsibilities.

It shouldn't matter to him what happened to her or Adela. But it clearly did.

Because he was a good man.

If she must marry someone, she would rather it be Josiah than anyone else in their party. He would take good care of her and her sister.

But he didn't love Mattie.

She glanced over her shoulder at him, standing tall and unwavering, a solid rock of dependability in a desert of shifting sands. Ready and willing to provide protection, no matter the cost to himself.

How could she allow him to make such a sacrifice?

How could she not?

If it were only herself she had to consider, she wouldn't ask it of him.

But for Adela's sake she must.

There was no other way that would see them safely to their relatives in Oregon Country.

Remorse heavy in her heart for what her deception had wrought, she turned away from Josiah and back toward the river. She had to put the needs of her sister above her qualms about taking advantage of Josiah's generous nature.

Still, her mind fought against the inevitable, like a wild bird beating its wings against the bars of the cage that imprisoned it. Searching for a route that would set her and Josiah free.

But it was futile.

To keep trying would lead to nothing but a broken wing.

Josiah watched Mattie struggling to come to terms with the situation. After all she'd gone through to make it this far, she would do whatever was necessary to make it the rest of the way. He had no doubt. And there was only one path forward.

Yet, she hesitated.

Why did the notion of tying herself to him give her pause? Would she react the same way to the prospect of taking *any* man as husband on such short notice and without a proper courtship? Or was it him in particular that she had an issue with?

He was sharply reminded of her lack of faith in him before the river crossing. Perhaps she doubted him still, despite his explanations and her subsequent apology. If she didn't believe him—didn't believe *in* him—there was nothing more he could do to convince her of his integrity.

Growing up, he had been ridiculed as his mother's illegitimate shame, and he'd gotten a bellyful of feeling that he didn't measure up to others' standards of morals and decency. Now, here was a woman who knew nothing of his family history, and still it seemed as if she judged him lacking.

Was his birth a stain that people instantly recognized despite all he'd done over the years to rise above it? Was that why Georgiana had chosen his best friend, instead? Because she'd seen something in Josiah that turned her away from him and toward William? It wasn't the first time he'd wondered such a thing. But going over the past, trying to make sense of it, wouldn't change the outcome; it only brought pain.

He turned his mind away from questions he had no hope of answering and moved to stand at Mattie's back. "We've spent enough time talking about this. Are you ready to proceed now?"

Turning to face him, she chewed on the corner of her lip as she considered him for a long moment, her pleated brow attesting to the weight of her inner turmoil. Finally, she nodded.

He let out a sigh of relief. Though he hated the thought that circumstances were forcing her into a marriage against her will, the harsh truth was that her feelings didn't matter.

And neither did his. No matter how much her obvious reluctance lacerated his pride. "I'll let everyone know we're ready to begin."

"I—" Her mouth worked, but nothing else came out. She turned her face away and took a deep breath.

Reaching for her hand, he offered her a commis-erating squeeze. "We don't have a choice, Mattie. I'm sorry."

She didn't meet his gaze, her lashes lowered to shield whatever emotions lurked in the amber depths. "I'm the one who's sorry."

He released her hand as if it had burned him.

That she didn't want to marry him had already been made apparent by her hesitation; now her words were like a knife thrust, driving home the point.

But he didn't want to marry her, either. Not in the truest sense, anyway. So, why did knowledge of her antipathy throb like a thorn embedded under his skin?

Chapter Ten

Mattie clenched her hands together at her waist while the preacher's words washed over her. They didn't bring calm; nor did the faint roar of the nearby river.

She looked out across the open landscape past the preacher's shoulder, squinting slightly against the bright glare of sunlight on the pale canvas wagon bonnets a dozen yards away. Endless miles of rolling hills carpeted in waving sage-green grasses stretched out before her; yet, she felt hemmed in, surrounded by the other members of their group.

A warm breeze caressed her skin, and a trickle of perspiration rolled down her temple. Reaching up, she wiped away the moisture and shifted restlessly.

The preacher droned on about the responsibilities of husband and wife, and the sanctity of marriage, when all Mattie wanted was for him to finish it as quickly as possible. She bit her lip to keep back a demand that he skip to the end.

She glanced up at Josiah to gauge if he was plagued by the same impatience, but his eyes were focused on the other man and his face was impassive. Unable to read anything of his thoughts, she could only guess what he was feeling.

Did he resent her for what was happening here now—this marriage, which had become a necessity due to her foolhardy actions?

The breeze lifted a lock of his hair, and the sun's rays picked out the colors of flicking flames among the strands. He stood with feet braced apart, ignoring the men at his back, who it seemed acted not so much as wedding guests but rather as guards against any last-minute resistance from either the bride or groom.

Whether or not undue outside pressure had been brought to bear on Josiah to coerce his agreement was unclear, as he'd been sparing with the details of the men's discussion. Perhaps he was following nothing more than the urging of his conscience.

That thought caused a twinge in her own conscience. After everything he'd done for her, it wasn't right that she should take and take while giving nothing in return. But what could she do to mend the one-sidedness of their relationship? How could she ever adequately compensate for all he'd sacrificed for her? How many of his hopes and dreams for the future would be forever out of reach to him now? Because of her.

No doubt he'd pictured himself marrying a woman he loved or at least felt some measure of affection for beyond mere obligation. After all, what man would aspire to a marriage of convenience if given the choice?

And this wasn't even particularly convenient for Josiah, when it came right down to it.

But perhaps she could do something about that.

Over the last several weeks, he had revealed bits and

pieces of the life he envisioned for himself, once they reached the end of the trail. When he'd talked about his plans for a ranch in Oregon Country, he hadn't mentioned a wife. But surely he desired a family— children to one day inherit all he would work long and hard to create.

He'd need a woman by his side who was up to the challenges ahead. And the past month had shown Mattie just how strong and capable she truly was. She could be an asset to Josiah, an extra pair of hands to lighten his load. She wouldn't shy away from any chore, no matter how difficult or dirty, and she could help him with his horses, besides.

But it would be much more than the mere aiding of a friend.

Even though Josiah had claimed nothing would change between them, and he didn't expect Mattie to think of him as her husband, she suspected he'd said it to ease any worries she might harbor over the immensity of what he was truly offering in order to save her.

Such selflessness wasn't to be disregarded. She silently vowed to be a good wife to him. And prayed that was enough to ensure he never came to regret their loveless union.

The preacher broke into her musing with a request to repeat after him. Hearing the sacred words of the marriage vows, Mattie felt their gravity. The promises she made today weren't just promises to Josiah, but to God, as well. She sensed His presence even now, guiding her toward this path. Had this been His plan for her all along?

She'd heard that marriages of convenience were

commonplace out west, and a good many worked out splendidly. She prayed it would be so for her and Josiah.

Taking a deep breath, she spoke the words that would bind her to him for the rest of their lives. Then it was his turn.

"I will," he solemnly promised in answer to the preacher's prompting, his voice clear and strong.

A few short minutes later, David Linton said the final words of the marriage ceremony. "What God hath joined together, let no man tear asunder."

It was done. They were married.

The preacher closed his Bible and beamed a smile. "You may kiss your bride, Josiah."

He bent toward her and pressed a light peck on her cheek. It was over in an instant. Then he was moving away to thank the preacher and accept his brother's congratulations.

Mattie experienced a curious prick of disappointment that he hadn't given her a real kiss to seal their vows. As if she'd been denied something significant.

Lifting her hand, she touched the place where his lips had so briefly rested and felt the small scar that marred her skin.

He had kissed it, though she was certain that hadn't been his intention. He'd probably never even noticed the slight imperfection, which served as a physical reminder to her of the disastrous marriage she'd narrowly avoided.

To have her new husband seal their wedding vows with a kiss on precisely that spot…

Was this God's way of telling her she was meant to be with Josiah?

All her life, she'd dreamed of a union that was a true

partnership, bound together by love and caring, as her parents' had been before her mother's untimely passing. Marriage to the one God had made just for her.

Was Josiah that man?

Would deep and abiding feelings grow between them if she only had the patience not to rush things, as she had in the past?

The possibility brought a lightness to her heart, filling her with hope and optimism for the future and their marriage.

The wagon train made camp for the night a few hours later. Rebecca prepared a special supper for the newlyweds and offered Mattie a sincere welcome into the Dawson family, seemingly determined not to focus on the way it had come about. Mattie was grateful for the other woman's support.

Josiah appeared likewise appreciative of his sister-in-law's efforts, if his hearty appetite was anything to judge by. After two helpings, he declined Rebecca's offer of more.

Stretching his arms over his head, he covered a yawn. "Well, I don't know about the rest of you, but I'm ready to call it a night."

Rebecca glanced up from the dish she was wiping clean. "Adela is welcome to stay with me tonight to give you two some privacy." She shifted her gaze to her husband. "You don't mind sleeping outside for one night, do you, dear?"

Elias opened his mouth to answer.

But Josiah cut across his brother before the other man could speak. "That's not necessary. There's no need for any shuffling. I'll bed down where I usually do. And everyone else can do the same."

"But it's your wedding night," Rebecca protested.

"No, it's not," he refuted. "This isn't a normal marriage. Therefore, the usual traditions have no place here. Our union is a means to protect Mattie and her sister during the journey. Nothing more. Once we reach Oregon Country, the marriage will be annulled."

Stunned by this declaration, Mattie gaped at Josiah. He hadn't said a word to her about annulment earlier.

She snapped her mouth closed, her cheeks heating at his unexpected rejection. It was painful to think that he was so obviously opposed to his marriage to her lasting a lifetime. He was already anticipating their union's demise. Had been even before he spoke his vows.

As much as Mattie feared the thought of being permanently tied to a man who might never love her, she should now be feeling relieved that she wouldn't be trapped in a loveless marriage forever. Grateful to Josiah for providing a convenient out. But she found she was curiously wounded, instead. Because he wasn't making this choice for her sake, but for his own.

It hurt to learn his desire to rid himself of his unwanted wife was so great that he planned to see Mattie gone from his life at the earliest opportunity.

But after all the trouble she'd caused him, was it truly so surprising that he would be glad to see the last of her? Sadly, his attitude was all too understandable. Her heart contracted at the thought.

Perhaps she should have guessed his intent from the start. Should've realized he didn't mean to marry her until death. Not when he'd been compelled into it by a sense of moral obligation rather than any deep affection for her.

Remembering their earlier conversation by the side of the river, she realized that he'd truly meant it when he had told her not to think of him as anything more than a friend.

She thought of her ridiculously starry-eyed dreams of just a few short hours ago—how she'd taken such encouragement in believing the specific placement of a simple kiss held some great significance. Reading entirely too much into mere happenstance.

She had arrived at a false conclusion based on very little real proof, building her future on a foundation as insubstantial as wisps of cloud. Again. She was always too quick in making assumptions and inevitably acted unwisely as a result.

When would she ever learn not to rush headlong into things, galloping ahead at breakneck speed, without first testing the footing for possible quicksand?

Even now, she still believed Josiah was a man she could love, given half a chance. Thus, it was imperative she guard her heart against him. Because he had made it clear he would never come to love her in return.

"I'll see you all in the morning." Josiah beat a hasty retreat, no doubt anxious to escape before his sister-in-law had a chance to voice any more opposition.

Rebecca turned to Mattie, dismay plain in her expression, while Elias's gaze was full of compassion for his brother's scorned bride. Adela just looked wide-eyed and bewildered.

With her feelings in jumbled confusion, Mattie wasn't up to further conversation, most especially as it looked to include well-meaning but unwanted

platitudes from her new—and very short-term—
in-laws. After bidding them a quick good-night, she
disappeared into her covered wagon with Adela in tow.

"Are you all right?" the younger girl asked, distress
plain on her face.

"I'm fine."

Adela worried the corner of her lip. "How can you
be fine when today was as far from the wedding day
of your dreams as it's possible to get? Never mind that
your marriage won't ever be the love match you've
prayed for."

Preferring not to be reminded of things over which
she had no control, Mattie ruthlessly pushed such
thoughts from her mind. "That's not important. All that
matters is reaching our relatives safely. By whatever
means necessary." She grasped her sister's hands. "I
appreciate your concern, but there's no need for worry.
I promise. Remember what Papa always used to say?"

"Things happen according to God's plan," Adela
recited. But her eyebrows scrunched together, marring the pale skin above the bridge of her nose. "Do
you truly believe that? Even now?"

"Especially now." Mattie delivered a comforting
squeeze to Adela's fingers. "We need to get to Oregon
Country, and He provided the way."

"I guess you're right."

"Of course I am." Mattie reached up to smooth the
creases on Adela's forehead. "Now, no more fretting."

"I just want you to be happy." Adela wrapped her
arms around Mattie in a tight hug.

Mattie stroked the younger girl's silky hair and then
pulled back so she could look into her face. "I can't

help but be happy when I have such a sweet and caring sister as you."

That coaxed a small smile from Adela.

"Come on, it's time to turn in."

As Mattie prepared for bed, she could hear Rebecca and Elias in quiet conversation a short distance away. At first, their words were so softly spoken as to be indistinguishable.

But as Rebecca's emotional state increased, so too did the volume of her voice. "Wedding vows are sacred. Josiah promised to love and honor her, in sickness and health, through good times and strife, as long as they both shall live—"

Elias said something too low for Mattie to catch.

"I didn't intend to repeat the entire marriage ceremony," Rebecca answered back. "But your brother promised 'till death' in the presence of man and God, and I just don't understand how he could do that and then speak so causally of breaking that vow. Marriage isn't something one jumps in and out of willy-nilly. And don't you shush me, Elias Dawson." But, despite her command, she heeded her husband's admonition.

Mattie could make out nothing else that was said after that.

Other sounds drifted to her, indicating the couple was moving around their wagon and getting things stowed away. After a few minutes, she heard the creak of wood as someone climbed onto the tailgate. Then the heavy tread of a man's steps passed by, and the light from the campfires cast his shadow on the canvas above Mattie's head.

She surmised that Rebecca had been the one to climb inside their covered wagon.

The other woman had made her opinion plain, but Mattie wondered what Elias thought about his brother's plans. Had he known all along that Josiah didn't intend to make a lifetime commitment to Mattie?

Josiah heard footsteps approaching and opened his eyes to find his brother walking toward him. Pushing into a sitting position, he waited for Elias to sink down next to him on the ground.

The older man sat with one arm hooked around his up-drawn knee, but long minutes passed without him speaking.

"Well?" Josiah finally broke the silence. "Did your wife send you out here?"

"Nope."

"Then why are you here?"

"I thought you might want to talk."

"Not particularly." He dropped back to a horizontal position and closed his eyes.

But Elias didn't leave. Josiah could feel his gaze resting on him.

Lifting an eyelid, he met his brother's look. Then heaved a sigh, opened both eyes and sat up again. "What do you want me to say?"

"I don't know. Maybe you can tell me when you decided that your marriage to Mattie was only temporary."

"That was the plan all along."

"Really? You never mentioned it to me. And Mattie seemed caught off guard by your announcement."

"Did she?" He thought back over the scene, trying to remember her expression. But he couldn't. He'd been focused on Rebecca at the time and hadn't glanced in Mattie's direction.

"Yes, she did," Elias confirmed.

Struggling to recall exactly what he'd said to Mattie earlier while standing on the bank of the river, Josiah again drew a blank. "Maybe I didn't say it in so many words. But she knew marriage was at Miles's behest. I assumed she realized this union was simply to meet his terms, and then only for as long as it was necessary."

Would she have reacted differently if he'd made his intention clear? If she'd understood she wasn't required to bind herself to him permanently, would her resistance have instantly vanished? Might she have accepted without argument or delay and thus saved him from witnessing her hesitation, which had ripped open old wounds? There was no way to know. He couldn't go back and do things over again.

"Well, don't worry. You've certainly made yourself clear now. No one's in any doubt."

"That's all to the good."

A slight frown tugged down the corners of Elias's mouth. "So, you're not willing to give this marriage a chance?"

He shook his head and scrubbed a hand over his face. "To what end? This marriage wasn't of our choosing. Neither Mattie nor I want a true union."

Elias considered him, his gaze steady and direct. "How can you know for sure what she wants? Did you ask her?"

"I didn't have to." Her opinion was all too apparent in her reluctance to wed him. "You weren't there, but trust me. It wasn't necessary for her to say the words to my face. She made it plain she doesn't want me for a husband."

And he didn't require further proof that he wasn't the type of man women wished to marry. Didn't care to be reminded that he could never measure up. His hand curled into a fist against his thigh.

It was a good thing his heart was walled off, or Mattie's protracted hesitation would have cut even deeper into something of much more importance than his pride.

He turned his attention back to his brother. "Now, if you don't mind, I have to be up early in the morning, and I'd like to get some sleep before then."

"Maybe some sleep will improve your disposition." Elias stood and moved away.

"There's nothing wrong with my disposition," he called after his brother.

Elias didn't look back or comment. He just kept walking, leaving Josiah alone again.

Grumbling to himself over interfering siblings, Josiah reminded himself it was best that the marriage was only temporary. That they didn't have expectations of love growing between them. That would never happen. And the last thing he wanted to do was cause Mattie pain.

But judging by her actions, there was little chance of that. Little chance that she'd weave fairy tales around him. Or that she might start hoping for more than he could give.

That last thought should have taken a weight off his mind. Should have made him feel less constricted.

So, why didn't it?

* * *

Lying in the quiet of the early morning hours, Mattie watched the inside of the wagon gradually lighten as dawn neared. This was the only time when she could just be still. When she didn't have to be constantly on the move, either walking along the trail or performing a myriad of tasks at the beginning and end of each day.

The tranquility didn't last long, however. Over the sound of Adela's soft snoring, Mattie could hear people moving around outside the covered wagon, signaling that it was time to get up and start the day. As soon as the morning meal was over, everything would be packed back into the wagons, the teams hitched up, and they'd get under way.

The same as any other day on the trail, despite the extraordinary events of yesterday. So, there was no point in dwelling on them.

Mattie tossed back the covers and collected her clothes, then changed out of her nightgown. She felt hobbled by her full skirt after weeks spent wearing men's trousers and figured it would take some time to become accustomed to dresses again. Running a brush through the short strands of her hair, she was done in seconds. Though she missed her long locks, their absence made quick work of her morning routine.

Donning a bonnet, she bent over her sister and gave her a gentle nudge. "Wake up, Adela. It's time to get up."

The younger girl rolled over onto her back, then sat up and hid a yawn behind her hand. "I'm up."

Satisfied that Adela wouldn't fall asleep again, Mattie lifted the canvas flap and ducked outside. A pearly-gray sky greeted her, showing hints of orange and pink on the eastern horizon. She breathed in the fresh air and caught a hint of wood smoke.

Climbing to the ground, she rounded the end of the wagon and found Rebecca stirring coals from the previous night's fire. "Good morning."

Rebecca returned her greeting, then continued, "If you want to make the coffee, I'll get breakfast started. There's no sense tending two campfires and cooking separate meals now we're family."

Mattie chose not to dispute the other woman's claim even though they were family only in the strictest sense of the word.

Moving to start on the task of brewing coffee as Rebecca had requested, they worked side by side in silence. Whatever her new sister-in-law's thoughts on the state of Mattie's marriage—and she had a good idea from the conversation she'd overheard last night—Rebecca chose to hold her peace.

For which Mattie could only be thankful. It wasn't that she disagreed with the other woman's viewpoint, but no more would she allow foolish emotion to guide her actions. Each time she heeded her heart over her head, it led her astray. From here on out, that was at an end.

Adela appeared shortly thereafter and asked what she could do to help. Once given instructions, she quickly got to work assisting in the meal preparation.

Sarah Jane came bounding over, with her mother following behind at a slower pace. Edith Baker exchanged a few pleasantries with the three women before reminding her daughter she could only stay until breakfast was ready, and then needed to rejoin her family to eat.

"Be sure to mind Miss Adela and Miss Rebecca. And Miss Mattie, too," she added belatedly, not yet used to including her in the group.

"Yes, Mama," the little girl replied obediently.

With a smile and a wave, Edith left them to return to her own campfire.

Soon bacon and potatoes sizzled in a skillet, while the rich aroma of coffee filled the air. Josiah and Elias appeared, no doubt drawn by the smell. Mattie poured two cups of coffee and handed one to each man.

Josiah smiled his thanks and leaned against the wagon wheel, his elbow propped on the rim. The dawn light illuminated his beard-stubbled face, and a slight breeze lifted strands of his red-gold hair.

She didn't know what to say to him, so she remained silent and let the others carry the conversation. Although there'd been many times when "Matt" had opted not to speak, she'd never been at such a loss for words before. What was different about today that she suddenly couldn't string together two syllables? It couldn't be the marriage, since it hadn't changed anything between them. At least, it wasn't supposed to have changed anything.

Still, she couldn't deny that a distinct shift had taken place. She didn't feel like the same person she'd been before yesterday. She wasn't "Matt" anymore. Or even simply Mattie. She was Matilda Dawson. A wife, however temporarily.

But she had no idea how to act like one. Especially as Josiah clearly didn't expect the normal wifely gestures. Didn't want them. Yet their arrangement meant that he'd eat food she helped cook, wear clothes she washed and mended. Rebecca had taken care of those things for him up till now, but that was when he was a bachelor. It wasn't fair to leave the burden on her when Mattie was perfectly capable of doing the tasks. Would Josiah think she was overstepping?

The only thing that was certain was she shouldn't read anything into his silence. As she'd already discovered, it wasn't always indicative of his inner feelings.

The morning meal was consumed quickly, in deference to Miles's desire to make up for time lost the previous day.

Once Mattie finished eating, she turned to her sister. "Will you help Rebecca with the cleanup while I go take care of the oxen?"

Adela nodded her agreement and accepted the dirty plate Mattie handed her. Standing up, Mattie moved around the campfire in the direction of the livestock.

Josiah stopped her with a hand on her wrist. "I can hitch the oxen up to your wagon for you." Forking up one last bite of food, he washed it down with a swig of coffee.

Her skin tingled where his fingers had briefly made contact, and she rubbed the spot in an attempt to erase the peculiar sensation. "That's not necessary. I'm perfectly capable of doing it myself."

"You'll get no argument from me on that point, but the whole purpose of yesterday was so you wouldn't have to take on everything by yourself anymore."

It was a tempting thought…and a dangerous one. She couldn't allow herself to become reliant on him, knowing that he would leave her behind in a few months' time when they reached Oregon Country. Growing accustomed to Josiah's help and support would be a hard habit to break, if she was foolish enough to let it form.

"I appreciate the offer, but—"

"You're not going to accept it," he finished for her, appearing unsurprised by her refusal. Almost as if he'd been expecting it, but had felt duty-bound to extend the offer anyway.

She nodded in acknowledgment of his words. "I've gotten used to the daily routine. There's no call to go changing it now. Besides, I don't want to take you away from your horses." He had a regimented training schedule that she hated to disrupt.

"Miles will give the order to move out soon, so I'd best see to my oxen, as well," Elias remarked.

Before heading away from the campfire, he paused to give his wife a lingering kiss goodbye. His behavior was sweetly sentimental, as he wasn't going very far and would be back by Rebecca's side in a matter of mere minutes.

Clearly, he was of the opinion that a man didn't need a reason to shower his wife with loving gestures. And Rebecca appeared to agree wholeheartedly. They shared a tender look filled with caring and deep affection.

Mattie felt as if she was intruding on a private moment simply by witnessing it, and she turned away. Her gaze landed on Josiah's back, already several yards away and rapidly widening the distance between them. But it wasn't as though he had any cause to wait for her.

The contrasts between the other married couple and Mattie and Josiah were marked. That was only to be expected, however, given the dissimilarities in their relationships. Elias and Rebecca loved each other, and it showed in their every action when they were together.

Though Mattie desired a marriage like that for herself, one of shared looks and warm embraces, she didn't fool herself that she would find it with Josiah.

For a brief time—the space of a few hours—she had deluded herself otherwise, but he'd quickly set her straight.

Josiah didn't see her as a true partner and helpmate. And he never would.

Neither had her ex-fiancé.

Would she ever find a man who truly wanted to spend his life with her? A man who saw the person she was deep inside and loved her? Would she ever experience that kind of love, sharing a bond with another that went soul deep? As strong and lasting as the one connecting her mother and father?

It seemed she'd searched for it forever. Had run after it, only to find what she'd been chasing was nothing more than an illusion that had led her off course.

What if it simply wasn't meant to be? Perhaps, it was time to stop searching. Time to let go of her impossible dream.

Sensible or not, her heart rebelled at the thought.

Chapter Eleven

"It doesn't look like she's learned who the boss is yet."

Josiah pulled his eyes away from Mattie and skewered his brother with a glare. "What?" Belatedly, he noted the other man's gaze was focused on Josiah's mount, not his wife. "Oh, you mean the horse."

The mare jerked her head up, attempting to pull the leather reins from his gloved hand. Almost as if she'd understood their words and wanted to show she was in charge.

He tugged on the reins to bring her head back down. "It will take a bit more conditioning before she accepts she's not the one calling the shots." Reining her in as she pranced to the side, he narrowly avoided a collision with Elias and the unhitched team of oxen he led. "The trick is not to break her spirit, only gentle her."

He'd been working with all his horses, rotating which ones he rode each day. But this little piebald had a stubborn streak that brought a certain woman to mind.

Turning his gaze back to Mattie, he found she'd

finished unhitching her oxen and now prodded them in this direction, toward the designated grazing area for the noon stop.

He was more than happy to do that job for her, as he'd told her several times over the past few days since their wedding. But she hadn't backed down from her stubborn insistence on handling it herself, and always completed the task before he could get his horses settled and return to the covered wagon.

As she neared him, he swung his leg over the saddle to dismount. The horse sidestepped away from him unexpectedly. He lost his balance and dropped like a stone, instead of the controlled descent he'd intended. His right foot hit the ground hard, taking the brunt of his weight, and his ankle rolled. Pain lanced through it.

Grabbing the saddle horn to maintain his balance while on one foot, he tightened his hand on the reins and held the mare in place. "Whoa, easy," he murmured when she tried to shift away, clearly displeased at him using her as a prop.

He glanced over the horse's back, thankful to discover that neither Mattie nor Elias was paying him any mind just now, as both were occupied staking their respective oxen.

But they wouldn't be kept busy for long. Best to assess the damage while he still had a few moments without an audience.

He put weight on his right leg to test it and immediately regretted the action. A hiss of pain slipped past his lips.

Elias straightened and turned toward him. Had he heard Josiah? Clamping his mouth closed, he blanked his expression.

The other man didn't appear to notice anything amiss. "Hurry up and unsaddle your horse. Rebecca will have dinner ready soon, and we don't have time to dawdle. Miles keeps a tight schedule."

"You and Mattie go ahead without me. I'll be there in a minute." Josiah stood motionless, silently urging them on their way. But they didn't move. "What are you waiting for?"

"I was just about to ask you that," Elias returned, rounding the back end of Josiah's horse.

Mattie's eyebrows furrowed. "Is something wrong?"

He sighed, knowing neither would budge until he answered their questions. "I turned my ankle. But it's no big deal."

Elias gave him an once-over, taking in his one-legged stance. "If it's no big deal, let me see you walk on it."

Mattie moved to the mare's head and took charge of the reins.

Left with no choice, Josiah released the leather and obeyed Elias's order. He took a step with his good foot then another much quicker one with his other to keep his full weight off the injured ankle as much as possible. Normal step, quick step, normal step, quick step, he strode along and hoped his brother wouldn't notice his uneven gate. "See, I'm fine."

"Except for the grimace twisting your face and the fact that you're limping around like a lamed horse." Elias stepped forward and placed an arm around Josiah's waist. "Come on, lean on me, and I'll help you over to the wagon."

"Wait. I need to tend to my horse first." He made a move away from the other man.

Elias tightened his grip, but that didn't deter Josiah.

At the same time, Mattie stepped toward him. At least *she* was willing to cooperate.

But instead of handing over the reins as he'd anticipated, she put her palm against his shirtfront, halting him in his tracks. "I'll take care of the horse. You go with your brother. And do what he says." She lowered her arm and led his mount away.

It rankled that he'd been ganged up on. "I could have seen to the horse myself," he grumbled as he stretched an arm across his brother's shoulders.

"And crippled yourself worse, no doubt." Elias maneuvered them in the direction of the campsite, where Rebecca and Adela were preparing the noon meal.

Rebecca glanced up and saw them coming. Her eyes widened in surprise, and she quickly jumped into action, clearing off the top of a wooden crate. "Sit him down here," she instructed.

Elias ducked out from beneath Josiah's arm, but maintained a grip on his elbow to steady him. Hopping on one foot, Josiah positioned himself with his back to the seat, then braced his hand on the edge of the crate and dropped down onto the wooden surface.

Concern shone in Rebecca's gaze. "What happened?"

Elias related the incident as he squatted in front of Josiah. "Let's have a look and see what kind of damage you did."

Josiah opened his mouth to protest it wasn't necessary.

But his brother's stern expression forestalled him. "If we don't get this boot off before your foot starts to swell, I'll be forced to cut it off."

"You'd cut off his foot?" Adela gasped in horror.

"The boot," Josiah explained. "Elias meant he'd have to cut off my boot." He turned his attention back to his brother. "I'd rather you didn't do that. I don't have a spare pair." Raising his leg, he presented his foot. "Have at it."

Elias took a firm grip on the boot heel, then flashed a look of compassion at Josiah. "Sorry, but this is likely to hurt."

"Just do it." Gritting his teeth, he bit back a groan when the boot was tugged free.

As the other man probed and prodded, Josiah curled his hands into fists. Sweat popped out on his forehead, and he swallowed a gasp of pain.

Out of the corner of his eye, he spotted Mattie's arrival. But he didn't glance fully at her. She'd already distracted him once today, and that was quite enough. He needed all his concentration to keep from visibly reacting to the torture his brother was inflicting on him.

"It doesn't seem to be broken, but you have a bad sprain," Elias pronounced. Finished with the examination, he lowered Josiah's foot to the ground. "You'll need to stay off it as much as possible until it heals. I'll wrap a bandage around it to restrict movement and provide support for the weakened joint." He stood up and headed to his wagon for the necessary supplies.

Staring down at his swelling ankle, Josiah berated himself for his stupidity. He knew better than to let his mind wander when he was working with a green-broke horse. That moment of distraction would cost him dearly. How was he supposed to do all the things that needed doing with this bum leg?

He glanced up and found Mattie watching him,

sympathy shadowing her eyes as if she'd read his thoughts. She moved past him and lifted the cover from the water barrel, then filled a dipper.

Returning to his side, she extended it toward him. "Have a drink."

"My leg's not broke. If I want a drink of water, I'll get it myself." He pushed the dipper away.

It slipped from her fingers and tumbled to the ground, sending water flying in all directions.

An expression of fear flashed across her face. While it was quickly masked, he knew he hadn't imagined it, though he wished he could explain it away so easily.

What nightmares tormented her that his feisty Mattie would react in such a way to his momentary fit of temper? She had stood toe-to-toe with him during their previous disagreements, unafraid to challenge him.

But now she'd retreated several paces. "I'm sorry. I was only trying to help."

His guts twisted at the knowledge that he'd made her feel even an instant of fear. "Please, don't apologize, Mattie. I'm the one who's sorry." A sorry excuse for a man.

He tried to push himself up and go to her, but his injury hindered his efforts. Subsiding, he reached out his hand to her, instead.

She straightened her shoulders and placed her fingers in his without hesitation, as if the past few moments had never happened. But they were etched into his mind and not easily erased.

He drew her forward and guided her down to sit on his good leg so their faces were on the same level. Though she held herself stiffly, she met his gaze without flinching.

He prayed she would see the sincerity in his eyes. "I'm sorry I took my frustrations out on you. It was wrong of me, and I humbly beg your forgiveness."

"Why?"

"Why should you forgive me?" He shook his head. "I don't know. I certainly don't deserve it. My behavior was uncalled-for and inexcusable."

"No, I didn't mean that. Why did you react that way over a dipper of water?"

His arm curved around her back as he rested his hand on his knee, next to her hip. "I was angry with myself and feeling a fool for making a mistake like a greenhorn his first day on the trail."

She cocked her head to the side and pursed her lips. "I don't recall any greenhorns in this group falling off their horses."

He grinned at her sass, glad to see her back in fighting form. "Well, at least I didn't knock myself on my rear, firing a rifle for the first time. I seem to recollect that happening to a certain greenhorn. Now, who was that again?"

"If you want her to forgive you, you're going about it all wrong," Elias butted into the conversation. "Apologies work better when they don't involve digs against the person you're apologizing to. You've already got one foot in your mouth, but I'm sure you could get the other to fit, too. I'd let you try, only I need to wrap your ankle first." He hunkered down next to Josiah's right side.

Mattie had relaxed into his loose hold, but she sprang off his lap at Elias's last comment.

Josiah grabbed her hand before she could escape completely. "I was just teasing her," he explained to

his brother. "She can't stay cross at me when I do that."
Waggling his eyebrows at Mattie, he tugged playfully
on her fingers. "Isn't that right?"

She shifted, giving Elias space to work, but didn't
pull her hand away. "Just because it worked before
doesn't mean it will work again now."

"I stand corrected."

"No, you *sit* corrected. Which is why I forgive you
for roaring like a lion with a thorn in his paw. Now, let
me go help Rebecca and Adela." She wiggled her fingers, reminding him that he still held them in his grasp.

He didn't want to let her go. And that simple fact
had him hastily releasing her hand. Glancing past her,
he spotted Rebecca giving them an indulgent look and
Adela wearing a sappy expression on her face.

His own face heated at the realization that he'd been
so focused on flirting with Mattie he'd forgotten the
other two females present. They had clearly been an
avid audience to the little scene he'd just preformed.
He lowered his eyes to the ground.

Mattie drew his gaze as she bent to retrieve the dipper. Cleaning the dirt from it, she hooked the handle
over the rim of the water barrel.

His mouth felt parched, and the muddy patches at
his feet seemed to mock him. But he wouldn't ask her
to bring him another dipper of water after he'd behaved
like a fractious child over her offering before. Going
thirsty seemed a fitting punishment.

Though he wasn't used to sitting still and doing
nothing, surprisingly, the inactivity didn't bother him.
He watched Mattie helping Rebecca and Adela with
preparations for the noon meal, her movements grace-
ful and assured. He much preferred to see her working

at domestic tasks rather than taking on a man's job. Not that she couldn't do it. But she shouldn't have to.

She was a fascinating bundle of contradictions. Raised in an affluent household with servants, she'd still somehow managed to learn the skills necessary to tend her own mount.

Brave and daring most of the time. And yet he'd frightened her with a small, thoughtless action.

A rare and precious jewel, more fragile than he'd realized, she had facets he was only just discovering.

Mattie could feel Josiah's eyes on her, tracking her every move.

What must he think of her? She had reacted to him as if he was a vicious blackguard when he'd done nothing to warrant such a strong response.

Glimpsing temper sparking in his eyes and his hand coming up, she'd flashed back to another time. The present had receded, and she was once again in a dark formal parlor, face-to-face with her ex-fiancé. His open palm swinging toward her face, a large ruby ring glinting on his third finger.

In the next moment, the image had vanished. She was back on the sun-washed prairie amid covered wagons. And feeling absurd for her overreaction.

She wasn't ordinarily one to cringe and cower. Certainly not from a man whose honor and decency she trusted as completely as Josiah's.

It was small comfort that it had been an involuntary reaction to flinch away from him. Remnants of the past bleeding into her present.

She'd left that life behind, but still it seemed to color her every thought and interaction with Josiah, no matter how unconsciously. All on the basis of another man's misdeeds.

Although she had finally discovered that Josiah *did* have a flaw, it was far from what she'd suspected during their first few weeks on the trail.

He lacked patience with his own weaknesses and made no allowances for himself, though he was always forgiving the shortcomings of everyone else.

The knowledge didn't diminish her opinion of him. If anything, it made her respect him more for the way he showed such consideration for his fellow man. Herself included.

She was reminded of how he'd rushed to offer an apology to her after his surliness. His strong arm had wrapped around her back, not letting her go until he'd made amends for the small fright he had unintentionally caused.

Within his embrace, she'd felt safe and protected. Comforted by his closeness and the steady beat of his heart, in those fleeting moments when she had leaned against his chest.

She didn't want to think about why it was a bad idea for her to allow herself to feel such things around him. The thought lingered in the back of her mind as she worked, that he had the power to affect her.

The noon meal was a hurried affair, and once everything was packed back into the wagons, it was time to hitch up the oxen, then continue on the trail.

Elias indicated his intention to head to the grazing area and collect his animals.

Mattie planned to be right behind him, but the sight of Josiah reaching for his boot diverted her. "What do you think you're doing?" she queried.

He glanced up at her, one eyebrow raised. "What does it look like I'm doing? I'm putting my boot back on, so I can saddle a horse."

"Oh, no, you're not." She made a grab for his boot.

But he guessed her aim and moved it out of her reach. "What's that supposed to mean?"

She stepped back, refusing to be drawn into a childish game of keep-away. "Well, for one thing, you shouldn't walk on that foot. And for another, you definitely can't ride with it."

"Oh, no? Just watch me."

Crossing her arms, she proceeded to do exactly that.

He attempted to pull the boot past his swollen, bandaged ankle and grimaced with the effort.

"Having a little trouble?" she questioned sweetly.

A glare was her answer.

She waited. He'd have to give up eventually. Even she could see that he wouldn't be able to force his foot back into the boot. It wasn't going to fit, no matter how hard he tried. And he did try. For a solid five minutes. She gave him full marks for persistence.

Finally, he growled in frustration and dropped the boot to the ground.

By this point, Elias had returned with both sets of oxen, and Mattie moved her team into position in front of her covered wagon, while Elias did the same with his. Then he returned to help his brother climb onto the bench seat of Mattie's wagon.

Josiah immediately balked. "Thanks, but no, thanks. I'll ride one of my horses."

Mattie opened her mouth to protest.

But Elias was quicker. "Those green-broke horses are high-strung and unpredictable. You try to ride one of them, and you'll make your injury worse. Is that what you want?"

Mattie pressed her lips together, her gaze shifting back and forth between the two men. It seemed prudent to let the doctor handle his brother. Elias was bigger than her and able to move Josiah bodily, if necessary.

Their war of wills stretched on for several charged seconds, but the older brother had the advantage since Josiah wasn't at full strength. Left with no option but to concede the field, he did so grudgingly.

Several days later, his disposition was little improved.

He shifted restlessly on the wooden seat. If he was searching for a better position, he wouldn't find it. Covered wagons weren't designed with the comfort of passengers in mind.

Since Josiah was driving her oxen, she'd taken over his duties, herding his string of horses. The decision hadn't gone over well with him, but he didn't have much choice in the matter. Someone needed to see to the responsibility in his place. It was a switch, him having to rely on Mattie, instead of the other way around.

She reined in beside him. "We'll be stopping to make camp about a mile up ahead."

He grunted in response, reminding her of a sulking little boy vexed at having his favorite toy taken away. The corners of her mouth curled up at the thought.

Catching her expression, his eyebrows pulled together. "It seems to me that you're enjoying my current predicament a mite too much. But don't get used to it. The swelling in my ankle has gone down, and tomorrow I'll be back on a horse. No matter what Elias has to say about it. I've had about all I can take of choking on trail dust and bouncing around on this hard wooden seat."

Though she worried whether his ankle was healed enough to withstand the strain, she didn't attempt to dissuade him. She was frankly surprised that he'd submitted for this long. Only the fact that his stern-eyed brother was driving the wagon directly behind him had kept Josiah in check.

Meanwhile, Mattie had taken full advantage of the opportunity to ride away from the line of covered wagons and the cloud of dust kicked up by twenty-five teams of oxen.

There was a sense of freedom while on horseback that nothing else could compare with. Moving as one with the animal, the wind whipping past, it seemed as if all her cares were left far behind. She'd missed that feeling over the past weeks of walking.

She gave the horse's neck an affectionate pat. "I had a mare with this coloring, back in Saint Louis."

The corner of Josiah's mouth quirked up in amusement as he glanced in her direction. "Which you no doubt rode sidesaddle while wearing a fancy getup that matched your horse's pale yellow coat."

He wasn't wrong about her past life—leaving out the part about color-coordinating her riding habit and her mount. Her lifestyle back then was a far cry from her present position sitting astride the palomino, with her simple lavender cotton skirts hiked up to her knees and a pair of her father's trousers sticking out from beneath, covering her lower legs.

Figuring he was simply trying to get a raise from her with his comment, she didn't take the bait. "My father purchased her when I was twelve. And I begged and pleaded for him to let me ride her. He kept refusing, saying she was too much for me to handle until I got a little bigger, and the horse had additional training."

"Let me guess," Josiah cut in. "You ignored his dictates."

"I might have...*forgotten* that he'd forbidden me," she allowed.

"Why am I not surprised? So, what happened when you disobeyed your daddy and tried to ride the horse?"

"Well, I wasn't strong enough to lift the saddle onto her back or tall enough to get the bridle over her head. But I couldn't ask for help, since all the stable hands knew of my father's restriction. Therefore, I decided to do without. It didn't seem a problem—she was docile as could be when I led her out of her stall. This gave me great confidence, and I climbed onto the mounting block, certain I would shortly show my father he was wrong about both of us." She paused, wondering why she had started telling Josiah a story that ended in her humiliation.

"Well, go on," he prompted. "What happened next?"

Sighing in resignation, she continued. "The moment I sat down on her back, she bucked. Before I knew quite how it had come about, I found myself in the water trough. Wet, but unharmed."

His eyebrows arched in alarm. "You could have been seriously injured."

"That's what my father said. He was furious. But the Good Lord was watching over me. And I told my father so. Still, that didn't stop him from banning me from the stables for an entire month. He hired a trainer to work with the mare, and afterward gave her to me for my thirteenth birthday. She was sold, along with all our other horses, before we left Saint Louis." When her father could no longer afford the upkeep for a full stable and needed money to finance their overland trip.

She didn't want to dwell on that and turned the focus back to Josiah. "When you reach Oregon Country and start your horse ranch, will you train other people's horses, besides selling the ones you've gentled?"

"Most likely," he answered, accepting her change of subject without comment. "There's sure to be a need. Too many people are of the opinion that the job's done once they're able to get a saddle on a horse and ride it around a couple times. But that mount wouldn't be suitable for an inexperienced rider. Or a child." He gave her a significant look.

"I'm not twelve anymore," she reminded him.

He flashed a charming grin. "I had noticed. And you're certainly more than capable of handling any saddle-ready horse now." His gaze shifted briefly to his string of horses, then returned to her.

Her cheeks heated at the admiring look in his eyes, while his praise caused a warm glow to spread through her.

"Will you hire other trainers to help you?" she queried, in an attempt to bring the conversation back to its original focus.

"Why do you ask? Are you intending to apply for the position?"

"Of course not." She'd given little thought to her future beyond reaching her relatives. "I was only curious."

"Well, to answer your question—no, I won't be hiring other trainers. At least, not right away. The ranch will be small to start, but I want to build it up to include breeding and raising horses, as well as training them." He outlined his plans in more detail, his face animated as he spoke of everything he hoped to accomplish.

His return to good spirits was a welcome relief. Mattie had come to expect his ready smile, and she'd felt its absence over the past few days.

She refused to look too closely at what that might mean.

Chapter Twelve

"What's wrong?" Adela asked a few nights later as they sat by the campfire after supper.

Mattie pulled her finger away from her mouth to answer. "I stabbed myself with the needle." For the third time. She was commencing to feel like a pincushion.

Rebecca had revealed she was in the family way, and Mattie and Adela were helping stitch garments for the coming child, which was expected to arrive in just over three months' time, somewhere around the beginning of October.

But Mattie's mind wasn't on the task. Instead, it circled round and round why Josiah's mood mattered to her so much. His happiness shouldn't have the ability to affect her that way. But it did. And she didn't like the implications.

Despite her steadfast faith in his character, she couldn't let down her guard. In fact, she had to be even more vigilant now that she'd recognized the emotional danger he posed to her. Because no matter how wonderful he was, Josiah was still the wrong man for her.

He wasn't offering forever, only a temporary union.

He'd made his position on the matter clear. He didn't want to be joined to her, didn't consider her as his wife. This marriage was nothing more than a means to an end.

And if she gave her heart to him, she'd be left with a gaping hole when they parted ways.

Still, her eyes were drawn to him. At the moment, he sat with his head bent over the saddle scabbard for his rifle, repairing an area where the stitching had come loose. She watched his strong hands work the supple leather. When he finished the job, he glanced up at her, almost as if he'd sensed her gaze on him.

Caught staring, she rushed into speech. "I was thinking I should learn the proper way to handle a rifle. It's an important skill to have out here on the trail. And I want to know I can protect myself if the need should ever arise."

"That's a very practical mind-set," Rebecca replied, then turned to her brother-in-law. "Why don't you teach her, Josiah? The two of you can go a little ways from the wagon train, where she doesn't have to fear that she might hit someone by accident."

Mattie silently groaned in dismay. She'd said the first thing that popped into her head without giving a thought for where it might lead. Rebecca had spotted the perfect opening to get Mattie and Josiah off alone together, and she'd seized it.

Mattie wanted to protest against the suggestion, but that would seem odd after she'd brought up the subject herself. She silently willed Josiah to refuse.

He didn't seem to receive her message. After nodding his agreement, he glanced at the sky. "We have about an hour of daylight left. I can give you a quick lesson now. Unless you'd rather continue with your sewing."

Rebecca reached over and plucked the material from Mattie's lax grasp before she had time to accept the reprieve. "There's plenty of time for Mattie to work on this later. The baby won't be here for several months yet." She tucked the half-finished garment away in her sewing basket. "Now, off you go."

"Maybe we shouldn't. Won't people worry if they hear shots?" Mattie argued in a bid to avoid Rebecca's obvious attempt at matchmaking.

"I'll let Miles know it's only a little target practice and no cause for alarm," Elias offered. Setting aside his knife and the small chunk of wood he was carving into a cross, he pushed to his feet to seek out the wagon master.

Mattie turned to her sister. "You should come with us, Adela." The younger girl could use the lessons, since she was even more clueless about guns than Mattie. More importantly, she could act as a buffer.

Adela thwarted her efforts, however. "No, thank you. I saw what happened to you the last time you shot Papa's rifle."

Mattie could have done without that reminder, which increased her dread for the coming event. But out of excuses to delay, she headed to her wagon and retrieved the rifle.

Surely, she was fretting over nothing. Rebecca might hope for something to happen between them, but that didn't mean it would. Mattie had been alone with Josiah on a number of occasions and nothing of a romantic nature had occurred.

That was before she'd lost a bit of the armor surrounding her heart, however. But no matter. She would simply strengthen her fortifications and ensure her emotions were well protected. It shouldn't be too difficult a task.

But despite her optimistic thoughts, she couldn't ignore the fact that she felt vulnerable as they set out together. He took the rifle from her, his fingers brushing against hers, and she quickly pulled away from the contact.

She and Josiah exchanged greetings with several people while making their way through camp, but they didn't stop to chat. The notes of a fiddle and harmonica, playing a jaunty tune, drifted above the hum of conversations and the occasional burst of laughter. None of this served to lessen her anxiety, however. The sounds faded as she and Josiah moved away from the circle of covered wagons, their footsteps crunching on the sandy soil.

Over the past week, the landscape had changed as the wagon train left the plains behind and moved to a higher elevation. Here, the ground was littered with large boulders and shrubby bushes.

It was to a cluster of these bushes that Josiah led her. "This looks like a good spot, far enough away from the wagons." He turned his attention to the rifle and checked it over.

"It's not loaded," she explained. "After I fired it, I didn't know how to reload the powder and shot." Her cheeks heated at the admission.

An incredulous expression enveloped his features. "Are you telling me you continued to go on guard duty with a gun that wasn't loaded? Never mind. The answer is obvious."

She was stung by the insinuation that she had done something which could have endangered their group. "Well, would you have wanted me to try to take a shot even if there had been trouble?" she demanded, feeling the need to defend her actions.

He didn't take so much as a moment to consider before he answered. "No. You likely would have caused more trouble than a whole gang of outlaws. It's a good thing for you there wasn't anything that needed shooting. Or perhaps I should say, it's a good thing for me. I might have stood in a place that should've been well out of range yet somehow still managed to be in your line of fire."

"I'll have you know that I wasn't actually aiming for that cute little bunny rabbit," she shot back, indignant.

He skewered her with a skeptical look. "So you say now."

"It's the truth!"

"Nonetheless, I should have thought to go over the basics with you long ago. It's not as if we had anything better to do with our time when we were on guard duty. I don't know why it didn't occur to me before this. I was remiss, but no more. Loading the rifle will be your first lesson."

She extended the bag that contained the necessary items, and Josiah took it from her.

"I'll show you how to do it the first time, then you can try it yourself after that." He began his instruction, walking her through the process step by step. "Guns are useful tools, but you have to handle them with the proper caution."

She kept her mind focused on his words rather than the shape of his lips as he spoke. And she paid heed to what he was doing instead of allowing herself to be distracted by the flexing motions of his hands.

Finding that it only took a bit of mental discipline to stay focused, her tension drained away. This wasn't the ordeal it had seemed a short while ago. She'd simply blown it out of all proportion in her head.

Once the gun was loaded, he handed it to her. "I want you to aim for that clump of brush over there." He pointed a short distance away, to an area where five large scrub bushes were bunched together, covering several feet of ground.

"Any one in particular?"

"Nope. For now, let's just concentrate on getting your shot in that general vicinity. Once you've done that, then you can try aiming for a specific target. Now, bring up the rifle and fit the stock against your shoulder." He moved in close behind her and explained how to sight down the barrel.

Reaching around her, he placed his arms alongside hers to make a slight adjustment in her positioning, and for a minute she lost track of what he was saying. It took a determined effort to bring her mind back to his words.

"…don't rush your aim before pulling the trigger. You only have one shot, and then you'll have to reload. If you miss your target the first time, it's not going to wait until you're ready to shoot again. And seeing a wild animal bearing down on you can lead to panic and fumbling, which often prevents a person from getting off another shot. So, no matter what else is going on around you, remain calm and steady. Make your first shot count. Or it might be your last."

She nodded her understanding, but staying calm and

steady was easier said than done. A distracting male standing too close seemed to have a similar effect on her as facing a hostile attack.

Unaware of her dilemma, Josiah continued. "I'm sure I don't need to remind you that this rifle's got a kick like a green-broke horse."

"No, you don't. It's not something I'm ever likely to forget after the last time."

"You're going to feel it, even with the gun sitting tight against your shoulder. Be ready for it. Brace your legs a little farther apart. Right before you squeeze the trigger, take a deep breath in and hold it, otherwise the movement could throw off your aim. Now, pull back the hammer to cock the gun, and fire whenever you're ready."

He backed off a few paces, giving her some much-needed space, which allowed her to focus on the task at hand. She aimed at the center of the group of bushes and tried to do everything exactly as he'd specified. Preparing herself for the loud blast that would sound in her ear, she pulled the trigger.

Though she was fully aware the kick was coming, it still knocked her back a couple steps. She came up against the solid wall of Josiah's chest, and her finger accidentally jerked on the trigger again. She thanked God the gun was a single shot. If not for that, she could have easily ended up with a piece of lead through her foot.

Josiah put his hands on Mattie's upper arms and shifted his body away from her. Once he was certain she wouldn't stumble without his support, he released his hold.

He'd thought he was handling himself well, ignoring the sweet scent of her soft skin and not letting her proximity affect him. But then she'd practically fallen into his arms, and he couldn't delude himself any longer.

When she was near, he felt emotions he didn't want to feel. Hadn't thought he *could* feel anymore. Not with a heart that he'd done his level best to bury away.

Mattie was stubborn and fiercely determined to have her own way, but she was also courageous and protective of those weaker than her.

He, in turn, wanted to shield her and keep her safe, so that she never knew a moment of pain or heartache. But it was different from the brotherly affection he felt for Rebecca. And more than the caring of a mere friend. He felt an emotional connection to Mattie unlike anything he'd experienced before—even with Georgiana.

Holding Mattie close had seemed right and natural. But it wasn't. She might be his wife on paper, but she would never belong to him, could never be his wife in his heart.

Clearing his throat, he glanced away from her and toward the spot where her shot had kicked up a tiny cloud of dust behind the bushes. "Not bad. You hit your target."

He considered cutting the lesson short and returning to camp, but he'd promised to teach her. Showing her how to load the rifle and allowing her to take only one shot wasn't enough to satisfy his obligation.

Besides, there would come a time when she might have need of the knowledge. In a few short months, he wouldn't be around to look out for her anymore. True, she had family waiting for her in Oregon Country, complete with a fancy life in a grand house. But the future was uncertain and things didn't always work out the way a person hoped or planned. He knew from painful personal experience that the unexpected happened all too often. And he didn't want Mattie to be without resources, as his mother had been years ago.

Maybe he shouldn't be so quick to move on when they reached the end of the trail. Of course he had no intention of staying married to her permanently. But perhaps he could stick around until he was sure she was safely settled.

She'd probably see that as him overstepping, however, the same as she'd viewed his previous attempts to help her. Better that he carry through with his original plan.

Mattie wouldn't need him once they arrived at their destination. She didn't need him now except to meet Miles's terms. She had proved she was capable of overcoming most any circumstances. And he had little doubt she'd do the same in the future.

She wrinkled her nose at his compliment. "From this distance, it would have been hard to miss. It's a fairly big target."

"So it is. Reload and fire again. Only this time, pick a specific bush to aim for." He made sure to stay a few paces back from her and didn't move close to correct her positioning. Rather than touch her again, he simply told her what changes were needed.

She followed his directions and squeezed off another shot, which hit a branch on the center bush, sending a spray of small leaves to the ground. And she only staggered backward a step before catching her balance.

"Was that the one you were aiming at?"

"Yes." She didn't look at him as she reloaded the rifle.

Was she being deliberately evasive? "Would you tell me if it wasn't?" he wondered aloud.

Her eyes came up to meet his. "Yes. But if you doubt it, you can pick the next target."

He cocked an eyebrow at her. "The base of that second bush."

She turned back toward her makeshift targets. "The second one from the left or the right?"

"Left."

She took her time aiming, then pulled the trigger.

A clod of dirt flew into the air, indicating where the lead had landed, directly in front of the bush he'd specified.

Though impressed, he didn't let on. "That was a little low. Try again."

Her subsequent shot was better. And she followed it with several more that were right on the mark. She seemed to have a natural aptitude.

Next, he tested her skills on a small clump of grass a bit farther out.

Her aim was a little to the right, but she hit it on her second attempt.

Though she didn't voice any complaints, after firing the rifle a dozen times, she must be feeling the effects. "How's your shoulder holding up?"

"I doubt I'll ever get used to the kick," she admitted. "But it's nothing like the first time."

"We should probably be heading back anyway." They were losing the light as the sun sank behind the mountains toward the west.

"Should I reload the rifle first?"

"That's up to you. Most men keep their weapons ready, in case they need it in a hurry. But bouncing around in a covered wagon can sometimes cause the gun to go off accidentally. Weigh the necessity of being able to shoot quickly against the potential dangers. Are you comfortable having a loaded rifle in your wagon when Adela's nearby?"

"No. I guess I'll leave it empty for now."

As they walked back to their campsite, she didn't suggest a second practice session at a later date. But neither did he. Her reasons were a mystery. And his own? Well, he didn't want to examine them.

Nearing the circle of wagons, they met Elias heading out to guard duty. "How did it go?" he asked.

"Fine." Mattie offered nothing more as she passed him and continued on her way.

Elias's eyes followed her for a moment before he turned back to Josiah. "What's the matter? She seemed a little out of sorts."

"Nothing's the matter." At least not with her. But his answer came out sounding curt, which he hadn't intended.

Of course his brother picked up on the tone. "Apparently, Mattie's not the only one who's out of sorts. She didn't almost shoot you, did she?"

"No. With a little more instruction, she'll be a decent shot, actually." But he didn't want to talk about it.

Mattie had affected him in ways he hadn't expected. She shouldn't be able to touch his emotions when his heart was encased in ice. Yet she had somehow found a crack in a wall he'd believed was impenetrable.

He had to keep her from reaching further inside. She would never love him, didn't want to be married to him. And he'd never again open himself up to the hurt of having his affection rejected. Never again allow himself to feel something for a woman who found him wanting.

Perhaps it would be wise to stay away from Mattie for a time, until he could seal off the cracks in his defenses. But changing his behavior would be admitting that she posed a serious hazard to his heart. She didn't.

He blocked out the disquieting voice in the back of his mind that whispered otherwise.

Chapter Thirteen

Josiah watched Mattie walking in his direction, back-lit by the setting sun. Her gaze focused downward, she picked her way across the uneven ground.

Several nights had passed since they'd been alone together. And while he hadn't deliberately avoided her, when a legitimate excuse presented itself—in the form of a wound on one of horses—he didn't hesitate to seize it.

He'd asked Elias to relay a message to the women that they shouldn't wait supper on him. One evening free from the tension of sitting across a campfire from Mattie had seemed a welcome respite. Now here she was, disturbing his solitude. He would have preferred that she leave him in peace.

She carried a plate of food, and his stomach growled as he caught a whiff of the tantalizing aroma of roasted meat and vegetables. She was behaving almost like a real wife, seeing to her man's needs. That should bother him, as it wouldn't be wise for either of them to become too comfortable with this arrangement. But he couldn't deny he felt a surprising spurt of pleasure at her actions.

"Rebecca asked me to bring you some supper," she explained.

His momentary joy was snuffed out by her words, which was just as well. He took the plate from her. "Tell her 'thank you' for me."

"I will."

He expected her to quickly return the way she'd come, her errand complete.

Instead, she moved toward his horse. "Elias told us that you were concerned about a scrape on Goldie's leg," she said, referring to the palomino mare. "What happened?"

"I'm not sure. But I want to keep an eye on her to-night and watch for any signs of infection." He forked a bite of food into his mouth, savoring the rich flavors.

Mattie bent down to inspect the injury for herself. "I don't feel any heat around the area."

He chewed and swallowed before answering. "Elias gave me some salve to put on it and that seems to be helping."

"Good." She straightened and gave the mare's neck a pat, then walked toward his other horses, which were staked slightly apart from Goldie.

The wind caught her skirts, swirling the hem around her ankles. She moved with an innate grace that drew his eyes against his will. What was it about her that captured his attention and refused to let go? Sure, she was a beautiful woman with delicate features and strik-ing eyes. But she was hardly the only attractive female he'd ever encountered.

Yet, she alone had the ability to so distract him that

everything else around him seemed to disappear into insignificance. Not even Georgiana had inspired such a strong reaction.

Mattie's effect on him was unsettling and unwanted. He had little control over it, however.

Which made it dangerous to spend too much time in her company. "Shouldn't you be getting back to your own meal?" he questioned.

She didn't glance at him as she replied, "I already ate." Greeting each of his horses in turn, she gave them all a bit of attention.

"Well, I'm sure you have other things to do, so don't let me keep you."

"Oh, you're not keeping me from anything. Rebecca and Adela were seeing to the cleanup when I left, but they'll be done by now. Besides, Rebecca asked that I wait and bring back the plate once you've finished your meal."

He shoveled several forkfuls of food into his mouth in rapid succession.

Glancing over the back of one horse, Mattie caught his actions. "That wasn't meant to be a hint. Please, take your time. There's no hurry."

He paused and considered her words. The quicker he finished, the quicker she would depart. But it didn't sit well with his digestion when he wolfed down food. Better to be a little uncomfortable for the short time until Mattie left than to suffer with an aching belly for the rest of the night.

As he carried on eating—but at a slower pace this time—his eyes continued to track her movements. Goldie butted her head against his shoulder, knocking him off balance, and he almost dropped his supper on the ground.

Mattie stifled a laugh behind her hand. "I guess she doesn't like being ignored."

He turned and gave the mare a stern look. She lowered her head, as if she'd understood the silent rebuke.

"It's amazing the way you can communicate with her," Mattie marveled. She returned to Goldie's side to stroke her pale coat—a move which also brought her nearer to Josiah again. "How did you get to be so good with horses?"

"My mother used to say that I inherited blue eyes and horse sense from Zechariah Barlow." He speared a chunk of potato and lifted it to his mouth.

Mattie's eyebrows pulled together in confusion. "Zechariah Barlow?"

Why had he mentioned his birth father, Zechariah? Josiah never talked about his childhood with anyone. Not even Elias. It served no purpose and only dredged up painful memories. Most days, he'd rather forget that time in his life. He had spent years pushing it so deep down inside that it wouldn't impinge on his conscious mind.

But there might be some benefit in telling Mattie about his family history. Then maybe she would understand why he wasn't husband material. He'd thought she had figured it out already, based on her reaction to his proposal, but in the time since then she'd seemed more than willing to go along with Rebecca's obvious matchmaking attempts.

He guessed Mattie was about to discover a reason to begin circumventing the other woman, however. Once she learned the sordid details of his background she wouldn't want to spend any more time in his company than was absolutely necessary.

Which was fine by him. It was exactly what he wanted, in fact.

He gulped down the bite of food before responding. "Zechariah Barlow was my father."

"But your last name is Dawson—" She abruptly cut herself off, doubtlessly having arrived at the logical conclusion.

"My mother wasn't married to my father," he confirmed.

Her cheeks reddened. "Forgive me for bringing it up." Her hand had stalled against the mare's neck, but now she resumed stroking the short hairs.

"You're hardly the first person to do so. My father wasn't one to settle down, and I'm like him in a lot of ways." He might as well warn Mattie off completely while he was at it, though he suspected his illegitimacy would be enough. "He worked as a wrangler capturing wild mustangs. Horses were the only thing he knew. He had no real home—not for years. He was just passing through when he met my mother, who was married to Elias's father at the time. When her husband found out about her affair shortly after I was born, he couldn't forgive her for shaming him in front of friends and neighbors, and he abandoned her."

He glanced up, expecting to find disgust on Mattie's face, but saw only sympathy and compassion.

"What happened to you and Elias and your mother after that?"

"Elias and I didn't grow up together—he was raised by his father. Mother wrote to Zechariah about her situation, and he came to look after her—us—as best he could. My father did what he had to in order to support us and put a roof over our heads and food on the table. But he was gone for long stretches at a time. He died when I was thirteen.

"Then it was just my mother and me. She had to work to provide for me, but the only job she could find was as a laundress. The backbreaking labor took a toll, and she became sick. We couldn't afford a doctor— we could barely afford food from the bits of money I was able to earn. But 'decent' folks looked down on us, and there was no one we could turn to for help. When she died I had to sell a brooch that had been in her family for four generations, just so she could have a proper burial."

He fell silent and waited for Mattie's reaction.

Mattie was saddened by Josiah's description of his childhood. It seemed people were the same everywhere— turning their backs on those they condemned for some wrongdoing. Why did they never see that willfully ignoring the suffering of others was the real sin against decency?

Her own experiences had taught her that there were two sides to every story. And the majority viewpoint wasn't always right or honorable, though the leaders of society worked hard to make everyone else believe it.

There was no disputing the fact that Josiah's mother had made mistakes. But Mattie had made her fair share of them, too. She knew how a single error in judgment— such as trusting the wrong man—could lead to endless regrets and community censure.

Poor Josiah had been an innocent child at the time.

He'd done nothing to deserve the disdain of others, yet she knew he'd felt it all the same.

Though he had kept his words matter-of-fact, she could still sense his hurt even now, years later. After everything he'd just told her, she was surprised by the generosity of spirit he'd displayed toward her and Adela. Most in his position would treat others as they themselves had been treated—never lending a hand to anyone because no one had ever done so for them. Instead, Josiah lived by the creed: do unto others as you would have them do unto you.

"That's why you helped me right from the start, isn't it? Because no one was there to help you and your mother."

His mouth turned down at the corners. "There was nothing I could do when I was a child. But I can do something to help others now."

And she had thrown that kindness back in his face so many times. Though she'd had her reasons, she could have been more affable toward him. On a few occasions, she'd been downright hostile in her refusal, painting him as a villain with nefarious motives. Which had been vastly unfair to him.

She reached out and placed her hand on his forearm. "I've never properly thanked you before. But I want you to know that even though I often turned down your help, I always appreciated you making the offer. Thank you for everything you've done for me." Up to and including marriage. There was no way she could adequately repay him for that. "Maybe I should explain why—"

He shifted, causing her hand to fall away from his arm. "There's no need for explanations. I can understand how you must have felt, living with the constant worry of inadvertently giving away the truth."

It went much deeper than that, but Josiah plainly wasn't interested in hearing her personal revelations. She hadn't missed his earlier hints that he'd rather be left alone, preferring the company of his horses over hers.

He took one last bite of food and handed the empty plate to her. "Thanks for bringing me supper."

Without giving her a chance to utter so much as a polite "you're welcome," he turned his back and focused on his horse. A move she recognized as a dismissal. Did he regret telling her something so private about himself? Just when they were getting a bit more intimate, he'd pulled away.

As she returned to the covered wagons, thoughts of him predominated. He was so steady and strong, she'd never stopped to consider what emotional scars he might carry from his past.

It seemed they'd both had experience with circumstances being held against them. In her case, she had played a part—however unintended—in creating the situation. But for Josiah, he'd been judged through no fault of his own, merely the small-mindedness of others. She would have liked to tell him he wasn't alone, that people had turned their backs on her, too. There was no point, however.

Having something in common could have served to draw them closer together, except Josiah didn't want that. And neither should she, if she hoped to keep her heart whole when they parted.

* * *

"Thunderstorm's heading toward us," Elias commented after they finished supper one evening.

A week had passed since the night Josiah spent by Goldie's side, and Mattie was relieved the mare's minor injury hadn't become a serious issue. She didn't want him to lose anything else that mattered to him, and he set great store by his horses, hanging all his future plans on them.

Though the wagon train had passed the halfway point, the most difficult part of the journey was still ahead of them. There were countless dangers out on the trail, not the least of which were the elements.

Josiah glanced at the sky. "Yep. We're in for a soaking."

Mattie watched the dark clouds roll in, dimming the last rays of the setting sun. A chill wind blew through the camp, catching the women's skirt hems and acting as a bellows on their cooking fires.

Rebecca started collecting empty plates and mugs. "We better get things packed up and inside the wagons before the rain gets here."

Mattie moved to help her as lightning flashed across the darkened sky. It was followed closely by the boom of thunder overhead, and she flinched at the loud noise.

The weather could change so fast out here, and there was nowhere to escape from nature's fury, except the meager protection of the covered wagons. She didn't miss much about Saint Louis, but she'd never feared thunder and lightning like this while tucked securely inside a solid and sturdy brick building.

Josiah placed a hand on her back. "Summer storms come on quick, but they move on just as swiftly."

The words, combined with his comforting touch, helped to ease her nerves. She felt safe with him near.

And bereft when he removed his hand and shifted away. "I better go see to my horses. This storm is liable to spook them, and I don't want any to bolt."

"You should probably grab a rain slicker if you don't want to get drenched," Elias advised.

"Good idea." Josiah switched direction and made a beeline toward the wagon.

Mattie followed behind him, her concern for the horses equal to his. "I'll come with you to check on them."

"I can handle it on my own." He tempered his refusal with a slight smile as he retrieved his slicker. "There's no sense in us both getting wet. Wait out the storm in your wagon with Adela, where you'll stay dry."

Jumping at a second thunderclap, she nodded her agreement. It was probably just as well he'd declined her offer. Skittish horses needed a calm and reassuring tone, which she doubted she could provide right now.

Josiah guided her back to her own wagon and assisted her up onto the tailgate. As she joined Adela inside, the skies opened, and the first fat drops of rain landed on the parched ground.

Josiah shrugged into his slicker and fastened the buttons. "Will you and Adela be okay on your own?"

Though she didn't want him to leave, the horses needed him more than she did. "We'll be fine," she reassured him. "Besides, Rebecca and Elias are close by."

He nodded and turned to leave.

"Be careful," she called after him.

"I will," he promised.

Pulling the wide brim of his hat down to shield his face, he headed out and quickly disappeared into the gloom and sheets of rain.

Another flash of lightning forked across the sky and brightened the inside of the covered wagon for a split second, then darkness descended once more. Mattie lit a lantern to dispel the shadows, but it did nothing to lessen her anxiety.

The storm was doubtlessly making the horses restive and edgy. Even as experienced and skilled as Josiah was, an accident could still happen. What if he was kicked? Or if an animal reared and trampled him?

Please, Lord, protect him from harm.

The wind gusted and rocked the wagon while raindrops fell faster, hitting the canvas covering above Mattie's head. And Josiah was out in the inclement weather.

She prayed for the squall to pass quickly.

Unlike Mattie, Adela didn't seem a bit bothered by the downpour. She occupied herself embroidering an intricate pattern of leaves on the hem of a tiny gown intended for Rebecca and Elias's baby.

Mattie admired her talent though she couldn't hope to replicate it. Her sewing skills were passable, but in no way compared to her sister's deft hand with a needle.

And even stitching a simple seam was beyond Mattie just now. Though she tried, she couldn't settle to the task. She returned her own unfinished baby garment to the sewing case and drummed her fingers on the wooden top.

Adela shot her a look. "Must you do that?"

Yanking her hand back, she curled her fingers into

a fist then tucked the offending appendage into her lap. "Sorry."

"Why don't you read from the Bible? It will get your mind off the storm."

Taking her sister's suggestion, Mattie lifted the lid on her trunk and retrieved the Bible, which rested atop her folded clothes. The cover was worn around the edges and the cross on the front was faded. But the imperfections were a reminder of the countless hours Daniel Prescott had spent reading the word of God aloud to his daughters.

Running a finger across the gold lettering on the spine, Mattie opened the book and flipped to one of her father's favorite passages, then began to read.

The Lord is my Shepard; I shall not want. He maketh me to lie down in green pastures: He leadeth me beside the still waters. He restoreth my soul: He leadeth me in the paths of righteousness for His name's sake.

After a few minutes, the rainfall seemed to taper off and the thunderclaps sounded as if they were moving away from the wagon train.

But she wouldn't breathe easy until she knew Josiah was safe.

It was a while before the rain and thunder stopped completely.

Shortly after that, Josiah's whispered voice drifted through the gap in the canvas flaps. "Mattie?"

Setting the Bible aside, she shifted to the end of the wagon and pulled back the material. By the grace of God, Josiah stood there, wet from head to toe, but seeming otherwise unscathed. The knots in her stomach loosened and her heart rate slowed to a more normal pace.

"Your horses are all right?" she checked.

He nodded and water dripped off the brim of his hat.

"You should change into dry clothes."

"I'm not too damp. The slicker kept the worst of the rain off me. It's getting late, and I'm going to head for bed now. You should do the same. I'll see you in the morning."

"Good night." Mattie released the canvas flap, allowing it to fall back into place, and moved toward her trunk to collect her nightclothes.

But once she was tucked under the covers, the lantern extinguished, sleep didn't come.

Though she was warm and dry inside the covered wagon, she couldn't stop thinking about Josiah—forced to make his bed on the wet ground. And the oilskin he put down as a barrier would do little to keep the chill from seeping into his bones.

Turning onto her side, she folded her hands under her cheek and tried to banish thoughts of his certain discomfort. Her mind refused to give her peace, and she turned over onto her other side.

Adela's voice reached her. "I can't sleep with you flip-flopping like a landed fish. The whole wagon shakes every time you turn over."

Mattie rolled onto her back and turned her head to peer at her sister through the darkness. "Sorry," she apologized.

But a slight smile tugged up the corners of her mouth at the mental picture Adela's comment produced. A few months ago, the younger girl wouldn't have made such a reference, as she'd never seen anyone catch a fish, much less done so herself.

"Why are you still so fidgety when the storm's long gone?"

Remembering the reason for her restlessness, Mattie's amusement quickly faded. "I was thinking about Josiah. He must be cold outside in the damp night air."

"So take him a blanket. Then you can stop worrying about him, and I can get some sleep." Adela covered a wide yawn with her hand.

Mattie sat up, the covers falling to her lap. "That's a wonderful idea. Why didn't I think of that?"

"Is that a rhetorical question? If not, I can't help you. I haven't a clue how your brain works. We're so different that most days it amazes me how we can even be sisters," she groused.

"All right, grump, go to sleep. I'll try not to bother you any more tonight." Sliding from the bed, Mattie dug through one of the trunks for a spare blanket. Then she pulled on her father's enveloping coat over her nightgown, stuffed her feet into her boots and ducked outside.

After all Josiah had done for her, this was the least she could do in return. Though he wasn't a lost little boy anymore, he still deserved compassion and caring. She could show him that sort of kindness without involving her emotions.

She wouldn't let it become anything deeper or more meaningful. Her heart was in no danger.

And once she'd seen to his well-being, she should be able to find rest for both her mind and body.

Josiah was trying to locate an agreeable position on the hard ground when he heard footsteps, too light to belong to a man. It came as no surprise to see it was Mattie approaching, though he did wonder what she was doing out here. Sitting up, he put the question to her.

"I thought you might need this." She held out a folded woolen blanket.

His eyebrows rose in astonishment.

Her demeanor had bewildered him since he'd revealed the details of his past. First, when she didn't display shock, scorn or any of the other reactions he had come to expect from others. She hadn't treated him as if he would sully her simply by being near.

And now she was braving the chilly night in consideration for his comfort.

But why?

He searched her eyes for answers, but the darkness prevented him from reading her expression.

Accepting the blanket from her, he laid it across his lap, over the top of his bedroll. "Thanks. It is a bit colder out tonight than normal."

"Will you be warm enough now?"

"That matters to you so much?"

"Well, of course. You're no good to me if you freeze to death."

Her tone was teasing, but he couldn't help thinking there was more than a grain of seriousness in her words. She needed him around until they reached Oregon Country.

Not that he believed she would wish misfortune on him if she had no need of his continued presence. But that didn't make him exceptional. She wouldn't wish misfortune on anyone.

She shivered, even bundled up in a large overcoat.

"You should go back to the wagon."

Nodding, she turned to retrace her steps.

A feeling of warmth spread through him as he watched her disappear. It had less to do with the woolen material covering him than the fact that Mattie had been the one to provide it.

She'd done much more for him than that, however.

Without realizing it, he had allowed memories of his childhood to fester and eat away at him, at his confidence, his sense of self-worth. He'd been convinced that no one would respect him if they knew of his past.

Mattie had proved him wrong. Talking with her hadn't erased the painful recollections. No one and nothing could do that. But she'd listened without any apparent signs of judgment.

In his experience, that was a very rare thing.

Chapter Fourteen

The days on the trail seemed to run together, each the same as the last. Filled with chores at the beginning and end of every day and hours of monotonous walking in between.

Time passed unnoticed as Mattie trudged along beside the oxen, the glare of the mid-August sun beating down on her and perspiration beading on her skin. But with every turn of the wagon's wheels, they moved closer to their destination.

"Rebecca, come back here!" Elias commanded.

Mattie glanced over her shoulder and saw the other woman walking at a good clip away from her husband, her enlarged belly leading the way.

Rebecca slowed her pace only when she reached Mattie and fell into step beside her. "I love that man, but he's driving me mad," she huffed out in exasperation. "I mentioned that I had a teeny-tiny little backache, and now he thinks I should be riding in the wagon so as to not overexert myself. He acts as if I'm the first woman with child to ever make this journey.

But I'm not. I'm not even the only one in our group in a delicate condition."

"Rebecca!" Elias had caught up to them and tried to take his wife's arm.

She pulled away from him. "I'm fine, dear. Don't fuss."

Concern clouded his eyes. "You need to take it easy, sweetheart. You should be resting."

"I prefer walking to riding on a hard wooden seat, bouncing over every bump in the trail. You go on back to our wagon while I chat with Mattie for a bit."

He seemed reluctant to leave her side though he would be less than a dozen yards away. He could still keep an eye on her from there.

Giving him a peck on the cheek, Rebecca shooed him on his way, and he finally dropped back in the line.

"The poor man." She tsked. "As a doctor, he's aware of all the things that could go wrong. But if I let him have his way now, I'll be spending the next six weeks confined to the wagon."

Though she hid it well, Rebecca must share his worries, at least in part.

Mattie couldn't imagine what it must be like for the other woman, facing the most treacherous part of the journey over steep mountain passes and rafting down the Columbia River while big with child. Fretting over the possibility of delivering early, before they reached Oregon Country. Fearful that something might happen to her or her child.

Rebecca linked arms with Mattie as they walked. "Let's not talk about it anymore. As I've told Elias, there's no sense borrowing trouble. And besides, there's something much more interesting I'd rather discuss."

"What's that?"

"You and Josiah, of course. It's been a while since the wedding. How are you two doing?"

"Fine." She hoped her succinct answer would keep the conversation from veering any further down that particular path.

But the other woman refused to be put off. "Come now, you can do better than that, surely. You've had several opportunities to spend time alone together."

"Yes, thanks to you."

"Oh, there's no need to thank me," Rebecca replied airily, waving a dismissive hand. "I'm simply doing my part to help the course of true love run smoothly."

Mattie had to fight against rolling her eyes. "It's not a love match."

"Maybe not yet. But I'm sure you don't want to end the marriage. And I don't think Josiah truly does, either."

That certainly wasn't the impression he'd given Mattie. So, how had Rebecca arrived at such a conclusion? Was she willfully ignoring the obvious, seeing the situation through a romantic, rosy haze?

Not once had Josiah mentioned anything that even hinted at love or affection for Mattie. He felt an obligation toward her. Nothing more.

And a coerced union was hardly a recipe for future happiness and marital accord.

Rebecca guided Mattie sideways slightly to avoid a rock in their path. "I'll admit it wasn't the most auspicious beginning. But that doesn't mean you can't have a good marriage. Or that you shouldn't try. It will take effort, but the rewards are well worth it. Josiah's a good man, kind and caring. He'll be a wonderful husband to you."

"I'm sure he would." She kept her lashes lowered, her gaze fixed on the ground, preventing Rebecca from reading anything in her eyes. "But that's beside the point."

"I don't think it is. I believe that God brought you two together for a reason. And not simply to help you get to Oregon County. Every day I pray for you and Josiah to find happiness together."

"And what if that's not part of God's plan for us?"

The other woman's expression remained serene. "I have faith. There's still plenty of time before we reach the end of the trail."

Time for what, exactly? Josiah had stated his intentions plainly—to annul their marriage. And he hadn't said or done anything to indicate he might be reconsidering.

"You could offer him a bit of encouragement."

Mattie looked askance at Rebecca. "Excuse me?"

"He might be waiting for some sort of sign from you. Did you ever think of that?"

"I can't say that I have."

"Well, consider this. Perhaps, he planned for an annulment because he thought it was what *you* wanted. After all, he knew you weren't given a choice whether or not to marry him. It's up to you to show him you want more than a temporary marriage for convenience's sake. To prove you're committed to the union, that you wish to be a wife to him. And leave the rest in God's hands."

"But I don't—"

Rebecca placed her hand over Mattie's. "Love can grow between you if you only give it a chance. I've noticed a subtle change in Josiah recently. In you both, actually."

Mattie ignored that last part in order to mull over the rest of what Rebecca had said.

Could it be true that Josiah was developing feelings for her? She hadn't sensed a shift in him, but Rebecca did have the advantage of longer acquaintance. Could she see inside his heart to a place Mattie couldn't?

She swung her gaze toward Josiah, riding on horseback a short distance out in front of the wagon train. He sat tall in the saddle, wearing an olive-green cotton shirt with a tan vest over it, his hat pulled low to shade his eyes from the sun.

He looked as strong and handsome as always. But he was too far away for her to read anything in his expression.

Rebecca might believe she saw signs of deeper emotion in Josiah, but Mattie was left with doubts. If she revealed more of her own feelings in the hope of reaching him and Rebecca turned out to be wrong, then Mattie would be the one left heartbroken. Though the other woman was only trying to help, Mattie couldn't follow her advice. The risk was too great.

She focused her attention back on her sister-in-law and opened her mouth to say as much. The words remained unspoken when she noticed Rebecca had a hand braced against her lower back, a slight grimace twisting her features.

Suddenly, Mattie's issues vanished from her mind, replaced by concern for her friend.

Resting her hand on Rebecca's shoulder, she could

feel the tension knotting the other woman's muscles. "Are you all right?"

"I'm fine. It's not surprising that my back is bothering me with the extra weight I'm carrying." She cupped a hand over her distended stomach.

"Regardless, maybe you should tell Elias—"

"No. I don't want him to worry. There's no cause for alarm. I felt a bit of pain for a moment, but it's gone now. Please, don't desert to Elias's side. One fusspot in this outfit is enough. And promise you won't say anything to him about this."

"All right," she agreed reluctantly.

But she watched Rebecca for further hints of pain or discomfort. And saw more than one before they stopped for the noon meal.

She dithered in indecision. Should she break her promise by going behind Rebecca's back to Elias? Or was she worrying over nothing, as the other woman had insisted?

During the noon meal, Josiah noticed that Mattie seemed troubled. Her eyebrows pleated, while lines of strain bracketed her mouth. And she contributed very little to the conversation.

Something was clearly sitting heavy on her mind. But what?

She didn't volunteer any information or explanations. Which left him with two options. He could act like he hadn't perceived anything amiss. Or he could take Mattie aside and get answers from her.

On the one hand, it was probably none of his business. And she likely wouldn't thank him for sticking his oar in. But there was a piece of him that couldn't let it go without trying to make things better. And that part won out.

"Would you all excuse us for a minute?" he requested of Elias, Rebecca and Adela. "I'd like to speak to Mattie alone."

"Of course." Rebecca gave him a smile, then turned to Mattie, sending her a significant look.

Though Josiah didn't understand what message she was communicating, he had more important things on his mind than figuring it out.

Taking Mattie's arm, he led her far enough away from the others to gain a bit of privacy.

"What is it?" she queried.

"Please tell me what's bothering you."

Her eyebrows arched in surprise.

"You didn't think I'd notice?"

"I..." Her tongue darted out to moisten her lips. "I wish you hadn't," she revealed.

"Why? Is it something to do with me?" Though she shook her head, he kept talking, convinced he'd hit on the truth. "If I've done something, or *not* done something, that has upset you—"

She put her hand over his mouth, cutting off his words. "It's nothing like that."

Grasping her wrist, he drew her fingers down to rest against his chest. "Then what is it?"

She remained silent for a moment, and it was apparent she debated with herself about what to say to him.

His gaze steady, he looked deep into her eyes, urging her to share the burden she carried.

Her breath gusted out, and she pulled her hand from his hold. But she didn't walk away as he'd expected.

Shooting a quick glance over her shoulder, she kept her voice low. "I'm worried about Rebecca."

The comment took him by surprise. His eyes shifted to his sister-in-law, but nothing stood out to him as cause for concern.

He brought his gaze back to Mattie. "Why?"

"She's been having some pains."

That sounded ominous, but there was no sense panicking when he didn't have all the facts. "What kind of pains?"

"I believe it's in her back, mostly. But what if it has something to do with the baby? What if there's something wrong?" She shook her head. "Or maybe I'm fretting needlessly. Perhaps it truly isn't anything of significance, as Rebecca maintains. I've never been around an expectant mother before. Except my own mother, when she was carrying Adela. But I was only four years old at the time. So, I don't know what's normal and what isn't." A frenzied note had crept into her voice, which didn't match her logical words.

"Calm down, Mattie." Reaching for her hand, he found it curled into a fist. He rubbed his thumb over her clenched fingers. "Getting all worked up won't help the situation."

"You're right. I'm sorry." She took a deep breath, then released it. "All right, I'm calm." But her hand remained fisted, belying her assertion.

He didn't point that out to her, however. "Good. Now, Elias was acting more solicitous than usual toward Rebecca over dinner, but he didn't seem to feel the need for any additional precautions beyond that. If he's not overly concerned, then the pains probably aren't a serious issue—" He broke off when Mattie shook her head.

"Elias doesn't know about all of them," she explained. "Rebecca didn't want him to worry. And she wouldn't let me tell him, either." The hot wind caught strands of her hair that were too short to be pulled back into a bun or braid and blew them across her face and into her eyes.

Reaching up, he grasped the wayward locks and tucked them behind her ear. "Elias has a right to be informed about any possible problems with his wife and child, no matter how large or small."

She bit her bottom lip in dismay. "I promised Rebecca—"

"That you wouldn't say anything to Elias," he finished. "And you won't. *I* will."

Her expression didn't clear. "You're splitting hairs. Either way, I'll still have broken her confidence."

"Would you rather break your promise, or keep silent and risk tragic consequences?"

Distress filled her features. "Do you really believe it might come to that?"

"I don't know." He prayed not, though he couldn't be certain. "I'm not a doctor."

Her gaze dropped to the ground. "But Elias is…" She stated what Josiah had left unspoken.

"You know he's the best person to make a determination on Rebecca's condition. And that's more important than her desire to shield him from worry."

The words brought Mattie's eyes back to his. "I guess you're right."

"I'd best go talk to him now, before we get back on the trail."

Though she still looked unhappy, she didn't attempt to stop him.

Mattie trusting him enough to share her worries caused a peculiar sensation in his chest. Her actions seemed proof she believed in his ability to make things better. Even knowing about his past and how he'd failed to save his mother from a life cut short by back-breaking labor. Could it truly be possible that knowledge of his shame-filled childhood hadn't adversely altered her opinion of him?

Despite the gravity of his errand, his heart felt less burdened as he left Mattie's side and went in search of his brother.

"Do you think Rebecca has forgiven me yet?" Mattie questioned Elias as she walked beside him after tending to their teams of oxen at the night stop.

He nudged his hat back and scratched his forehead where the headwear had left a slight indentation. "It's hard to say. She kicked up a fuss when I put my foot down about her riding in the wagon this afternoon. But she fell silent pretty quickly once we were moving. I suspect she spent most of the time sleeping. When I left the wagon a few minutes ago, she still wasn't awake."

At least Rebecca had taken the opportunity to get some rest.

But that didn't relieve Mattie's guilt. She sighed, hoping her friend had gotten over her anger. Not for Mattie's own sake, however, but for the other woman's. She hated to think she'd piled additional stress on the expectant mother.

"Why don't you come with me to check on her,"

Elias suggested. "If she wakes up, you can ask her yourself."

Mattie hesitated. If Rebecca was still angry, Mattie would rather not confront her. But it was cowardly to decline on that premise. Besides, if her temper hadn't yet cooled, it might benefit Rebecca to vent her displeasure, enabling her to move beyond it more quickly.

Taking her courage in hand, Mattie kept pace with Elias until they reached the Dawsons' covered wagon. Then she stood back while he pushed aside the canvas flaps.

She had a clear view past him, and she gasped at the sight that greeted them.

Rebecca's eyes were closed, but not in peaceful slumber. Her face was screwed up in pain, her fists gripping the quilt spread over her. Though she was breathing heavily, her mouth was clamped shut, and she didn't make a sound.

"Sweetheart, what's wrong?" Elias pulled himself onto the tailgate and scrambled to his wife's side, placing his hands over hers.

Mattie stood frozen, looking on helplessly.

Something must have caught Elias's attention, because his gaze suddenly jerked from Rebecca's face to her midsection. Shifting, he ran his hands over the large mound of her belly. His frown deepened.

Rebecca didn't respond to her husband for several seconds, until the pain released its hold on her. She slumped back, her fingers relaxing their grip on the blanket. "That was a bad one."

Sweat beaded on her skin, and Elias brushed a damp tendril of hair from her brow. "You told me the pains were only minor." Accusation colored his voice, the harsh tone at odds with the visible gentleness of his touch.

Apology filled Rebecca's gaze. "They started out that way. But they got worse shortly after the noon stop."

Mattie guessed the other woman hadn't been sleeping all afternoon as Elias had assumed. Instead, she had more likely fallen silent in order to keep her husband from learning of her deteriorating state.

"Why didn't you tell me?" Elias spoke the question that was on Mattie's mind.

"There was nothing you could do, and I hoped they would stop. But they haven't." Tears shimmered in her eyes. "The babe's coming, isn't he?"

"Yes."

A tear spilled over her lashes and rolled down her cheek. "But it's too soon. Our baby isn't due for another six or seven weeks."

Elias stroked his thumb across her skin, wiping the teardrop away. "Don't cry, sweetheart. Everything's going to be all right. I'm here." He lifted her hand to his lips and pressed a kiss to her knuckles. "I won't let anything happen to you or our child."

Mattie cleared her throat. "What can I do?" she asked when Elias turned toward her.

"Can you sit with Rebecca? I'll likely be delivering the child tonight, and I need to get things prepared." He started to shift away from his wife.

Mattie stopped him. "You stay with Rebecca. Tell me what you need, and I'll take care of it."

He smiled in gratitude and resumed his previous position at his wife's side. "There are linens in that trunk in the corner. And could you fetch a bowl of water?"

"Boiling water?" she checked.

He shook his head. "That will come later. For now, I simply want to bathe Rebecca's brow with a damp cloth."

Mattie moved to fill a bowl from the water barrel, then climbed into the wagon to collect the other required items. Following Elias's instructions, she laid everything out in readiness.

She paused once to give the couple space when another pain hit, then quickly completed the list of tasks the doctor had given her. "Is there anything else I can do?"

"Can you allow us some privacy, please?" Elias requested. "I need to examine Rebecca to check her progress."

"Of course. I'll go see to supper. If you need anything, just holler." Climbing to the ground, she headed to her own wagon to begin the meal preparations and found that Adela had gotten there before her.

The younger girl had already lit a fire and was industriously chopping vegetables to add to the pot suspended above the flames.

Mattie gave her sister a quick hug. "Thank you for doing this on your own."

Though Adela generally helped with the cooking, it was a combined effort on most days and not left to just one person.

"You're welcome." She returned the hug before continuing with her self-appointed job. "I knew you were busy helping Elias tend to Rebecca, so I figured I should get started without you."

"I appreciate it." She kissed the crown of her sister's head, then moved to assist the younger girl.

By the time Josiah arrived at the campfire after seeing to his horses, their supper was ready.

"Where are Elias and Rebecca?" he inquired.

"They're in their wagon." Mattie related the current state of events and then turned to her sister. "Adela, can you take these two plates to them while I dish up food for the rest of us?"

Though Mattie doubted either Elias or Rebecca would actually eat anything, she wanted the nourishment available to them.

Once Adela returned and everyone was served, Josiah said grace, adding an extra prayer for the health and well-being of Rebecca and her baby.

"Amen," Mattie echoed.

She merely picked at the food, her stomach too knotted up to allow her to eat. Josiah tried to engage her in conversation, but her mind wasn't focused on what he was saying.

Instead, it was with Rebecca and Elias. Throughout the meal, she kept glancing in the direction of their wagon, her ears straining to hear any sounds. She caught the soothing murmur of Elias's voice speaking low to his wife and a few pained gasps, but nothing else.

Word of the situation traveled through the camp, and several of the other women stopped by to inquire about Rebecca and offer their assistance. But, for the time being, there was nothing anyone could do other than wait.

After supper was over and the cleanup complete, Mattie headed to the Dawsons' wagon to check on them.

She knocked on the wooden frame, and a moment later Elias poked his head between the canvas flaps.

"How's Rebecca doing?" she queried.

"As well as can be expected. She's been brave during the pains thus far. But the baby won't be here for hours yet." He was silent for a minute, as he looked at the sun sitting low on the western horizon before bringing his focus back to Mattie. "I know it's early, but you might try to get some sleep now, in case I need you later on, when it's time to deliver the child."

Mattie faltered. She knew nothing about delivering babies. "Maybe another woman would be better. One who has been through childbirth before."

Elias started to reply, but his wife's voice halted him. "I would rather it was you, Mattie, than anyone else," she stated. "I'll feel more at ease with you by my side."

Mattie couldn't refuse in the face of Rebecca's appeal. "All right," she agreed.

Returning to the campfire, she gave Josiah and Adela an update, though there wasn't much to tell.

He folded his arms across his chest and shifted his stance. "I have the second shift for guard duty tonight. But maybe I should switch with one of the other men, so I can stay nearby."

"There's no call for that. You can't do anything for Rebecca—the women and Elias will see to whatever needs doing. And there's nothing you can do for your brother, either. You can't sit with him to keep him from dwelling on what his wife's going through, the way you would with a man who's not a doctor."

He nodded his understanding. "I guess I'll take my turn at guard duty as planned. But if you need me, send someone to let me know, and I'll come right back."

"I will."

Adela voiced her intention to turn in for the night and disappeared inside the wagon.

Too stirred up to rest, as Elias had suggested, Mattie remained by the fire and searched for something with which to busy herself. But she couldn't settle to any task for more than a few seconds and ended up pacing in an attempt to relieve her agitation.

Josiah caught her as she passed him for the dozenth time and pulled her against his chest. Wrapping his arms around her, he rubbed a hand up and down her back. "Try not to worry. Rebecca's in good hands. Elias will take care of her."

"I know." A large part of her frantic energy dissolved as she melted into his embrace, gaining comfort from his strong arms holding her close.

All too soon he moved back, but he pressed a kiss to her forehead before releasing her. "Go on to bed now. I'll be around for a while yet. I don't go on guard duty until midnight."

Doing as he had directed, she climbed into the covered wagon and prepared for bed. But once she crawled under the covers, she couldn't sleep. Though she closed her eyes, her brain wouldn't switch off.

She lay awake, apprehension gnawing at her nerves.

Chapter Fifteen

In the early hours of the morning, Mattie was jerked from a sound sleep. She remained motionless for a moment, trying to figure out what had disturbed her. Then a woman's pained scream rent the night air.

Mattie shot upright in bed, her mind still clouded by sleep and struggling to make sense of what was happening. Something brushed against her arm, causing her to jump.

But it was only Adela shifting next to her. "What was that?"

"I'm going to find out." She already had a strong suspicion, however.

She didn't bother with the lamp, searching for her coat and boots, instead. It took her only a matter of seconds to locate the items in the darkness, then she pulled them on. "You stay here," she instructed her sister.

The younger girl stretched out a hand and stopped Mattie from leaving. "Is it Rebecca?"

Her worry was apparent, though Mattie couldn't see her face clearly.

"Most likely. But Elias is with her." She wished she

had time to offer more assurances, but responding to Rebecca's cry and reaching her side was of greater importance. "I might be gone for a while. Go back to sleep, if you can." She pulled her arm from her sister's grasp.

Exiting the covered wagon, Mattie found that others had been awakened, too, and now milled around the dying campfires. She didn't stop to speak to any of them as she moved toward the Dawsons' wagon.

A lantern burned inside, illuminating the canvas covering, but she could see nothing of what was going on within. It was left to her imagination to supply the details. Not one of the mental pictures brought her ease.

She wished for Josiah's presence. Though he could be of no practical help in the situation, he would have calmed some of her fears simply by being near. But he had a job to do.

As did she.

Walking to the end of the covered wagon, she didn't hesitate before she climbed inside.

Elias glanced over his shoulder at her entrance. "It's time. Come and sit by Rebecca's head and hold her hand."

Mattie did as he'd bidden. Rebecca's grip was painful, but Mattie didn't protest.

It seemed as though there was a lot of blood. Mattie had no way of knowing if that was out of the ordinary, and she didn't want to bring it to Rebecca's attention by asking Elias about it.

The doctor was steady and strong as he worked to deliver the baby, remaining solid as a rock for his wife in her time of need. But as the minutes passed, his expression became more and more grim.

It worried Mattie. There was nothing she could do but pray.

Finally, the child arrived, screaming a protest against being ripped from a warm, dark little cocoon to be unceremoniously thrust into this cold and glaring new world.

"Here, take the baby," Elias demanded, practically shoving the infant into Mattie's arms once he'd cut the cord. "Take it outside and clean it up." His use of the impersonal pronoun made it evident that he hadn't even taken a moment to determine whether he had a son or a daughter.

That, more than anything else, spelled out just how dire the situation had become.

Sparing a quick glance at the child, Mattie bent to whisper in her friend's ear. "You have a beautiful baby girl, Rebecca."

The other woman smiled weakly at the words, but her small show of joy quickly faded.

With one last look back, Mattie exited the wagon and lowered the canvas flap on the scene inside.

Rebecca had looked frighteningly pale and listless. And she hadn't made any attempt to stop Mattie from taking her baby from her. Those were not encouraging signs.

A few women approached with happy expressions on their faces, but their good spirits slipped away as they realized all was not well.

Without being asked, the preacher's wife volunteered to get water to wash the child while Edith Baker went to retrieve some milk to quiet the babe's cries. Mattie gratefully accepted their aid.

As the baby girl was cleaned and fed, Ruth Carpenter, the wagon master's wife, tentatively suggested that someone should return to Rebecca's side to assist the doctor. But Mattie believed it best not to interrupt unless Elias called for them to come. And the others accepted her judgment.

Once the child was swaddled in a cotton blanket, everybody except Mattie dispersed to give the Dawsons some space. But the other women were only steps away if their presence should again be required.

Mattie watched as the newborn drifted off to sleep, clearly tuckered out from her recent activities. With one finger, Mattie gently caressed the delicate skin on the infant's cheek.

Though tiny, she was perfect, with ten fingers and ten toes. And no visible indications of any health issues brought on by her early arrival.

Shifting her gaze, Mattie focused her attention back toward the wagon where the baby had been born. What was going on inside? Surely, if Elias needed another pair of hands, or anything else, he would have called out.

But all was eerily silent.

Though she wanted to believe everything would turn out all right, she had a sinking feeling in her stomach. Turning her eyes to the heavens, she sent a prayer to the Lord that He would heal and restore Rebecca, delivering her from pain.

The other woman had a brand-new daughter depending on her. An innocent babe who needed her mama.

* * *

Josiah returned from guard duty in the dark hours just before dawn and found Mattie pacing outside, with a newborn clenched in her arms. Though she wore her father's oversize coat, her white nightgown was visible beneath it.

Something was obviously not right. Her dishabille, as well as the expression on her face, told him that much.

Lantern light revealed deep lines of strain marring the skin between her eyebrows, and her mouth turned down at the corners.

When she spotted his approach, she rushed to his side. Shifting the baby to one arm, she wrapped the other about his waist and burrowed her face against him, her hand gripping the back of his shirt.

His arms automatically closed around her, returning the hug. "What's wrong?"

She kept her head tucked beneath his chin as she answered. "I don't know for sure. But after the baby came, Elias sent me away while he saw to Rebecca. And he hasn't come out yet. It's been too long. I feel something terrible has happened."

He tried to move back so he could look at her, but she refused to loosen her hold. "You haven't checked on them?"

Her cheek rubbed against the front of his shirt when she shook her head. "I couldn't. I was too afraid to face it. As long as I don't go in there, the possibility remains that Rebecca's just fine."

Josiah shifted his gaze to his brother's child, who slept serenely, unaware of the conversation's significance. "I'll go."

Once Mattie released him, he walked to the covered wagon. Hoisting himself onto the tailgate, he hoped for the best—but braced for the worst—as he pushed aside the canvas material.

Elias turned toward him, his face devoid of emotion. "She's gone."

It felt as if a stone was sitting on Josiah's chest and his throat closed up, making it difficult to breathe. He mourned for a life ended too soon. For the loss of a woman he'd come to love like a sister.

And his heart wept for what his brother was going through. Elias had been all alone when his wife passed.

Josiah felt immense guilt over that. He had failed his brother. After years on the receiving end of the older man's unwavering support, Josiah hadn't been present when Elias needed *him* the most.

I should have been here, Lord, he silently cried out.

But he was here now. Moving to his brother's side, he put an arm around the older man's shoulders.

Elias sat stiff and unyielding, refusing to accept the comfort offered. Staring blankly at his wife.

Rebecca's lowered lashes formed dark crescents against her pale cheeks. One might have mistaken her stillness for slumber if not for the blood staining the white fabric of her nightgown.

Josiah noticed rust-colored streaks on his brother's clothing, as well.

Elias's hand fisted against his thigh. "It wasn't meant to be this way. Maybe if I had done something differently, I could have… She wasn't supposed to give her own life for her child's."

Josiah gave his brother's shoulder a consoling squeeze. "You did everything you could."

"It wasn't enough!" Elias shrugged off Josiah's hold and slumped in defeat. "It wasn't enough," he repeated in a softer tone.

Josiah wished there was something he could do to ease his brother's suffering. It wasn't in his power, but it was in the Lord's. "Let's pray."

Bowing his head, Josiah asked for strength and guidance to accept His ways, though they couldn't understand them now. For the Lord to watch over the ones who had been left behind. To comfort them and give solace for their loss.

"We know Rebecca's in a better place now, Lord— she's with You. And we'll see her again one day, when You call each of us home. Bless us, Lord, and keep us safe. Amen." He raised his head and discovered that Elias hadn't joined in.

Instead, the other man remained focused on his wife's body. Had he heard a word Josiah spoke? Judging from his demeanor, it didn't seem as though he had.

Josiah wanted to lighten his brother's burden in some way, but so far Elias had blocked him at every turn. He wouldn't give up, however.

His mind shifted to practical matters, and he placed a hand on Elias's back to gain his attention. "I'll get some of the woman to attend to Rebecca."

"No. I'll do it myself." He didn't glance in Josiah's direction.

"All right." Arrangements had to be made. "I'll speak to the preacher."

Elias didn't acknowledge the statement.

"Don't worry about the baby. Mattie's looking after the little mite." Josiah realized he didn't know if the child was a boy or girl.

Elias's closed expression didn't invite inquiry. And mention of the newborn hadn't roused any visible emotion in him.

Josiah was at a loss as to how he could help his brother. Perhaps the other man simply needed a bit of time alone.

Leaving the wagon, Josiah looked toward Mattie. Tears streamed unchecked down her face. He opened his arms to her, and she flew into his embrace.

Gut-wrenching sobs shook Mattie's slight frame as Josiah rubbed her back. "You heard."

Too choked up to speak, she simply nodded.

She'd tried not to cry. But the door she kept her emotions locked behind had been breached. One thing after another had piled up against the barrier until it was too much for her to withstand. She'd lost too much already. And her grief, too powerful to be contained, had burst through.

These were the first tears she'd allowed to fall since her father's death, and now that the floodgates had been opened she couldn't seem to stop the surge.

Josiah gathered her close and rocked her in his arms, with the sleeping baby nestled securely between them. His low tone was a soothing whisper in Mattie's ear. "Rebecca's with the Lord now. Her pain is gone. She's at peace."

When there were no more tears left, she pulled away from Josiah and wiped the traces of moisture from her face. Straightening her spine, she drew her mantle of control back around herself. "I'm sorry I fell apart like that. It won't happen again," she assured him.

"You don't have to be strong all the time. It's not

weakness to admit when you're hurting or in need of help. There are others more than willing to lend a hand, to prop you up when you falter. If you'll only let them."

She recognized that he was talking about himself, first and foremost. He had never forsaken her, through all the ups and downs of their unconventional association.

But she couldn't become used to leaning on Josiah. He wouldn't always be around. Only until the end of their journey.

The preacher began the funeral service for Rebecca at the side of the trail, just as dawn was breaking in the east. The rising sun seemed a fitting tribute to a woman who had brought joy to countless others during her short time on earth.

Sunrise usually filled Mattie with a sense of renewed optimism. But on this morning, though the sun cast a radiant light over the gathering and painted the sky above in stunning shades of orange and pink, her mood was dark and despairing.

Clinging to her elbow, Adela sniffled softly and pressed a handkerchief to her tearstained face.

Josiah's arm encircled Mattie's waist, and she stiffened. He didn't draw back. Remembering his earlier words, she relaxed her stance and leaned into him for support. Just this once.

She held Rebecca's daughter cradled against her, taking comfort from the infant's warm weight. Looking down into the baby's sweet face, pain filled Mattie's heart at the thought that this little girl would never know her mama and would grow up without Rebecca's loving care. It had been snatched away from her while she was too young to comprehend the magnitude of the loss.

But it was not for Mattie to question why a young mother was taken from her child and family.

She glanced up at Josiah and saw moisture shimmering in his blue eyes. Scanning the small crowd, she noticed there were only a handful of dry eyes. Surprisingly, one set belonged to Elias. He wore a stoic expression on his face. But though he didn't show any outward signs, he must feel deeply bereft. How could he not? The woman he loved was gone.

Brushing a tear from her cheek, Mattie focused on the preacher's words.

"Find joy in whatever time we have together on this earth. However long or short a time that may be given to each of us. Whether counted in days, weeks or years—all time is precious. We cannot predict when we might be separated in body.

"But though we mourn the loss of Rebecca's physical presence, she is with us still. 'For God so loved the world, that He gave His only begotten Son, that whosoever believeth in him should not perish, but have everlasting life.' John 3:16."

It amazed Mattie anew, the ways of the Lord. How He could deliver the exact message she needed to hear to strengthen her. Reminding her that she should focus on His blessings, and not on what was gone.

The preacher offered a final prayer, ending with, "We ask that You protect us, Lord, and lead us on the path of righteousness as we continue to journey west to our new lives. Amen."

"Amen," Mattie echoed along with the rest of the group.

After offering their condolences, the others trickled away until only Mattie and Josiah remained by Elias's side. The baby had been handed temporarily into Adela's keeping.

Several minutes passed in silence.

Finally, Josiah put a hand on his brother's shoulder. "It's time to go."

Everyone else was already back at the covered wagons preparing for their continued exodus. The Dawsons had no choice but to do the same.

Despite the recent tragedy, they couldn't stop to grieve. The group had to get back under way. To push on and keep moving forward. As they had with the other passings, which had come before.

God willing, there would be no more.

A short time later, Miles Carpenter gave the order to move out. Mattie looked back at the fresh mound of turned dirt on the hillside and the lone wooden cross silhouetted against the vast and endless blue skies.

"Goodbye, my friend. Until we meet again, I'll keep watch over your daughter." Her whispered words were carried away on the wind.

But Mattie knew Rebecca heard them, and smiled.

Chapter Sixteen

"I need to speak with you, Josiah."

He released the horse's hoof and patted the animal as he straightened to face his wife. "Sure. What's on your mind?"

Mattie was frowning. "A small wooden chest appeared in my wagon this afternoon. A chest filled with baby things Rebecca stitched. And I'm guessing Elias was the one who delivered it."

Uncertain where she was heading, he gave a noncommittal response. "That's a fair assumption."

Reaching up, she whisked an errant lock of hair off her face. "I didn't mind taking charge of the baby for a few days. But I hadn't expected it to become a permanent arrangement."

"It's just for a little while."

"So, you knew about this?" Her frown deepened.

"Yes. Elias thought it best that a woman continue to care for the newborn for the time being. But if you don't want to do it, I'm sure we can find someone else who's willing. Perhaps Tessa Linton."

She propped a fist on her hip. "It's not a matter of

wanting to or not. Elias is her father, and he's choosing to ignore her."

"He's in a bad place right now."

Crossing her arms, she narrowed her eyes. "And that makes it acceptable for him to shunt his child aside?"

"Of course not. But he's not himself, and I'm willing to make allowances when he lost his wife less than a week ago. Please, try to understand."

She abandoned her militant stance and confusion took the place of anger on her face. "But why wouldn't he wish to have the baby near? Shouldn't she be a comfort to him during this time?"

In all honesty, Josiah was worried about his brother's behavior—toward the baby and everyone else. Except for the few words Elias had uttered in the covered wagon after Rebecca's passing, he'd been close-mouthed about his feelings and had kept his emotions hidden, bottling them inside.

"Everyone deals with grief in their own way." And who was Josiah to tell his brother the proper way to do it?

God alone knew how Josiah would react if he were in the other man's shoes. Though Josiah had also lost the woman he'd loved, it hadn't been to death. She simply hadn't wanted to be with him, had never truly been his. But his pain was tempered by the knowledge that she was alive and well.

And if it had been Mattie—no, he refused to even think along those lines. Though he didn't love her, he wouldn't tempt fate by playing a morbid game of what-if.

And it wasn't a fair comparison in any case. Elias and Rebecca had been devoted to each other, while

Josiah's marriage to Mattie was nothing more than a temporary arrangement.

"Elias needs our patience and forbearance. Can I count on you to look after his daughter until he's himself again?"

"Of course. I'll do whatever I can to help."

"Thank you. I want to make this situation as undemanding on him as possible, but I can't do it alone."

"You're a good brother."

"He would do the same for me. I was truly blessed the day he reentered my life. It was just after my mother died, and I thought I had no family left who was willing to acknowledge me. Then Elias appeared, the older brother my mother had told me stories about, but whom I'd never known."

Compassion shone in her amber eyes. "How awful for you. I can't imagine what it would have been like to grow up without Adela. You must have missed Elias terribly."

"It wasn't as bad for me as it was for my mother. I had no memories of him. But my mother pined for her eldest son for the rest of her life. She sent countless letters to him, and never received any reply. She died believing that was the way Elias wanted it. She didn't know that Samuel Dawson had made sure their son never saw her correspondences."

"How were you eventually reunited?"

"When she knew the end was near, Mother wrote to her former husband, begging him to take me in after she was gone. He refused, but Elias discovered the letter, and he came. He arrived days too late to say a final farewell to our mother.

"Before he explained everything to me, I believed

he was every bit as uncaring as the man who'd sired him, and I was hostile and belligerent toward him. But Elias didn't give up on me, and I'm not going to give up on him now. I'll find a way to reach him." Somehow.

Tears filled her eyes. Were they brought on by thoughts of the events in his past or by the current situation? Most likely it was a combination of both. Though Mattie tried to act tough, he'd seen glimpses of the softness buried beneath her prickly exterior.

When a single teardrop slipped down her cheek, he reached out and brushed it away. He was standing close enough to her that he could see a previously unnoticed scar marring the skin slightly below her cheekbone.

He rubbed his thumb across it. "What happened here?"

At first he didn't think she would answer, but he saw in her eyes the moment she changed her mind. Maybe his own sharing of confidences had allowed her to open up to him in return.

"My fiancé took exception when I called off our wedding. He slapped me and the heavy ruby ring he wore on his finger left its mark. It was the first time he raised a hand to me. And the last."

Josiah wanted to hunt down the man who had done this to her, but the cad was more than a thousand miles away. At least that put him far enough from Mattie that he would never hurt her again. "You made a timely escape."

"I know. And though that wasn't the reason I ended our engagement, it served as proof I had made the right decision. But my family suffered for my choice." Lowering her gaze to the ground, she bit the corner of her lip.

"In what way?" He dipped his head down in an attempt to regain eye contact, but her lashes acted as a screen, hiding her thoughts from his view.

"My ex-fiancé was the son of my father's boss, and Papa lost his job as vice president of the Worthington Steamboat Company as a result of my actions."

She fell silent, but he reckoned there had to be more to the story than that. Taking her hand in his, he entwined their fingers and waited for her to continue.

The direction of her stare shifted to focus on their joined hands as she pressed on. "Mr. Worthington Senior used his influence to ensure that Papa couldn't find decent work. Then some bad investments wiped out our savings." Once more, she worried her bottom lip. "Crippled by unpaid debts from the canceled wedding, in addition to our everyday expenditures, we were forced to sell our family home."

Barely stopping for breath, she rushed to finish the telling. "That's what led us to Independence, Missouri, and the promise of a new life in Oregon Country. But if not for me, and my decisions, Papa wouldn't have lost his job. There would have been no reason to leave Saint Louis." Guilt was thick in her voice.

With a gentle hand under her chin, he brought her focus back up to his face. "You shouldn't blame yourself, Mattie. You did the only thing you could."

"Not according to the society matrons." Shadows darkened her eyes, hinting that the memories troubled her still. "The heir to the Worthington fortune was considered an excellent catch. Even when I revealed what I had learned of his lecherous and debauched behavior, it was deemed of no consequence. And certainly not just cause to break off the engagement. His own mother told me that men will be men. Then she took pains to instruct me on what society expected of a proper wife, and how I should turn a blind eye." Indignation filling her tone, her glance beseeched him for the understanding she hadn't received back then. "But I couldn't do that."

"Of course not." And shame on the arrogant woman who had tried to convince her otherwise, as well as anyone else who had looked down their nose at Mattie. "I'm sorry you were made to feel as though you were the one in the wrong. Or in any way responsible for what followed afterward." Leaning down, he kissed her cheek, directly over the small scar, then drew back and looked into her eyes.

He hated seeing the traces of regret in their depths. When her bottom lip trembled slightly, he lowered his head and caught her mouth under his.

Then immediately wondered what had gotten into him.

He ended the kiss and retreated, releasing her hand.

She stared up at him, her gaze liquid pools of shimmering gold filled with questions that he didn't want to answer in his own mind, let alone out loud.

"If you'll excuse me, I need to finish up here."

Though the questions lingered in her eyes, she didn't voice any of them. "I should be getting back to Adela and the baby anyway."

Josiah turned toward the horses and didn't watch Mattie's departure.

He never should have kissed her. But he quickly excused his impulsive action as an offering of comfort only, not anything more significant.

His emotions hadn't been engaged. It wasn't possible when his heart was walled off.

And if he'd felt something in that kiss, he refused to admit it.

Or examine what it might be.

Walking back to the covered wagons, Mattie put a hand to her mouth, where the imprint of Josiah's lips seemed to linger. Why had he kissed her? What did it mean? Was it evidence that he was developing tender feelings for her, as Rebecca had claimed? Perhaps he did have some affection for Mattie beyond his innate need to protect those who were at a disadvantage.

Was she throwing away an opportunity for something wonderful due to fear? Because the truth was that she remained afraid to risk her heart. And she no longer had her friend to give her encouragement. At the reminder, her eyes filled with tears, and she blinked several times to stem them.

When Josiah arrived at the campfire for supper a short time later, she tried to ascertain the answers from his expression. But his face was curiously blank.

Once everyone had a plate of food, Josiah asked a blessing and then they began to eat. Several minutes passed in silence, with the scraping of forks against enamel and the crackle and pop of flames the only sounds heard around their campfire.

Conversations and laughter drifted to them from the nearby families, but it was as if the Dawsons and Prescotts had been struck mute. Not even the baby cried from her place inside the small open-top crate that had been repurposed as a bassinet.

Searching her mind for something to say, Mattie

said the first thing that came to her. "Have you decided on a name for your daughter, Elias?"

He put his half-full plate aside and stood up. "I'm going for a walk."

Stunned speechless by his sudden action, Mattie's mouth worked, but she didn't find her voice until he had disappeared from sight on the far side of the covered wagon.

She turned to Josiah, feeling immeasurable guilt. "I'm sorry, I didn't mean to drive him away. I didn't realize that a simple mention of the baby would have such on effect on him."

Josiah reached over and caught her hand, entwining his fingers with hers as he had done earlier. The show of support brought her emotions back to a more even keel. Without him speaking a word, she knew that he didn't hold the thoughtless inquiry against her.

A few days later, the baby still didn't have a name. And that fact bothered Mattie. Josiah had taken to calling her Sweet Pea, but the child needed a Christian name.

And Mattie said as much to him.

He didn't look up from the chunk of wood he was carving. "What do you suggest?"

"Can't you talk to your brother about it?" She tried to keep exasperation out of her tone, but feared she hadn't been entirely successful.

"I doubt it would do any good." Turning the piece of wood over, he squinted his eyes and examined it from a different angle. "If you're so set on her having a name, you'd be better off picking one yourself."

"I couldn't do that!" It wasn't her right and seemed highly insensitive besides.

Lowering his hands to his lap, Josiah held the knife motionless as he focused his full attention on her. "It's either that, or she will henceforth be known as Sweet Pea."

Mattie refused to accept the latter, and her conscience rebelled against the former. "Under different circumstances I might suggest calling the baby after her mother, but I fear that would push Elias even further away from the little one. If only Rebecca had mentioned a girl's name she preferred. But she was certain she was carrying a boy and had settled on Elias Junior."

"I guess you could call her Eliasa."

She huffed out a sigh. "Elias can't even speak of her—do you really think he would want her named after him?"

"You're probably right, at that." He lifted his arms and resumed carving.

Her gaze shifted to his hands. "I thought Elias was the whittler. I've never seen you doing it before."

"He taught me. But I'm usually too busy."

Lately, however, he'd been spending more time around the campfire. Staying close to his brother in order to pick up any slack, instead of working with his horses.

Though she might not agree wholly with Josiah's decision to stand aside and allow his brother wallow in his grief, she took heart from the knowledge that he had an unshakable personal code by which he lived. He wasn't simply taking an easy out by avoiding a confrontation with his brother. He was doing what he believed best. Rather than pressuring the other man, Josiah was helping in the only way he felt he could, giving Elias space free from everyday worries.

But Mattie's very nature chaffed against the soft approach. She'd never been one to sit idly back and let life happen as it may. She much preferred racing to meet it. But her propensity to take action without a thought for the consequences wasn't always the wisest course, as she'd come to realize.

Impatience still gnawed at her. Instead of yielding to it this time, however, she resolved to restrain her impulse.

Returning her focus to Josiah, she watched him for a few minutes and noted the growing pile of wood shavings at his feet. "What are you making?"

"I don't rightly know yet. I have to get a feel for the wood first, before it will tell me what it should be." He glanced in her direction. "What about choosing a family name?"

It took her a few seconds to realize he had circled back to their original topic of Elias's as-yet-nameless daughter.

"That could work." But after what Josiah had recently revealed of his past, she didn't want to use any names from the Dawson family—there was too much bad blood. "Maybe one from Rebecca's side. Do you know any of her relatives?"

He shifted and stretched out his legs in front of him. "I've only met a few, and only two who are female. Her younger sister, Abigail, and her mother, Emmaline. I'm partial to the name Emmaline myself."

"That's a rather large name for such a tiny girl." Folding her hands in her lap, she glanced toward the crate bassinet. "How about Emma?"

"Emma?" He considered the infant for a moment, as if trying the name on for size. "I like it."

Mattie's eyebrows pulled together in a frown. "But will Elias?"

"If he doesn't, he can say so."

The next morning Mattie found out what Josiah had been carving. He'd stayed up late by the fire, working on it long after she had turned in for the night, and now it was finished.

Her mouth dropped open in wonder. In his hand, he held a bundle of leaves tied with twine, and at the center was a tiny wooden horse.

Her eyes flew to his, delight welling inside her as she reached to take it from him. How long had it been since anyone had given her a present? Much less one crafted by hand with such care. "You made this for me?"

He nodded. "I wanted to show my appreciation for everything you've done for my brother and my niece."

"Technically, she's my niece, too," she pointed out.

He ignored her remark, however. "I left the wood raw because the light golden color is similar to a palomino's coat."

Returning her gaze to his gift, she stroked the smooth surface of the carving and marveled at the minute details. "It's beautiful. Thank you."

"You're welcome." Clearing his throat, he shifted from one foot to the other. "I need to, uh, see to the horses. The uh, full-size, uh…alive ones, that is." He pivoted and hurried away without waiting for a reply.

Her praise had clearly made him uncomfortable. But why? If the miniature was truly only a gesture of appreciation, as he'd claimed, surely he would have accepted her compliments with aplomb.

After placing the wooden horse and its nest of foliage on the tailgate of the covered wagon, she returned to cleaning up the remnants of the morning meal. But her gaze was drawn back to the tiny horse again and again as she wondered over Josiah's real reasons for giving it to her.

She knew how Rebecca would have viewed his actions. But Mattie was still hesitant to believe it.

Once she completed her chore, she climbed into the covered wagon to stow the gift before the wagon train moved out.

Adela was occupied dressing the baby, but glanced up at Mattie's entrance. "What's that?"

She handed the miniature to her sister. "Josiah made it."

"It's darling, and so tiny. You'd better keep it away from Emma." She passed it back to Mattie. "We wouldn't want her to choke on it."

"Don't worry. I'm going to put it away for safekeeping." Kneeling in front of her trunk, she lifted the lid and removed a cotton handkerchief to wrap around the carving.

After the ball of material was tucked back inside, she picked up the cluster of leaves to lay it atop her clothes. But she paused with it still clenched in her fingers, studying the veining in the leaves.

"Remember how Mama used to tell us that we could see God's work in the patterns of each leaf and petal in her garden? His greatness in a single blade of grass amidst the millions comprising the manicured lawn."

"And His glory when she looked into our eyes," Adela finished the familiar refrain.

One of the hardest things to leave behind in Saint

Louis had been the rose garden that had been their mother's pride and joy while she was alive.

Setting the leaves on her lap, Mattie reached for her Bible. Though they weren't a bouquet of wildflowers— it was too late in the year for those—she wanted to press the bundle between the pages of scripture.

She flipped to a spot near the beginning and laid the leaves inside. But before she could close the cover again, a verse caught her eyes.

Then the Lord God said, 'It is not good that the man should be alone; I will make him a helper fit for him.'

Had God guided her hand to that particular passage?

She traced the tip of the leaf that was acting as an arrow pointing toward the Lord's words. It felt as though her mother was seconding the advice Rebecca had given in days past. Encouraging her to take a chance.

And what better way for Mattie to honor her friend's memory than by giving her marriage to Josiah fair consideration.

If she opened her heart to the possibilities, would her courage be rewarded? Would love blossom between her and Josiah?

She didn't know what the future held, but one thing was certain. She would never find the deep and lasting affection she craved if she kept herself closed off and refused to allow her feelings to grow.

Josiah stood watching his horses. Though he needed to get them ready for travel, he risked another injury if he attempted to do so while he was distracted.

And he was undeniably distracted now, his thoughts on his last encounter with Mattie. Her reaction to his gift, the light in her eyes as if he'd given her a treasure beyond price, had been much more than the simple wooden carving warranted.

Then she'd made a subtle reference to their marriage by claiming a familial connection to Emma. Had he given Mattie the wrong idea with his friendly gesture? Because that was all he'd intended it to be.

But if she had begun to imagine there could be something permanent between them, had convinced herself that he wouldn't follow through with an annulment once they reached Oregon Country…how could he set her straight without being callously blunt?

He worried that problem over in his head for the better part of the day. But by the time they made camp in the early evening, he'd hit upon a solution. After supper, he started on a second carving.

"Do you know what that one is going to be yet?" Mattie questioned, a slight smile turning up the corners of her mouth.

"Yep. It's another horse."

"Oh? Are you planning to make a whole herd?"

"No. Just the one I made you, and this one, which I intend to give to Emma."

She was clearly surprised by his answer, and the smile vanished from her face. Had she assumed he was carving something else for her and now was deflated at learning otherwise?

Though he felt a pang at hurting her, it was a relief that she seemed to have gotten his message not to attach any special meaning to the carving he'd given her.

"That might not be the best present for an infant," she cautioned. "It's dangerous to give her any object that's small enough to fit in her mouth."

Was that truly her reason for protesting against the idea? It must be. Though she might be disappointed, he couldn't believe Mattie would hint that he should give the carving to her, instead. If the woman had a selfish bone in her body, he'd never seen any evidence of it.

And she did make a valid point. When he'd thought up this plan, he hadn't even considered the little detail of what was appropriate for a child who was barely a week old. He didn't have much experience with babies, but that was still no excuse for such an oversight.

It didn't cast him in a very good light. Mattie might not trust him around his own niece now. "I'm going to hold on to it for her until she gets a little older," he remarked, as if that had been his aim all along.

He tried to imagine how Emma might look a couple years from now—as an adorable toddler with big blue eyes and a dimpled smile like her mama's.

In his mind, he kept seeing her toddling toward Mattie, who scooped her up for a hug…and then turned to him to share in the moment.

It was a foolish thought. Mattie would be long gone from their lives before Emma learned to walk. And yet, the image of Mattie's radiant expression as she held Emma close seemed to be imprinted on his heart.

Chapter Seventeen

Although Josiah's gift didn't have the significance Mattie had attributed to it, she viewed this discovery as a minor setback only, not a reason to abandon her determination. She wouldn't be disheartened by the first bump in the road.

True and enduring love took time to grow. It happened in God's time, not her own. She had to be patient, though that wasn't a virtue she possessed in much abundance.

As evidenced a few days later when she sought Josiah out for a private moment to discuss his brother's troubling behavior again.

It wasn't a mere excuse, as she truly was concerned. "He hasn't held Emma since the day she was born, and that was only in the capacity of a doctor delivering her. He doesn't interact with her, doesn't look at her. Doesn't acknowledge her existence in any way. He never so much as commented on the fact that you and I gave *his* child a name."

If Elias had even noticed, he'd shown no signs of it. He didn't seem to be aware of much that was going on around him. It was as if he occupied a world all his own.

"He completely ignores his own child," Mattie continued. "His own flesh and blood." It was unnatural. The newborn was beauty, innocence and lightness. How could her father not have fallen in love with her the moment he laid eyes on her? "Something needs to be done about the situation."

Josiah released a weary sigh. "I thought we'd already settled this."

"Yes, I agreed to help until Elias can take over her care. And I'm not going back on my word." But the more time that passed without any change, the more bothered she became by the way things stood. Until she couldn't stay silent on the matter any longer. "I'm not heartless toward his bereavement. I miss Rebecca, too. But their child needs him."

Emma had already lost her mother. And right now her father was as good as gone, too.

Josiah shook his head in dispute. "All she needs for the time being is someone to feed her and change her, to hold her when she cries and rock her to sleep. It doesn't matter who that someone is. She's too young to know one person from another anyway."

"That doesn't make it right. Doesn't excuse Elias," she argued. "I know you said talking to him wouldn't do any good, but I think you should try."

Removing his hat, he ran his fingers through his hair, then resettled the hat on his head. "Pushing him is likely to do more harm than good. He's made his boundaries very clear, and we should respect them. Besides, I know the pain he's suffering. It's not something a body gets over quickly. Nor something that can be mended on command. Though the Lord knows you try."

What did Josiah mean, that he *knew* his brother's pain? He spoke as if he had loved a woman who was no longer in his life. "Are you saying you were married before? That you lost your wife, too?"

"No, I was never married."

She felt relieved that she had misunderstood his point and wasn't facing the impossible task of competing with the ghost of a lost love. Mattie's father had been forlorn when her mother died, and he had never remarried. No one could replace his beloved wife in his heart.

In the next moment, however, Mattie learned her feelings of relief had been premature.

"But I did lose the woman I love, when she married my best friend," Josiah went on to explain.

From the sounds of it, he loved her still. He had used the present tense, indicating he still had feelings for the woman in his past. Which meant he couldn't be falling for Mattie, as she'd believed.

She felt ambushed by this revelation.

And deceived, in a way. Not once, during all their conversations before now, had Josiah ever mentioned the other woman.

Which left Mattie wondering what else he might not have told her. Finding out that he hadn't felt inclined to share something of such significance reminded her sharply of events in her past. And brought up her old insecurities. Had she made another error in judgment?

But as soon as the thought had formed in her mind, she realized she was permitting panic to cloud her reasoning. The current situation had very little in common with what had happened back in Saint Louis all those months ago.

Josiah didn't owe her explanations about his past; it was his private business and nothing to do with her. So why had she imagined that he would have—or should have—apprised her? True, she had told him about her own failed romance. But that didn't put him under any obligation to reciprocate.

He hadn't deceived her. From the beginning, he'd made it plain that their union wasn't based on emotion or any deep and abiding feelings on his part.

Still, she had deluded herself. Blinding herself to reality. Again. She'd repeated the same mistake a second time, letting her dreams of love lead her off course as she chased after an illusion.

Rebecca had been wrong. Mattie had never stood a chance of winning Josiah's affection. There was no possibility for a happy future together. How foolish of her to believe for even an instant that love might grow from a forced union. It was best that they ended the marriage and went their separate ways once they reached Oregon Country.

As was Josiah's intention all along. That had never changed, though Mattie had allowed herself to forget it for a time.

So much so that she'd given him enough of an opening to sneak past her guard and into her heart. She was now paying the price for her carelessness. She hadn't realized how deep her feelings for him ran until this moment.

It was yet another thing she had blinded herself to. But she couldn't evade the truth any longer. She loved Josiah.

For all the good it did her. He would never return her love. That had been made clear by his last remark.

And the knowledge was like a knife in her chest. All her efforts to avoid heartache had come to naught.

Josiah would leave her once they reached Oregon Country. Go on to build his ranch and make a life for himself. Thoughts of Mattie would never cross his mind.

"I know you mean well," Josiah continued, blissfully unaware of the devastation he had wrought. "But it takes more than a mind-over-matter approach to move beyond heartbreak."

Mattie hoped he was wrong about that. For her sake as much as Elias's.

Lord, please, numb my wounds so I don't have to feel. Return me to what I was before, with a heart impenetrable to hurt.

But even as she silently cried out, she knew she was asking for the impossible.

She had merely imagined herself to be in love with her ex-fiancé, but her heart hadn't truly been involved. Thus, it had remained intact and whole.

But not any longer.

Please, give me the strength to endure this, Lord. Guide me, and show me Your way.

Awakened by a baby's cry, Josiah tossed back the covers and climbed from his bedroll. Glancing up at the dark sky, he noted the position of the moon and guessed it to be close to two o'clock in the morning.

He took only enough time to pull on his coat, then headed toward the campfire where Mattie was adding wood to the glowing embers in preparation for heating a bottle to feed little Emma. The fire snapped and crackled as flames licked along the dry kindling.

He watched her fill a pot with water and hang it above the campfire. His footsteps crunched across the ground as he neared her.

She turned at the sound and spotted him. "Did the baby wake you?"

"Yeah."

A grimace briefly twisted her features. "Sorry. Can you hold her while I make sure this doesn't get too hot?" She indicated the glass bottle in her hand and then moved to place it in the pot of water. "I know she's too hungry to be settled, but perhaps rocking her a bit will help. I don't want to wake up anyone else with her crying. There's been some grumbling about it."

Josiah knew exactly whom she meant. "Pay no attention to Hardwick. Most everyone else knows better than to expect a newborn to be silent."

Gingerly, he scooped up his niece from her makeshift bed, treating her as if she was fragile as the most delicate glass. The baby's face was scrunched up and flushed an angry shade of red from crying. Her mouth opened wide around pitiable squalls, exposing her toothless gums.

"Hush now, little one. Mattie will have your bottle ready before you know it." He swayed back and forth, as Mattie had requested, his eyes locked on the infant in his arms.

She was growing bigger every day, but even at almost three weeks old, she still seemed impossibly tiny to Josiah. Whenever he picked her up, he feared holding her too tight and hurting her. Nearly as much as he feared not holding her tight enough and dropping her.

He felt more than a smidgen of panic every time he was charged with her care. Not so Mattie.

Perhaps it was a strictly feminine attribute, an innate maternal instinct that all females possessed. Adela often lent a hand with the baby and appeared perfectly at ease doing so. Even young Sarah Jane Baker, forever trailing after Adela, seemed captivated by baby Emma, wanting to help take care of her as if she was a living doll.

Mattie retrieved the bottle and tested the temperature, then set it aside and reached for the baby. "I'll take her now."

Her hands brushed against his arms as she lifted Emma away from him and settled the child comfortably in the crook of her elbow. Picking up the bottle, she nudged the top against Emma's lips. The baby latched on instantly, her cries quieted at last, replaced by the sounds of her greedy sucking.

They made an arresting portrait, Mattie's delicate features warmed by the glow from the flickering flames and his niece's eyes closed in blissful contentment, her formerly scrunched-up face now relaxed and peaceful.

Mattie glanced over at him, the firelight reflecting in her amber eyes. "Thank you, but I can take it from here. You should head back to bed now. There's no need for you to stay any longer." She didn't bother waiting for a response before she turned her attention back to the baby.

Plainly, he was surplus to requirements. "I'll leave you to it, then. Good night."

As he made his way toward his bedroll, he tried to figure out why her dismissive attitude troubled him.

He should feel relieved she no longer protested caring for the baby in Elias's stead. Nor looked to Josiah to urge his brother to face up to his responsibilities.

Except she was still working toward that aim. She had simply cut Josiah out of the equation and now dealt with Elias directly. Thankfully, she was subtle in her appeals, recognizing that a hard-nosed approach would only push him further away.

In contrast, she appeared to be purposely pushing Josiah away. Why did that thought hurt so much? Wasn't that what he'd wanted? By his own choice, they would soon face a permanent split.

Yet, he no longer looked on it with the same equanimity he once had. Where before it had merely seemed the first step toward a new beginning, he now saw it for the ending it truly was.

But he couldn't change course now.

Days later, Josiah's muscles strained and sweat trickled down the side of his face as he held the rope that snaked through a pulley and connected to one of the covered wagons.

"Steady now, men," Miles instructed. "Let the rope out nice and easy."

Working together with several other men, Josiah helped to slowly lower the heavy weight down the steep side of a fifty-foot ravine. Around them, there were two other clusters of men doing likewise with two more covered wagons.

The group of travelers had reached the Blue Mountains of Oregon Country. The looming peaks to the west were the final obstacle standing between them and the Columbia River, which would carry them the last miles to their destination.

Shifting his eyes toward the bottom of the ravine, Josiah noted the men leading teams of oxen down the steep slope. And the group of women and children scattered about the surrounding area, watching the progress. Mattie wasn't among them. Even from this distance, he would have no trouble picking her out from the sea of bonnet-bedecked heads.

He scanned the landscape and spotted her, wending her way around large boulders partway up the hill, with Emma cradled in her arms. The pair had clearly been left behind, as everyone else was already at the bottom.

Josiah guessed that Mattie was taking her time, in deference to the little one she carried. Over the past few weeks, she'd been a good caretaker to the baby. Protective and loving, she was the kind of mother he wanted for his own children.

The thought brought him up short. Why had it even crossed his mind? He wouldn't have any children of his own because he didn't intend to stay married, or to wed ever again.

Mattie didn't belong in his picture of the future. It was true that his affection for her had increased over the course of their journey, but he didn't love her.

Their marriage was only temporary. He shouldn't have to remind himself of that. But, apparently, it was necessary.

They were heading in different directions. He had to accept that she didn't want to stay with him.

As they neared the end of the trail, she clearly anticipated a parting of ways. Already, she had pulled away from him.

It was a pretty impressive feat, the sense of distance she'd created between them, given the fact that they lived and worked in such close proximity. But it wasn't a physical distance, rather an emotional one. Though she still talked to him, their conversations were of casual, everyday matters. Nothing of any real meaning. She no longer shared her thoughts and concerns with him, and that left him feeling curiously shut out.

He was drawn from his musing by the sounds of men shouting, and his eyes darted around to ascertain the problem.

"It's fraying," one man yelled, his voice tight with alarm.

"It's not going to hold," another added, panic edging his tone.

Josiah realized almost immediately that they were talking about the rope keeping one of the other two wagons from careening down the steep grade.

A few men dashed forward to lend whatever aid they could, but most were like Josiah, who had his hands full maintaining control of a different covered wagon.

"Don't let go of that rope," Josiah ordered the teenage boy next to him, when it looked as if Cody was about to do just that.

There was nothing he or any of the other men around him could do to help with the fraying rope. Acting without thought and releasing their hold on their own rope could lead to a worse situation in which they had several wagons dangling precariously in imminent peril.

Suddenly, the frayed rope snapped, sending the wagon barreling out of control down the hillside.

And heading straight toward Mattie and Emma.

A wave of horror slammed into Josiah at the realization that he couldn't save them. Even if he were free to chase after the runaway covered wagon, he'd never get to Mattie and Emma in time.

He prayed for the Lord to spare his loved ones' lives, and the Lord heeded his cry.

Maybe it was by the wagon's wheels hitting a rock, which altered its path slightly. Or Mattie scrambling to the side to get out of the way. Or perhaps both of these things combined that kept them from harm. Josiah didn't know or care. He was simply relieved that disaster had been averted at the last second.

His heart filled with thanksgiving that his family was safe. *Thank You, Lord.*

He inhaled, taking a deep breath of air laden with the scent of pine. Sweat had chilled on his skin, and he swiped his arm across his forehead to remove the moisture.

Then he suddenly froze as his mind went back over his recent thoughts. Including the specific words of his appeal to God.

He had numbered Mattie as a loved one. And was shocked to realize it was true.

He loved her.

His knees buckling, he staggered slightly before catching his balance. His damp palms slipped on the rough hemp rope, and he tightened his grip.

But while he got his body under control, his mind continued reeling. He had believed that he'd built a wall around his heart so thick no other woman could touch it. And all the while Mattie had been slowly slipping past his defenses, with him none the wiser.

How had he not recognized his feelings before now? He was a fool.

When he remembered his efforts to discourage Mattie in weeks past…he could kick himself. They had worked all too well. If she had ever felt anything for him, she certainly didn't any longer.

He would be forced to let her go, allowing her to find happiness with someone else—a repeat of his past. Only it would hurt so much more this time because his feelings for Mattie were deeper, stronger than any he had felt for the woman back in Tennessee.

The covered wagon that had broken loose ended up smashed beyond repair against the rocks at the bottom of the ravine. Though one family had to abandon a good many of their possessions as a result, no one had been injured.

But Mattie was still shaken by the close call.

One good thing had come out of it, however. Elias had examined Emma to ensure she wasn't suffering any ill effects. Unfortunately, his involvement with her didn't extend past that. Still, it was progress.

Mattie could finally see a glimmer of hope on the horizon that things would get better. Elias had taken the first step toward building a bond with his daughter. He cared enough to worry over her well-being. By the grace of God, he would one day be healed and whole again, acting as a true father to her. Hopefully, before she was old enough to be conscious of his neglect and hurt by it.

A short time later, Josiah appeared. "I wanted to check on you two." Moving to the makeshift bassinet sitting on the tailgate of Mattie's covered wagon, he leaned down and stroked a gentle finger across Emma's cheek.

Mattie's thoughts traveled back to the early hours of the morning, a few days past, when he had appeared and joined her by the campfire. How he'd rocked his niece while Mattie readied a bottle. And the way the sight of the tiny baby nestled in his arms had stirred her emotions. Though tentative in handling Emma, his love for her was never in doubt.

His uncertainty had further endeared him to Mattie. She could easily imagine him showing the same tender regard to his own children someday. Cherishing them as welcome blessings from the Lord.

But she quickly blanked the mental picture. If he ever had any little red-haired sons or daughters, they wouldn't be hers. She and Josiah would never have children together.

Still, she prayed that God gifted him with a second chance at love. She didn't want him to be alone, forever mired in sadness and regrets. Though he yet cared for a woman who didn't return his feelings, Mattie hoped he might one day meet another who could reach his heart.

No other woman could possibly love him more than Mattie did, but, God willing, Josiah would find one who loved him just as much.

He straightened and turned toward her. "Emma seems none the worse for her misadventure. How are you doing?"

She had to bite her tongue to keep from begging him to hold her. She desperately wanted to feel the comfort of his strong embrace. To press close to him, her head against his chest, allowing the steady beat of his heart to calm her.

But any hug she received from him would be bitter-sweet with the knowledge that he didn't feel anything more toward her than friendship. Though he might pull her near for a few seconds, the gesture would never mean all the things she wished it did.

She moved away from him slightly, resisting the temptation to throw herself into his arms and sob her heart out. "We're both fine."

"Your quick actions in moving out of the wagon's path probably saved your life and Emma's. You protected her, as you have since the day she was born."

She glanced at the sleeping baby nestled in the blanket-padded crate. "She's too precious for me to willingly let anything bad happen to her."

Returning her gaze to Josiah, she found that he wasn't watching Emma, but had focused an intense scrutiny on Mattie, instead. He studied her in silence for long moments, and she shifted nervously under his piercing regard. What exactly was he searching for?

Finally, he seemed to reach some sort of determination. "I was thinking that maybe we should reconsider our plans for an annulment."

Her breath stalled in her lungs, and the world seemed suddenly brighter. Until she remembered that his words weren't prompted by love—at least, not love for her. How could she have forgotten that for even an instant? The air gusted out of her body, leaving her feeling light-headed.

Still, her brain had enough function left to work out a logical explanation for his abrupt about-face. "Because you need me to continue caring for Emma."

He hesitated for a moment before opening his

mouth, then closed it again without speaking, and merely nodded his head.

For the space of a single heartbeat, she contemplated accepting his proposal to continue their practical marriage of convenience. She'd give just about anything, if it meant she could keep him as her husband. But such an arrangement would kill her by inches, a little piece of her dying each day she shared with him, loving him but never loved in return.

If only there was a chance he could learn to care for her, a ray of hope that she could hold on to— No, she couldn't think like that. She had to stop torturing herself with impossible dreams of what might have been, if only things were different. No matter how much she wished it, those foolish dreams were never going to come true.

A clean break was best; one quick cut preferable to a thousand tiny pricks, which would leave her heart bleeding endlessly. Though it would hurt unbearably when they parted, the gaping wound would eventually scab over.

"I can't stay married to you. I'm sorry."

Chapter Eighteen

While working with his horses that evening, Josiah berated himself for bringing up the subject of their marriage. Had he really imagined that Mattie might want to remain his wife? That she would want *him*? That she would willingly choose the hard lot of a rancher's wife over a life of leisure in her uncle's house?

It seemed he was destined to love a woman who could never be his.

Hearing movement to his left, he glanced up in time to see the object of his thoughts heading off into the forest alone and without her rifle. Where did she think she was going? It was unwise to wander too far from the circle of covered wagons without a weapon for protection.

All Mattie carried in her hands was her Bible. Though Josiah didn't discount the power of the word of God, it was no match for the dangerous predators who called this area home.

Pulling his rifle from the saddle scabbard, he abandoned his horses without a backward glance and followed after Mattie. He didn't mean to disturb her, but he would ensure she didn't come to any harm.

When she reached a small, grassy meadow, he hung back inside the tree line and watched. Sitting down on the ground, she tucked her skirts around her legs and opened the Bible.

Josiah glanced around the clearing, on the lookout for any possible dangers. For the time being, all appeared peaceful. Birdsong echoed through the trees, and he could hear the gurgle of water trickling over rocks in a nearby stream.

He returned his gaze to Mattie. She was looking down at her Bible. She didn't seem to be focusing on the words but rather on something dark that rested against the white page. He couldn't quite make out what it was, and he squinted to get a clearer view.

His eyes widened as he realized it was the bundle of leaves he'd given her as a frame for the horse carving. The leaves were brown and dried now, but she had kept them. Why?

She picked up the bundle, but the brittle leaves couldn't withstand even her gentle handling, and they crumbled into pieces that were blown away by the wind.

Putting her hands over her face, Mattie's shoulders began to shake. And he realized she was crying. Surely, it couldn't be over the destruction of a few little leaves. Could it?

His heart contracting at the sight of her sorrow, he took a step forward. A twig snapped beneath his boot heel.

Mattie jumped at the sound and turned her head in

his direction. She quickly wiped the tears away as he approached. "What are you doing here?"

Ignoring her question, he sank down at her side and asked one of his own. "Why did you keep them?" It seemed like the sort of memento a woman would only care about if it came…from the man she loved. Could that possibly be true? Was there a chance he could get back what he had carelessly thrown away?

She sniffled several times, though she did her best to suppress them. "Because it was part of the gift you gave me. But it was a foolishly sentimental thing to do. It was just a bunch of dead leaves."

Then why had she been crying over them?

He took her hand in his. "I don't think it's foolish to be sentimental."

What *was* foolish was him staying silent about his feelings for her out of fear that he'd be hurt.

But all his life, he'd shied away from opening himself up to others because doing so would give them the power to wound him. He'd believed it better not to get too close to anyone and thus never risk the possibility that they might reject his feelings.

Even with Georgiana, he'd maintained a certain distance. Now he wondered if that might be the reason she'd preferred William over him.

Perhaps his problem was never that he wasn't good enough to be loved, as he'd always feared, but that he closed himself off too much to allow love to reach him.

Offering his whole heart carried risk, and he'd been hurt already when Mattie had shot down his attempt to renegotiate the terms of their agreement.

She hadn't rejected his love, however. Because *he* had never offered it to her.

He'd been a coward, taking the out she'd given him. Allowing her to believe the baby was the only reason he had suggested she remain his wife, instead of putting his heart on the line by admitting that he wanted Mattie for himself, not just as a nursemaid for his niece.

He looked at her beloved face. At her delicate features that could firm into such determined lines when her stubborn streak came to the fore. And her beautiful eyes that gave him glimpses into her thoughts while still keeping so much of her inner feelings a mystery. He noted how her hair had grown out a bit over the past months and now peeked below the edge of her bonnet, the silky strands curling against her neck.

All she'd gone through—the unexpected twists and turns life had thrown at her one right after the next—hadn't defeated her.

And it was her indomitable spirit that he loved most about this woman.

Lord, give me the courage to say what's in my heart.

Josiah wanted to be Mattie's protector, her partner. Her devoted husband. For the rest of their lives. If she would let him.

Looking deep into her gaze, he pulled down the final stones from the crumbling wall guarding his heart. "I love you, Mattie Dawson."

She tugged her hand from his grasp and shook her head. "You can't possibly. You told me yourself that you love someone else."

It wasn't the reaction he'd hoped for. But neither was it the rejection he had feared. Instead, it gave him insight into how she must have felt when he'd referred to his love for Georgiana.

So many mistakes he'd made. Would he be able to right them?

He shifted his glance to the surrounding landscape, mentally searching for the words to explain his actions in a way that she would understand and accept, so that he might yet have some small chance of creating a life with her.

He found no clues in the brightly colored autumn leaves on the trees or the mountain peaks rising majestically in the distance. Nor the flock of birds flying across the vast cloudless sky. Even the wind whispering through the tall grasses refused to give him any answers.

Bringing his gaze back in line with Mattie's, he snatched his hat from his head. His fingers shuffled along the brim, turning it round and round in his hands. "I thought I was in love before—but I was wrong. What I felt for her was merely an infatuation that I built up in my mind as something more."

Doubt shone in her eyes. "Why would you do that?"

He scarcely noticed his fingers as they flexed, crushing his hat brim. "To keep myself from falling in love with anyone else, as a way to protect my heart from another disappointment."

He'd used his supposed feelings for Georgiana as a talisman to ward off future heartache.

But it hadn't worked. His emotions toward Mattie had overridden the dictates of his brain.

Laying his hand atop hers where it rested on her lap, he refused to let her pull away again. "I want to stay married to you, Mattie. To live with you as my wife. For no other reason than because I love you."

When she remained silent, he feared she didn't believe his words. Or perhaps she did, but his love wasn't enough to satisfy her.

Most women didn't want to be isolated on a remote ranch like the one he planned to build, far from town and neighbors. Mattie was likely of the same mind. And after months on the trail, she was undoubtedly tired of backbreaking work and endless chores, and didn't desire more of the same as the wife of a rancher.

"We don't have to live on a ranch," he promised. Anything to sway her to consider the possibility of staying with him. "We can live in town, instead. I'm sure I could find a job, buy a fancy house. Dress in hand-tailored suits," he added with a slight smile.

It wasn't a future he had ever pictured for himself. But, to please Mattie, he would make himself over into a dandy if that was what it took.

Her eyebrows knit together over the bridge of her nose. "But the ranch is your dream. And though you can keep a few horses in town, you wouldn't be able to accomplish all the things you've planned." She cocked her head to the side, her gaze intent on him. "You would forfeit everything you'd envisioned?"

He didn't hesitate for even an instant before answering. "I'll do that and more, if living in town is what you want."

She shook her head. "I don't want to live with you in town."

His heart sinking, he turned his face away. He'd offered all he had to give, and still he couldn't measure up. What he could provide simply wasn't enough. Would never be enough.

Clearly, she wanted a husband who had a pedigree

to rival those back in Saint Louis. And Josiah's was sadly lacking.

He had to accept that her vision of the future didn't include him.

Realizing that Josiah had misunderstood her meaning, Mattie lifted her hand and placed it along his jaw. She turned his face back toward her and stoked her thumb over his cheek, enjoying the texture of the bristles covering his skin.

At first, she had mistakenly believed that his words of love were simply an attempt to manipulate her for his own ends. To get her to agree to stay married so that he wouldn't be left caring for the baby on his own. She'd received false declarations before, from a man who had been angling to gain her favor, and she'd been determined that she wouldn't be taken in again.

But that wasn't what Josiah was doing.

The moment he'd told her he would give up his dream in order to keep her as his wife, she had known he spoke the truth when he said he loved her.

He wouldn't make such an offer merely to gain a temporary caretaker for his brother's child. Eventually, Elias would move past his grief and take over the raising of his daughter. When that time came, Josiah wouldn't want to run the risk of being trapped in town with a job he didn't like and a wife he didn't need or desire.

Thus, there was only one logical explanation for his willingness to make such a sacrifice. He did love Mattie, just as he claimed.

Tears of joy welled in her eyes, and she blinked to

keep them from falling. "I want to help you build your ranch." Help him make his dream a reality.

His mouth dropped open, and she smiled at the look of stunned surprise in his gaze.

He reached up and snagged her hand, pulling it away from his face. "I don't understand."

Weaving her fingers between his, she rested their joined hands against her knee. "I don't need a fancy house, or a man in hand-tailored suits. I just need you, Josiah. I love you."

Uncertainty lingered in his eyes. "But you've been so distant recently."

"I was trying to protect myself. I'd realized I love you, but believed you would never feel the same way about me." To suddenly find that wasn't true after all seemed the greatest gift God could ever bless her with. It was enough to renew her faith that all things were possible with the Lord.

An effervescent happiness swelled inside her, and she felt as if it would burst free. The joy that filled her heart was too great for any body to contain.

"If that's true, why did you wait so long after I admitted my feelings before you said anything in return?" His expression held equal parts hope and fear that he'd be disappointed.

"It was only a few minutes," she argued, although she did feel guilty she'd left him to suffer in agony for even that short amount of time.

She well knew the pain of hopes unrealized and how difficult it was to take a risk again. To hold on to the optimism that this once, unlike all the others before, it might turn out differently.

And now, at last, it had. For both her and Josiah.

The corner of his mouth hitched up in a lopsided smile. "It seemed like an eternity to me."

"I'm sorry." Her gaze dropped to her lap. "I thought you were only telling me what I wanted to hear in order to get me to agree to continue looking after Emma."

His grip on her fingers tightened, transmitting his tension to her. "How could you think I would lie to you?"

Her heart ached that she'd wounded him with her groundless suspicions. "My ex-fiancé's duplicity left me looking for ulterior motives in all men's actions," she tried to explain. "Though you were steadfast and unwavering, it still took me a long while to believe I could trust you. To believe that you were the man you seemed, a man of honor and integrity. The kind of man who would stand beside me through all life's trials."

"Then, it was never anything against me personally?"

The question caught her by surprise, and her glance came back up to mesh with his. "Of course not. Is that what you imagined?"

Though he didn't answer in words, she could see it in his eyes. Just as her past had affected the way she viewed his actions, so too had Josiah's past influenced his perception of her behavior.

She placed her palm over their linked hands, her gaze steady and direct, so that he might read the truth of her words in her eyes. "I love you because of the man you are, Josiah. Everything that came before—it has all helped to shape you. If even a single aspect was missing or altered, you would be a different person."

"You don't know how often I wished for a different life. But not anymore." A huge grin split his face.

The corners of her mouth curled up in return. "It's time we both put the past behind us and focus on the future."

His smile dimmed a bit. "Are you sure you want to build a horse ranch together? We'll be starting out with very little. After building a small cabin and buying basic necessities, any money left over from the sale of the horses I've been training will have to be put straight back into the operation, toward making improvements. There will be several lean years before we're likely to see a profit."

Though she didn't discount the difficulties they would face, none of it troubled her mind. "As long as I have you, nothing else matters."

"That's exactly the way I feel about you." He pulled her close and captured her lips with his.

She could sense the love and emotion behind his kiss, and returned it in equal measure.

Epilogue

Willamette Valley, Oregon Country
Early May, 1846

Mattie paced to the front window for the fifth time in as many minutes, checking for Josiah's return. She was wearing a path in the wooden floor between the front window and the back in her impatience. He'd left early that morning to deliver a horse to its new owner but had promised to be back for dinner, and it was past noon already.

Looking out from the front of the house, she could see the road leading to town. But from the back window she had a view of the pasture where Josiah had turned out their horses to graze. From which direction would he come?

Josiah was on horseback, so he might not stay on the road when he could just as easily ride through a shallow stream and cut across the pasture in a more direct route, which saved time.

She turned from the window to retrace her steps in the opposite direction, and her gaze landed on the cradle where she'd laid baby Emma down for a nap. She found the infant wide-awake, her blue eyes shifting as if following something on the ceiling. But the moment Mattie entered her field of vision, she cooed and reached out her arms.

Leaning down, Mattie lifted the little girl from her nest of blankets. "Did you have a nice nap, precious?" She kissed the baby's downy head and inhaled her sweet scent. "Uncle Josiah should be returning soon, and we have the most wonderful secret to share with him. You're going to have a cousin! Isn't that exciting?"

Emma grinned as if she understood Mattie's words and approved.

Perching the little girl on her hip, Mattie ensured all was in readiness for Josiah's arrival. She had a basket packed with cold chicken, cheese and apples for their picnic dinner. And a folded quilt sat on the table next to the covered wicker basket, in anticipation of finding a shady spot under a tree where they could enjoy the food.

Then she would make her big announcement.

She turned her attention back to Emma. "Do you think it will be a boy or a girl? Now, I know you'd like it to be a girl—that way you'd have a playmate to share secrets with as you get older. But a boy would be just as welcome to Uncle Josiah and I. Either way, we'll have a child to inherit all we're working to achieve."

Emma chewed on her fist, her eyes bright and inquisitive.

Unable to remain still while eagerness bubbled up inside her, Mattie paced around the one-room cabin she'd helped Josiah build before the snow set in last winter. "If we're going to add another member to our family, we'll need a bigger home." She looked down at the child in her arms. "Don't you agree, Emma? Uncle Josiah will need to add another room. Or two. God willing, this will be the first of many children.

"Auntie Adela can help stitch baby things, like she did for you. Next time we travel to Oregon City, we'll share the happy news with her. And we'll tell your papa he's going to be an uncle when we visit him in town the day after tomorrow."

Thoughts of Elias dimmed her mood a bit, and she caressed the baby's soft cheek with one finger. Emma smiled in response, unaware of the dark turn Mattie's mind had taken.

Elias Dawson hadn't managed to move past his grief. Moreover, he viewed the loss of his wife as an unpardonable failure as a doctor and hadn't attended to a patient since. Still, the townspeople had allowed him to move into the house they'd built for him and Rebecca, believing he simply needed a bit more time before opening the clinic.

Heavy snowfall had kept Mattie and Josiah trapped at the ranch for several long stretches the previous winter, unable to reach town and offer him support. He seemed to prefer it that way, however, choosing solitude over their invitation to stay with them at the ranch. He'd claimed he didn't want to crowd them, but she suspected his true motive was avoiding any situation that had the potential to shake him out of his numbed state.

Sadly, there hadn't been much improvement when spring arrived, even though she and Josiah made it a point to stop by his house every few days. On Sundays, they went into town together and visited him after attending church. And Josiah usually checked in with his brother any time the delivery of a horse took him in that direction.

In addition, Mattie had taken to driving the five-mile distance with Emma at last once a week while Josiah was occupied with the horses' training. Each time, she hoped that seeing the baby, spending time with her, would have a positive effect on Elias. But as of yet, she'd seen few signs indicating any change.

It was now nearing summer. The clinic continued to stand vacant, and Elias was still too grief stricken by the passing of his wife to care for their child. Emma remained a constant reminder of what he'd lost.

Mattie prayed for them both every day. That God would heal Elias's heart. That he might one day rediscover the peace and happiness he'd once known. That he would find the strength to move past his loss in order to be the loving and attentive father Emma deserved.

The front door swung open, and Mattie turned to see Josiah framed in the doorway, a bouquet of wildflowers clenched in one hand.

Moving forward, he gathered her into his arms and kissed her. "I missed you."

"You were only gone a few hours." Laughter tinged her voice.

His eyes caressed her upturned features. "A few minutes are too long to go without seeing your face."

Her lips stretched into a grin. "I missed you, too."

He leaned down to give her another quick kiss, then handed the bouquet to her and took Emma in exchange. "And I missed you, Sweet Pea."

Inhaling the flowers' sweet fragrance, Mattie moved

to the sink and filled a glass jar with water. Once she had the blooms arranged to her satisfaction, she placed the jar on the windowsill and turned back to Josiah.

He was standing beside the table, an indulgent expression on his face. "I see you have a picnic planned."

"It's such a nice day I thought we'd eat outside, under the big oak tree out front."

"I don't understand your fascination with eating outdoors. Didn't you get enough of it while we were on the trail?"

"After being cooped up for most of the winter, I like to get out into the fresh air. Besides, it's a special occasion." She picked up the basket and quilt.

"What's the occasion?"

"It's a surprise. I'll tell you once we're settled outside."

"Then let's go." He wrapped an arm around her waist, guiding her out the door and down the porch steps.

They had chosen a beautiful spot for their horse ranch. A piece of wooded land with a stream running through it and the mountain peaks in the distance. There was something extra special about it this time of year, when the hills were carpeted with a profusion of bright spring flowers.

She couldn't imagine any place on earth she'd rather be than right here. With Josiah. Her husband, her soul mate, the man she would love for the rest of her days.

She set the basket down and took Emma from him, while he spread the quilt where she directed. Sinking to her knees on the colorful patchwork, she laid Emma beside her.

The baby rolled from her back to her stomach and pushed up on her stubby arms, lifting her torso from the ground and bouncing her legs. Her entire body wiggled with her movements. She gave them a proud grin, displaying two small baby teeth.

"You're such a clever girl," Mattie praised, then turned to her husband. "She's going to be crawling soon."

Josiah dropped down next to her. "Any day now. Is that what we're celebrating?"

"No. It's something even better. I was going to tell you after we finished eating, but I can't wait that long. We'll have a new addition to our family just in time for Christmas."

Josiah's eyes lit up. "A baby?" At her nod, he gathered her close in his arms and kissed her with all the love in his heart.

He pulled back, his gaze tracing the contours of her face. "I didn't think it was possible to be any happier than I've been with you these past several months, but I am. My joy is overflowing. God has blessed us."

"Yes, He has." She thanked God every day for the blessings He had given her.

And for setting her on the path that led her to Josiah.

All she'd gone through had been necessary to reach this point—and this man who loved her deeply, unconditionally, eternally.

If she hadn't made the mistakes involving her ex-fiancé, she never would have left Saint Louis. Never would have met Josiah.

Though she hadn't understood God's plan at the time, had questioned how certain things could be His will, now she could see clearly how He had worked in her life for a purpose.

To bring her and Josiah together.

* * * * *

*If you loved this Oregon Trail story,
be sure to pick up the* JOURNEY WEST *series:*

*WAGON TRAIN REUNION by Linda Ford
WAGON TRAIN SWEETHEART by Lacy Williams
WAGON TRAIN PROPOSAL by Renee Ryan*

Find more great reads at www.LoveInspired.com

Dear Reader,

Thank you for choosing to read *Wed on the Wagon Train*, my first Love Inspired Historical.

I've always been fascinated with Oregon Trail history. I've traveled to landmarks all along the route, including Scotts Bluff, Independence Rock, and the Blue Mountains. I've visited forts, stood on the banks at river crossings and walked in wagon ruts cut several feet into solid stone.

From the 1840s to the 1860s thousands of men, women and children left behind almost everything to embark on the difficult and dangerous two-thousand-mile trek. All for the promise of a better life. I believe there's a bit of that pioneer spirit in each of us.

I hope you enjoyed reading about Mattie and Josiah's journey.

Happy Holidays,
Tracy Blalock

REQUEST YOUR FREE BOOKS!

2 FREE INSPIRATIONAL NOVELS
PLUS 2 *FREE* MYSTERY GIFTS

Love Inspired® HISTORICAL

YES! Please send me 2 FREE Love Inspired® Historical novels and my 2 FREE mystery gifts (gifts are worth about $10). After receiving them, if I don't wish to receive any more books, I can return the shipping statement marked "cancel." If I don't cancel, I will receive 4 brand-new novels every month and be billed just $4.99 per book in the U.S. or $5.49 per book in Canada. That's a saving of at least 17% off the cover price. It's quite a bargain! Shipping and handling is just 50¢ per book in the U.S. and 75¢ per book in Canada.* I understand that accepting the 2 free books and gifts places me under no obligation to buy anything. I can always return a shipment and cancel at any time. Even if I never buy another book, the two free books and gifts are mine to keep forever.

102/302 IDN GH6Z

Name	(PLEASE PRINT)	
Address		Apt. #
City	State/Prov.	Zip/Postal Code

Signature (if under 18, a parent or guardian must sign)

Mail to the **Reader Service:**
IN U.S.A.: P.O. Box 1867, Buffalo, NY 14240-1867
IN CANADA: P.O. Box 609, Fort Erie, Ontario L2A 5X3

Want to try two free books from another series?
Call 1-800-873-8635 or visit www.ReaderService.com.

* Terms and prices subject to change without notice. Prices do not include applicable taxes. Sales tax applicable in N.Y. Canadian residents will be charged applicable taxes. Offer not valid in Quebec. This offer is limited to one order per household. Not valid for current subscribers to Love Inspired Historical books. All orders subject to credit approval. Credit or debit balances in a customer's account(s) may be offset by any other outstanding balance owed by or to the customer. Please allow 4 to 6 weeks for delivery. Offer available while quantities last.

Your Privacy—The Reader Service is committed to protecting your privacy. Our Privacy Policy is available online at www.ReaderService.com or upon request from the Reader Service.

We make a portion of our mailing list available to reputable third parties that offer products we believe may interest you. If you prefer that we not exchange your name with third parties, or if you wish to clarify or modify your communication preferences, please visit us at www.ReaderService.com/consumerschoice or write to us at Reader Service Preference Service, P.O. Box 9062, Buffalo, NY 14240-9062. Include your complete name and address.

LIHI5

"Are you going to be okay with the children?" Logan
asked.

Sadie bristled. "Of course I am."

"I expect the first night will be the worst."

"To be honest, I'm more concerned about tomorrow
when I have to leave the girls to teach." She looked back
at her living quarters. "They are all so afraid."

"I'll be back before you have to leave so the girls
won't be alone and defenseless." He didn't know why
he'd added the final word and wished he hadn't when
Sadie spun about to face him. He'd only been thinking of
Sammy's concerns—be they real or the fears of children
who had experienced too many losses.

"You think they might have need of protection?"

"Don't all children?"

Her lips trembled and then she pressed them together
and wrapped her arms across her chest in a move so self-
protective that he instinctively reached for her, but at the
look on her face, he lowered his arms instead.

She shuddered.

From the thought of him touching her or because of something she remembered? He couldn't say but neither could he leave her without knowing she was okay. Ignoring the idea that she might object to his forwardness, wanting only to make sure she knew he was concerned about her and the children, he cupped one hand to her shoulder. He knew he'd done the right thing when she leaned into his palm. "Sadie, I'll stay if you need me to. I can sleep in the schoolroom, or over at Uncle George's. Or even under the stars."

She glanced past him to the pile of lumber at the back of the yard. For the space of a heartbeat, he thought she'd ask him to stay, then she drew in a long breath.

"We'll be fine, though I would feel better leaving them in the morning if I knew you were here."

He squeezed her shoulder. "I'll be here." He hesitated, still not wanting to leave.

She stepped away from him, forcing him to lower his arm to his side. "Goodbye, then. And thank you for your help."

"Don't forget we're partners in this." He waited for her to acknowledge his statement.

"Very well."

"Goodbye for now. I'll see you in the morning." He forced himself to climb into the wagon and flick the reins. He turned for one last look before he was out of sight.

Don't miss
MONTANA COWBOY FAMILY by Linda Ford,
available January 2017 wherever
Love Inspired® Historical books and ebooks are sold.

www.LoveInspired.com

LIHEXP1216

SPECIAL EXCERPT FROM

Love Inspired®

*A promise to watch out for his late army buddy's
little brother might have this single rancher in over
his head. But he's not the only one who wants to
care for the boy...*

Read on for a sneak preview of the fourth book in the
LONE STAR COWBOY LEAGUE: BOYS RANCH
*miniseries, **THE COWBOY'S TEXAS FAMILY***
by Margaret Daley.

As Nick settled behind the steering wheel and started his
truck, he slanted a look at Darcy. "So what do you think
about the boys ranch?"

"Corey is much better off here than with his dad. He's
not happy right now, but then he wasn't happy at home."

"He's scared." That was why Bea had brought him to
the barn first to see Nick. "He'll feel better after he meets
some of the other boys his age."

"What if he doesn't?" Darcy asked.

"He's confused. He wants to be with his dad, and yet
not if he's always being left alone. He doesn't know what
to expect from day to day and certainly doesn't feel safe."
Those same feelings used to plague Nick while he was
growing up.

"I've dealt with kids like that."

"In a perfect world, Ned wouldn't drink and would
love Corey unconditionally. But that isn't going to hap

pen. Ned isn't going to change." He knew firsthand the mind-set of an alcoholic and remembered the times his dad promised to stop drinking and reform. He never did; in fact he got worse.

"How do you know that for sure?"

"I just do." He didn't share his past with anyone. It was a part of his life he wanted to wipe from his mind, but it was always there in the background. He never wanted to see a child grow up the way he had.

"Then I'll pray for the best for Corey," Darcy said.

"The best scenario would be the state taking Corey away from Ned and a good family adopting him. I wish I was in a position to do it." The second he said that last sentence he wanted to snatch it back. He had no business being anyone's father.

"Because you're single? That might not matter in certain cases."

"I'm not dad material." How could he explain that he was struggling to erase the debt that his father had accumulated? If he lost the ranch, he would lose his home and job. But, more important, what if he wasn't a good father to Corey? It was one thing to be there to help when needed, but it was very different to be totally responsible for raising a child.

Don't miss
THE COWBOY'S TEXAS FAMILY
by Margaret Daley, available January 2017 wherever
Love Inspired® books and ebooks are sold.

www.LoveInspired.com